The Jew Who Was Ukrainian

or

How One Man's Rip-Roaring Romp through an Existential Wasteland Ended in a Bungled Attempt to Bump off the Exceptionally Great Leader of Mother Russia

Alexander J. Motyl

Červená Barva Press
Somerville, Massachusetts

Červená Barva Press
P.O. Box 440357
W. Somerville, MA 02144-3222

www.cervenabarvapress.com

Bookstore: www.thelostbookshelf.com

Cover Design: William J. Kelle

Production: Jennifer LeBlanc

ISBN: 978-0-9831041-1-7

Library of Congress Control Number: 2011924368

The Jew Who Was Ukrainian

or

How One Man's Rip-Roaring Romp through an Existential Wasteland Ended in a Bungled Attempt to Bump off the Exceptionally Great Leader of Mother Russia

For Fanka Lacher, who became Sister Maria and always remained my Mother's best friend

Chapter 1

The master narrative begins logically, if insidiously, as Volodymyr comes face to face with a variety of deeply disturbing, and arguably unique, problems involving language, names, history, guilt, responsibility, hatred, assassination, and other mundane things

How a preposterous name got poor Volodymyr into hot water even before he was fully aware, or even capable of being fully aware, of just how hot hot water can really be and of just how unpleasant life can become in the aftermath of total immersion, not in a language or culture, but in hot water

Volodymyr Frauenzimmer's decision to rid the world of the exceptionally great leader of Mother Russia was made on a Friday, relatively late in the day, at a time that he usually felt remorse for not being in the least inclined to celebrate the Sabbath and, instead, devoted himself to cerebral pursuits—though generally not to thoughts of political adventurism. When he looked back on that fateful day—knowing full well that the word *fateful*, while quite accurate, was dreadfully hackneyed—he was always struck by the appropriateness of the passive voice. The fact was that he had not, strictly speaking, decided to eliminate the exceptionally great leader. Rather, the decision had been made for him. It was almost as if it had struck him like a bolt out of the blue (alas, another hackneyed phrase). Cast by whom or by what? That was easy: by God, by fate, by history, by his very nature. And, last but not least, by his preposterous name, the preposterous past it embodied, the tangled roots it had, and the preposterous present and future it entailed.

Volodymyr knew that his name was preposterous—almost an insult, if one thought about it for any length of time, and he thought about it all the time—so the preposterousness of his preposterous name couldn't fail to strike him as hard as Dempsey had struck Firpo. To be sure, Volodymyr fully appreciated its fine structure and rhythmic quality. Both his first and last names consisted of four syllables, and in both the emphasis was on the third. That, and the rhymed endings, made his name mellifluous. It didn't exactly trip off one's tongue; it flowed off it—not quite like milk and honey, but it flowed nonetheless, perhaps like the smoothly rounded pebbles that recede pell-mell into the ocean with a gentle wave.

What made the name preposterous was something else, and it was obvious to anyone who knew anything about the etymologies of names. Only a Ukrainian would call himself Volodymyr, and only a Jew could be called Frauenzimmer. Things became worse if one understood German, as then there'd be no avoiding the awful realization that Frauenzimmer was an antiquated, and somewhat pejorative, term for woman, or *Frau*. Volodymyr Frauenzimmer was thus Volodymyr the Pejoratively Designated Woman, and the real Volodymyr could hardly take comfort in a name that only radical feminists or medieval historians might admire. His discomfort would only be compounded, much like the return on a long-term municipal bond, when his dyslexic friends transposed the syllables comprising his surname and produced, of all things, *Zimmerfrauen*—or maids—a name that, Volodymyr suspected, even radical feminists could not love.

Volodymyr adopted various strategies for dealing with his preposterous name. At one point in his life he began introducing himself as V.F. and insisted that all his friends and acquaintances call him that as well. Vee-Eff appeared to have the ring of authority; it sounded like a moniker for some fat cat or well-heeled politico. But Vee-Eff worked only for a while, and Volodymyr noticed that something wasn't quite kosher when, one day, a turban-clad Sikh shopkeeper who had always treated him with unnecessarily exaggerated respect appeared sullen and morose. When Volodymyr asked him what the matter was, he replied gruffly (though in that inimitable South Asian sing-song that belied the gruffness and struck Volodymyr as excessively familiar and slightly preposterous), "Do you take me for a carrier of night soil?" Just what that meant Volodymyr didn't quite know, but he could guess that the shopkeeper's feathers had been ruffled and that he had become one sad Sikh.

Vee-Eff also provoked derision among his German friends, who pronounced it Fow-Eff and inquired how much he was being paid by the automobile manufacturer. Americans asked if he was a walking advertisement for a vegetable drink. A pal suggested he try Walter, but that seemed too mundane. Another friend suggested Wally, but that seemed downright silly, if not

Californian. A Russian *droog* proposed he go with Vlad or Vladimir, but Volodymyr tearfully replied, "That would mean turning my back on the essence of my being." Some Jewish chums marveled at Frauenzimmer and urged him to keep it, while others shook their heads in amazement at a name that reeked, as one put it, of "fried onions and boiled kasha." Would Volodymyr considering shortening it? a Finno-Ugric girlfriend named Bobo asked. But Frau or Frauen seemed even more preposterous than Frauenzimmer, and Zimmer—though more commonplace as a last name—produced, when appended to Volodymyr, an extended mumble, *volodimmerzimmer*, that seemed no better than Volodymyr Frauenzimmer. In the end, Volodymyr gave up and decided to accept the name he had, the name he had been given by his mother and by his father.

His parents were another source of deep concern. Volodymyr's mother was Ukrainian, and that accounted for the Volodymyr. And Volodymyr's father was Jewish, and that accounted for the Frauenzimmer. Volodymyr knew little about them, except that she had been a translator for the German Wehrmacht during World War II and that he had been a decorated officer of the Soviet secret police, the NKVD. They apparently met in less than auspicious circumstances, in the Nazi concentration camp at Auschwitz, and either fell in love or did not; in any case, they obviously made love, at least once, and the product of that crossing of both paths and loins was, nine months later, after the guns had stopped booming across Europe, Volodymyr Frauenzimmer. Volodymyr knew one more thing about his parents. His Ukrainian mother hated Jews, while his Jewish father hated Ukrainians. Despite his appreciation of how symmetry could enhance the aesthetic appeal of bad art in general and dreadful architecture in particular, Volodymyr instinctively knew that too much existential symmetry could result in vicious contradictions. He struggled with that dialectic, eventually resolving it by coming to hate the exceptionally great leader. Hating him was one thing; bumping him off was quite another, of course. But as Volodymyr reflected on his long and tortuous road to that fateful decision that struck him like a bolt out of the blue, he knew that his past, or more exactly his parents' past, or more exactly the past, was key to that step.

That road was tortuous, but it was also long and convoluted—comprehensible in its ultimate import only in hindsight as the product of a long and convoluted history. At no step of the way could Volodymyr honestly say that he knew, or even suspected, that developments might lead him to a decision to rub out the exceptionally great leader of an exceptionally great country. Indeed, as Volodymyr thought about that winding road— he liked to imagine it as curving through green meadows and cool forests inhabited by round-eyed does and bushy-tailed rabbits—he understood that nothing could have ever led him to such a course of action. Who was he? A nobody with an odd name. And who was the exceptionally great leader? A powerful man with suntanned friends in all the European capitals, with bank accounts in Zürich and the Cayman Islands, and with spacious villas and armies of silent servants on the Côte d'Azur and Palm Beach. And why should a Ukrainian-Jewish boy with a preposterous name and a twisted personal history feel impelled to knock off the Big Kahuna? *That* was the mystery. Volodymyr's name and parental background obviously had something to do with that decision. But not all. They couldn't have been all. Volodymyr knew that, even when he could construct a satisfying explanatory narrative with a logically connected beginning, middle, and end. History, Volodymyr suspected, was just an *ex post facto* rationalization of the contingent and unexpected. So why shouldn't he construct his own history in the same manner that historians—who actually get paid tidy sums for their measly efforts—do?

There were at least eleven key characters in the story and all had to do with long-past events: his parents (one Jew and one Ukrainian), the Ukrainian Katorga, the half-Russian, half-German, half-Jewish Putschkin, the Russian Dostaevsky, two dead assassins (one Jew and one Ukrainian), their three victims (all Ukrainians), and, of course, the man without a country—Lenin. (Deep down, somewhere in the bowels of his soul, Volodymyr instinctively knew that no story could ever be complete without the intercession of the great Vladimir Ilich—even if, or perhaps especially if, his presence was marked by his conspicuous absence.) These people and their pasts were, Volodymyr decided, the necessary and sufficient conditions of his non-decision to bump off the exceptionally great leader. To the charge that they didn't seem adequate to the causal job, Volodymyr invariably replied, "Who says? It's my history and I'm the only one who can say what's right and what's not." To the charge that an obsession with the past deprived him of what Beaubeau, a Parisian girlfriend with a penchant for betraying her hyperintellectual husband, called agency and subjectivity, Volodymyr countered, "Who says, Bozo? It's my fucking subjectivity and I'm the only one who can say that I'm a fucking agent or not." At that point, his interlocutors would usually abandon their protests—as much from indifference as from defeat and shock at his recourse to street language—and nod sagely. Volodymyr knew quite well that their nods signified nothing, that he had hardly persuaded them. But he didn't care, or at least he never let on that he really cared, which was arguably the same thing in a universe that both seemed to be morally relative and arguably was or was not.

Poor Volodymyr experiences humiliation and confusion piled, relentlessly and unforgivingly, on humiliation and confusion, while still managing to draw a few not wholly inconsequential moral lessons therefrom and thereafter, though definitely, quite definitely, not thereto

Volodymyr knew that assassins, terrorists, gangsters, and hit men were generally much younger than he was. It took not inconsiderable physical and mental agility to plan a hit, and even more to pull it off and make the escape. But, as Volodymyr's latte-sipping American friends never failed to remind him, sixty was the new forty, and Volodymyr not illogically concluded that a forty-something man had just enough experience and just enough maturity to execute a rub-out without looking or feeling too ridiculous. Naturally, feeling too ridiculous was something Volodymyr wanted to avoid at all costs. He already felt ridiculous because of his name, and he had felt ridiculous ever since his early teenage years, when it had dawned on him that Volodymyr Frauenzimmer had to be one of the most ridiculous names the world had ever seen, metaphorically speaking, that is. A dawning was not, he knew, the same as a bolt, but these metaphors didn't strike him as mixed or incompatible; indeed, he took pleasure in the way all the major developments of his life seemed to lend themselves to comparisons with natural phenomena, proof positive, if ever there was such a thing, of the rightness of his determination to rid the world of the exceptionally great leader.

Even worse than the intrinsically weird nature of his name was the ridicule his friends heaped on him. Ukrainians made fun of *Frauenzimmer*. One fat boy who rarely bathed and had a pronounced tendency to release farts at regular intervals taunted him by snickering, "Frauenzimmer, Frauenzimmer, you ain't worth a Cossack glimmer." Volodymyr had no idea what a Cossack glimmer was, and he suspected that it was just a nonsense phrase, but the rhyme hurt, perhaps because the prepubescent girls who congregated like geese on street corners found it sufficiently funny to warrant singing to the latest Alla Pugacheva hit. Jews made fun of *Volodymyr*, and one skinny Hasidic kid with long ear locks and a big black fur hat that he wore even at the beach teased him by saying, "Dimmer, dimmer, Volodymyr, oy vey, oy vey, dimmer, dimmer." That seemed to make a bit more sense, but the girls laughed just as hard, and despite the illogic of their mirth, Volodymyr felt mortified and would usually run home, tearful, snot-nosed, and red-faced.

But running home never helped. Unless occupied with getting seriously soused, Volodymyr's parents were usually casting ingenious invectives at each other—

"Stupid Ukrainian pig!"

"*Dirty kike!*"

"Killer!"

"*Exploiter!*"

"Pogromchik!"

"*Usurer!*"

"Collaborator!"

"*Boot-licker!*"

"Nazi!"

"*Stalinist!*"

"Peasant!"

"*Banker!*"

"Filthy peasant!"

"*Money-grubbing banker!*"

"Vicious anti-Semite!"

"*Rabid Communist!*"

"Fascist scum!"

"*Socialist scum!*"

"Stupid Ukrainian pig!"

"*Dirty kike!*"

—and, as they did so with increasing intensity and decreasing substance in the course of their acrimonious exchanges, their verbal matches would degenerate into endless name-calling that, as dusk turned to nightfall and the birds stopped their chirping, came to resemble a single sound—*youantisemiteyoudirtyjew* or, depending on who started the round, *youdirtyjewyouantisemite*—that, Volodymyr would have loved to have been able to say, resembled the roar of the ocean or the wailing of the wind, but that in reality sounded like nothing more than the histrionics of two meshugge people who obviously had nothing better to do with their lives than to play out, with infinite patience, their mutual hatreds and phobias and traumas. The funny thing was that, in contrast to most long-married couples, for whom alcohol tended to serve as a solvent of their self-restraint and as fuel for the resulting fire, Volodymyr's parents would, after drinking prodigious amounts of whatever happened to be on hand, fall into a dull state and actually stop their name calling. By then, night would have fallen and the poor boy, unable to complete his homework and hiding in the stained bathtub that also doubled as a wash basin, would crawl out and, his flat face as pallid as a worn-out cotton undershirt, slither into bed, but never without saying his prayers.

Alas, praying rarely brought the comfort that Volodymyr so desperately sought. Should he pray to Yahweh or to Christ? Should he pray in Ukrainian or in Yiddish or in Hebrew? A *Hail Mary* seemed too partisan, so he generally eschewed it, unless of course it was Mother's Day or his mother was ill or his father had been particularly abusive. An *Our Father* seemed much better, if only for its obviously patriarchal bent, but the prayer contained sentiments that didn't quite square with Judaism. Should he say the kaddish? Just read some Psalm? Or think of King David? Should he read the Hebrew Bible or the Old Testament? There were no obvious answers to Volodymyr's dilemmas, and, considering that he was just a pimply boy when he first realized that he was fully flummoxed by these questions, his solution—to invent his own prayers and to pray to all the holy people who populated the Bible—seemed wise and irenic and just. Was that when Volodymyr's overdeveloped sense of justice and morality and ethics and history first developed? Was that when he first divined

9

that the only way to combine incompatible things was to subordinate them to some higher notion, one developed by himself for himself? It's at least possible that Volodymyr's eventual non-decision to bump off the exceptionally great leader ultimately traces back to his dialectical resolution of the prayer dilemma. It's also possible that Volodymyr's fascination with the past and with words also had its roots in the first line of Genesis. Volodymyr's love of paradox surely emerged at this time. When bewhiskered Ukrainians said Jews were money-grubbers, Volodymyr would deny the charge and then grab their money. When bewhiskered Hebrews said Ukrainians were vicious anti-Semites, Volodymyr would vehemently say no and then punch them in the face.

Volodymyr's overdeveloped sense of right and wrong was something everyone noticed, if not immediately, then after a few brief conversations or a few large beers. Disinterested observers often remarked that Volodymyr had the sensibility of a Scholastic monk or a Talmudic scholar or a Jesuit missionary, by which they meant that he knew how to split moral hairs when confronted with tough choices. Should he inform the shopkeeper of his friend's theft of candy? Most children would have said yes or no and done just that. Volodymyr agonized for days, as he explored what could have driven his friend to the theft, what if anything could justify it, and what its consequences were likely to be. Little Volodymyr felt confused, but the adults who knew him appreciated that his young mind was trying to cope with essentialist and consequentialist approaches to morality. Small wonder that one family friend, a Polish plumber who had been deported from France for distributing grammatically incorrect anti-American leaflets to the working-class clientele of Les Deux Magots, bought him, for his tenth birthday no less, the complete works of Immanuel Kant and John Stuart Mill. Volodymyr was hoping for a soccer ball, so he threw the books into a corner and completely forget them for some twenty years, but, once he finally retrieved them—on a languorous day when he had slept late after reading Andropov's posthumously published bittersweet memoir, *Lubyanka, O My Lubyanka!*, in one sitting—he remembered the unusual circumstances of the gift and was pleased that the friend's wise choice had paid off—proof positive, if any were needed, that plumbers could be very sensible people, that both essentialism and consequentialism made eminent sense, and that lightning could sometimes strike very, very slowly.

Despite his parents' well-nigh incomprehensible unwillingness to communicate anything about anything at any time, Volodymyr acquires a deep respect for Russia and Germany and an unswerving commitment to the historical truth, the whole historical truth, and nothing but the whole historical truth

It could, at first glance, appear to the casual or uninitiated observer that Volodymyr's childhood was bereft of all amusement, but the reality, in this case as in most cases, was quite different from the surface appearance. Indeed, an obsession with the disjunction between surface appearance and reality, which eventually became one of Volodymyr's primary, even if unstated and arguably unconsciously held, concerns, probably had its origins in this formative period of his life—but not because the disjunction was a reality, but because the disjunction was both surface appearance *and* reality. Despite their detestation of each other, his parents did try, on very occasional occasions at least, to act as run-of-the-mill mothers and fathers do with the little boy, playing games, telling stories, squashing bugs, and teaching him their accumulated life's wisdom. Their ability to bracket their all-consuming hatred of each other and still pursue a more or less ordinary existence was, Volodymyr believed, testimony to their deep love of him—and, of course, to their equally deep hatred of each other. Was it the case, little Volodymyr often asked, that love and hate always go together and, perhaps, even form a useful partnership? There was something decidedly Kantian as well as decidedly utilitarian about this proposition, and, though still unfamiliar with the moral or political philosophy of either the young or old or even middle-aged Marx, little Volodymyr began acquiring his very first inkling—an odd word that would never give him any peace—of just what the dialectic was, of how it worked, and of what it entailed.

Volodymyr's parents had seemingly contradictory, though in fact mutually reinforcing, pedagogical approaches to the child. For reasons that little Volodymyr could not yet fathom—no bolt out of the blue was possible at such a tender age—both focused all their attempts at amusing, educating, and rearing the child on two

11

countries. As much as Volodymyr was beginning to feel the oppressive effects of creeping existential symmetry, he had no choice but to submit to the reality of their obsessions—his father's with Russia and his mother's with Germany. Papasha would turn misty-eyed when he related stories of the great achievements of Russia's great men and the great conquests of Russia's great tsars. Volodymyr could never be quite certain that his father wasn't exaggerating, but, being young, ignorant, and still incapable of judging a book by anything but its cover, he accepted his father's tales as true, even if tallish if not quite tall. Mamochka, meanwhile, would actually break down and cry when she regaled Volodymyr with stories of Deutschland's equally great Kaisers and their equally great achievements. Volodymyr suspected that each parent was, wittingly or not, trying to outdo the other in the fulsomeness of their praise, but he took their enthusiasm in stride, interpreting it solely as the manifestation of a deep and abiding love of greatness. And who could disagree with that? Certainly not an essentialist, for whom greatness was intrinsically great, and certainly not a consequentialist, for whom greatness promised great things.

"Russia," Papasha would intone, his eyes glistening with fanatical exultation and his hairy hand placed firmly on his heart, "is the most beautiful, most wonderful, most just, and most powerful country in the world. There is nothing like it; there has never been anything like it; and there never will be anything like it." When Volodymyr felt a tad peeved by his father's unconditional exaltation of a place he had never seen or been to and questioned his use of so many superlatives, his father would gruffly reply, "How dare you insult Mother Russia, you filthy little kulak? Don't you know that you wouldn't be who you are without her?"

Volodymyr wasn't quite sure what to make of that comment—partly because he wasn't quite sure who he was and mostly because he couldn't possibly imagine just how his being who he was, a preposterous little boy with a preposterous name that always provoked derision from his friends, could possibly be the doing of Mother Russia and just why, if that were indeed the case, it should evoke feelings of awe and wonder and gratitude in him. It was usually then, after Volodymyr turned the other cheek, that his father would relate stories from his life in Russia. "We built socialism in one country, my dear boy," he would say, exhausted from his extended forays beneath Mother Russia's historical skirts. "We brought an end to the past. We transformed the present. We lived in the future." When Volodymyr naively asked how time travel was possible, Papasha would respond with extended declamations of the speeches and writings of the great leaders that made Russia the great mother it was. When Volodymyr wondered how such great things could have been accomplished so quickly, his father would answer, "Lenin was a genius. Stalin was a genius. And you are a fool." At that point, confused and disappointed by his father's lack of faith in his God-given abilities, little Volodymyr would usually turn silent—and not infrequently leave the room and run to his mother.

Mamochka would immediately pounce on the poor boy and say, "Forget Russia, my pet. She is a whore, not a mother. Only Germany is great. Love it—love the Fatherland with your whole heart and your whole soul." When Volodymyr responded to his mother's exhortations by citing all the great Russian achievements extolled by Papasha, she would turn a bright crimson and, barely containing her anger, bark, "That man is a fool, Volodymyr. Russia is nothing. Germany is everything. It is absolutely *über alles*. I've been to both. I know." At that point, Volodymyr's mother would usually embark on ecstatic meditations on the greatness of Germany and its great leaders and, upon completing her *tour d'horizon*, remind Volodymyr that, if it weren't for the *Vaterland*, he wouldn't be who he was. Once again, Volodymyr felt confusion and dismay, wondering just how such greatness could possibly have engendered such smallness. Unbeknownst to him, of course, little Volodymyr was acquiring some of his first lessons in the mismatch between large causes and small effects and, by logical extension, between small causes and large effects. These lessons, as he eventually came to realize, would stand him in good stead in his later life's journey.

The upshot of these stories proved quite unexpected, especially for Volodymyr. His parents hoped only that their boy would acquire a perfectly understandable appreciation of the things they personally held dear—and who could possibly dispute the right of every mother and every father to pass on their values to the fruit of their loins?—but the ultimate consequence of Volodymyr's extended exposure to master narratives about the Mother and the *Vater* and their great offspring turned out to be, as so often happens on the paved road to hell, unintended. Not unexpectedly,

Volodymyr mastered both languages. Rather more unexpectedly, and far more importantly, he came to comprehend what the past was and how it worked. These would appear to be obvious lessons, but only at first glance and only to fools. After all, Volodymyr instinctively knew that he lived in the present. He wasn't sure what the present was, but he knew that it wasn't the future and it wasn't the past. But what exactly was the past was a question that he rarely pondered or even considered until sometime after his prolonged conversations with his parents. It was only then that, having become attuned to the importance of the dead to the lives of the living in such great countries as Russia and Germany, he was able to appreciate that the dead must be important to the lives of the living *always* and *everywhere*, especially to the lives of the insignificant living. It was in this manner that Volodymyr came to acquire a more sophisticated understanding of just what the past was—it was, as paradoxical as it might sound, the lives of the dead—and just how the past affected the present. Great Caesar's ghost, Volodymyr concluded, the dead must be alive in the present! But if that were so, were the living really dead to the past or were the living, like the dead in the present, also alive in the past?

Volodymyr had no idea, *no idea whatsoever*, what the answers to these perplexing questions were or could be, but he knew, or rather sensed somewhere in the depths of his heart, that these questions would never abandon him. As he contemplated the unanswerability of these unanswerable questions, Volodymyr came to appreciate two more things that, as this particular narrative will show, were of enormous importance to the way his life unfolded, the path it took, and the twists and turns it faced along the path it followed. First of all, Volodymyr saw that the answers to all questions, like the answers to these questions, depended on how the questions were formulated. This insight was no mean feat for a boy who barely communicated with his parents and whose primary exposure to the world was mediated by a preposterous name. It was never exactly clear, either to Volodymyr or to those who, like the thoughtful family friend who gave him the complete works of Kant and Mill, knew him well, just when and how he came to appreciate this truth, but no one would dispute that it was a truth the truthfulness of which he genuinely came to value.

To prove the point, Volodymyr would often ask himself simple questions—such as, for instance, "What is your name?"—and try to answer them in a variety of ways, always to discover that a question such as this permitted of one and only one answer, namely, "My name is Volodymyr Frauenzimmer." Or Volodymyr would ask himself, "Is Volodymyr Frauenzimmer a preposterous name?" and, once again, he saw that such a question could be answered only with "Yes, Volodymyr Frauenzimmer is a preposterous name." This insight—into the nature of language and its relationship to the world around him—struck Volodymyr as being of earth-shattering importance. "I understand how the world works!" he once cried upon waking from a moist dream in the middle of the night. "Get the words right, and the rest will always follow." Little did he know that the fetishization of concepts was a grievous ontological error committed many centuries ago by none other than Plato and repeated annually by most of humanity since the venerable Greek philosopher's death. But no matter: the insight proved insightful to Volodymyr, even if it might have been, or then again might not have been, completely wrong, or at least not quite right, or at least not as right as he thought it to be.

The other thing that Volodymyr came to appreciate was that both Russia and Germany were important to him in ways that were quite different from their importance to his parents. Although Mamochka venerated Germany and Papasha worshipped Russia, Volodymyr discovered—while hunting for mushrooms at a summer camp in Rapallo, as a matter of fact—that he neither venerated nor worshipped either country. Not that he didn't want to or couldn't appreciate the intrinsic value and utility of such love. No, the problem was more basic. He simply could not. As much as he tried—and he tried, by jingo, quite a lot—he just couldn't. That said, the Mother and the *Vater* did join in his consciousness to form an indivisible whole—a single family unit in space-time that determined the course of his being independently of his own volition. Russia and Germany dominated his entire existential *Lebenswelt*. They not only filled every nook and cranny and crevice of his present, but they also imposed themselves on every nook and cranny and crevice of his past. "Gadzooks," Volodymyr at one time roared, "I have two sets of parents!" Russia and Germany so thoroughly suffused his consciousness that it seemed to Volodymyr, at least on those days that life appeared to be hopeless

and the preposterousness of his preposterous name weighed on
him with the utmost heaviness, that he *was* Russia and Germany or,
more exactly, that they were him. This was a preposterous
proposition, of course, and he knew it, but that did not, alas,
necessarily make it false.

*Volodymyr's desperate and rather ill-considered attempt to escape grim reality
and find moral certitude in the manly ranks of a grand army exacerbates his
moral quandaries while also hinting at possible solutions that may or may not
be true solutions to anything, and least of all to moral quandaries*

Once Volodymyr reached adulthood—and that happened
when, prodded by his father who knew a good thing when he saw
it, he volunteered to serve in the Russian army—his sense of
morality began to blossom unhindered. And the Russian army,
which seemed like the perfect haven for a young man who couldn't
live with his obstreperous parents, also turned out to be the perfect
place for drawing fine moral distinctions. That was decidedly not
what Volodymyr expected. Whether from naiveté or ignorance or
both, Volodymyr thought that being a soldier would teach him
some basic life skills, enable him to discover his true self, and,
above all, escape from the stifling environment of an alcohol-
sodden and insult-permeated home. That German men, or *Herren*,
called their army a *Heer* also appealed to Volodymyr's fascination,
no doubt engendered by the ambiguities inherent in his own name,
with the fine line that separated gender from sex.
    Volodymyr actually expected the army to simplify his life
and his outlook on life. What complex decisions could one
possibly confront as a simple *russkii* grunt? One took orders, one
executed orders. One did whatever one's sergeants or superior
officers told one to do. If they said do pushups, he'd do pushups.
If they said clean the latrine, he'd clean the latrine. If they ordered
him to run double-time or triple-time or even quadruple-time and
sing the Horst Wessel Song while carrying a knapsack full of
bleached *zek* bones, he'd run double-time or triple-time or even
quadruple-time and sing the Horst Wessel Song while carrying a
knapsack full of bleached *zek* bones. Scholastic monks and
Talmudic scholars and Jesuit missionaries had no place in the army,

which, as he knew from the advertisements, was a *muzhik*'s world. Oh, how wrong he was!

No one at the Hermitage recruitment office had told him, in no uncertain terms at least, that the whole point of his training was to convert him into a killing machine—a fearsome weapon directed against the insubordinate subordinates who dared besmirch Mother Russia's purity and disrupt her composure. In retrospect, Volodymyr was impressed by that word, *convert*. Its obvious religious overtones underscored the actual depth of the change that the army expected him to undergo. It also suggested to him the extent of his resistance to that expected change. Being, or becoming, a machine with respect to the mundane things of life—doing pushups, cleaning the latrine, running double-time—seemed attractive, precisely because it eliminated the element of moral choice from things that could just as easily be viewed as not involving agonizing moral dilemmas as involving them. Why agonize, Volodymyr not unreasonably figured, over things that need not be agonized over? Such an attitude seemed perfectly appropriate, even desirable, as it promised to simplify his life, perhaps even impose some semblance of structure on it, without in any way undermining his fragile sense of moral order.

But Volodymyr drew a line at killing in machine-like fashion. It wasn't the killing itself, especially of cutthroats and hate mongers and historical falsifiers, whether dark-skinned or slant-eyed or round-faced, that troubled him. He could imagine circumstances in which leveling a village or cleansing a town might be necessary or desirable or inevitable, for both essentialist and consequentialist reasons. But to approach killing as a machine seemed fundamentally wrong. One should, he reasoned, be able to look one's enemy in the eyes—indeed, one should *want* to look one's enemy in the eyes—before pulling the trigger. Were one to kill, personalized killing involving moral agonizing seemed the only way to go. Abraham, after all, looked at Isaac as he raised the knife. And David knew that he was aiming at Goliath or, more precisely, at Goliath's forehead, which was really the same thing.

Needless to say, with thoroughly absurd and increasingly humorless thoughts such as these circulating with growing velocity in Volodymyr's mind, he made a very poor soldier indeed. He always did what he was told to do, and in time he developed short-cuts that lent him the aura of efficiency, but he was always just a

17

tad too slow in aiming his rifle, pulling the trigger, or jabbing straw saakashvilis with his bayonet. His superiors invariably regarded that hint of reluctance as insubordination and punished him accordingly. Very quickly Volodymyr became the undisputed barracks leader in cleaning the latrine; he also developed enormous biceps from the daily execution of several rounds of push-ups. In a word, he came to look like a model soldier. Whether or not the officers thought that the appearance of reality would eventually result in actual reality is something Volodymyr never knew. Some of them could read and write blindfolded, but it was hard to see through their steely visages and past their crew cuts and crooked teeth and catch sight, however fleetingly, of genuine human beings able to empathize or sympathize with his existential qualms.

The Moral of the Popcorn and how it got that way and what it means, assuming, of course, that meaning is a meaningful category that is attainable by normal human beings in normal human circumstances, especially with respect to as shockingly empty a signifier as popped corn

Volodymyr's own sense of what a human being was developed progressively, slowly, and without much assistance from most people's primary source of moral norms—parents. As we know, his mother (Ivanna) and his father (Solomon) rarely displayed any awareness of conventional morality in their everyday dealings. Quite the contrary, their eagerness to pour verbal filth on each other seemed limitless to the boy and, later, to the teenager and the man who, unsurprisingly, rarely had the opportunity to spend any quality time with both of them. That probably spared him the pain of witnessing psychologically disturbing outbreaks of structural violence, but it also meant that Volodymyr often had to do the same thing twice, once with each, an experience that initially struck him as reaching dizzying heights of ennui, until he realized that it gave him an unparalleled opportunity to examine the world in all its complexity from two, if not indeed three, completely different vantage points and, thus, perhaps reach something approximating the truth or the half-truth or even the one-third truth.

The down side of this particular up side was that poor Volodymyr would often hear diametrically opposed—even mutually exclusive—views on things, which, despite or because of their symmetry, precluded reconciliation or complementarity. There was, for instance, the time the family traveled to Brussels, with both parents occupying separate compartments in separate wagons and the poor boy shuttling between one and the other every thirty minutes. The procedure, while initially amusing and adventuresome—especially as Volodymyr observed the snaking tracks disappear beneath his little feet as he scampered from car to car—became tiresome after five rounds. Worse, Volodymyr's increasingly inebriated parents would become aggressive if he left too soon or arrived too late and—since Volodymyr had by then come to appreciate that physical objects required time to travel through physical space—he had no choice but to bow to nature's laws and either leave a few minutes before the thirty had expired or arrive a few minutes after the thirty had begun. Either way, one or both parents found his behavior infuriating and unbecoming for a child of Mother Russian or *Vater* German aspirations if not quite pedigree.

Fortunately, the train ride did eventually end and, after his parents checked into separate rooms in separate hotels in diametrically opposed parts of town, each declared a desire to show Volodymyr the great art in the National Museum. That's when his troubles really began. Volodymyr was certain that the inscription identified the canvas as David's painting of the dead Marat, but Papasha insisted that the figure was actually Lenin—draped over his tub, quill in hand, towel wrapped around his head, a smile on his face—in the aftermath of the Bolshevik seizure of the Winter Palace. In turn, Volodymyr's mother claimed that the figure was General Ludendorff, before the Great War, and that he wasn't really dead, only asleep—a habit he had apparently picked up during the Franco-Prussian War, when one dozed off where and when one could. Another painting, ostensibly by Magritte, was, his father said, really by Ilya Glazunov, and the dark street with dark houses and lighted street lamps and the bright afternoon sky was not an excellent example of Surrealism, but a socialist-realist depiction of Leningrad, a beautiful socialist city on which the sun never set and indeed had, since the time of Stalin, never dared to set. Mamochka then informed him that the painting was really of Thierschstrasse in Munich, home of the Führer-to-be in the twenties, and that the painter was—she lowered her voice several decibels—none other than you know who.

Unlike their neighbors, the Frauenzimmers didn't go to the beach or on picnics or even to the movies. One might have imagined that sitting together in a dark theatre could hardly provoke any altercations, but, *mirabile dictu*, it did. The popcorn inevitably became the bone of contention. If Ivanna held it, she'd never give any to Solomon. If Solomon held it, he'd never give any to Ivanna. And if the boy held it, neither parent would dare extend a hand lest it touch the other's buttery fingers and provoke a fit of revulsion of the sort one might feel upon stepping on a dead toad while walking barefoot in a dewy glen. Purchasing three bags of popcorn cost too much and, although a reasonable logistical solution to the problem, was out of the question. The moral of the popcorn—in an inspired moment, Volodymyr later came to refer to it with capital letters as the Moral of the Popcorn—wasn't lost on Volodymyr. Some of his unemployed Left Bank friends insisted that everything was political; Volodymyr knew from that and many other bitter lessons that everything was moral—more or less, of course, and most of the time, of course—and that all moral questions had no adequate answers, alas.

One day, as Volodymyr was hiking in the vineyards outside Volgograd, he experienced an epiphany—or, to put it in the language he might have preferred, a bolt out of the blue. It came to him—with the suddenness that the sight of the burning bush must have struck Moses—that the answers he was so desperately seeking—to life, to existence, to the universe—could not possibly be found outside himself. The Moral of the Popcorn was valid not because others believed in it, but because it made sense of life to Volodymyr. And, notwithstanding the morally relativist implications of such a stance, it would remain valid as a moral compass even if it made sense *only* to Volodymyr. When all was said and done, he remained, *mirabile dictu*, Volodymyr Frauenzimmer and no one else. Volodymyr understood that applying the Moral of the Popcorn to life meant embarking on a long and tortuous journey—perhaps through verdant meadows and cool forests inhabited by frolicking fauna or perhaps through arid grasslands and parched deserts inhabited only by wicked scorpions and slothful camels—to nothing less and nothing more than something as absurd and hackneyed as, of all things, *self-discovery*—

assuming of course that there was indeed such a thing as the self and that, even if there were, it could be discovered and not, say, imagined or invented or constructed or, heaven forbid, deconstructed.

Chapter 2

Volodymyr learns what may or may not be but, in all likelihood, probably is or could very well be the truth about the two people—his mother and father, of course—who made him who he is or, just as possibly, who he isn't

Despite being awe-struck and befuddled by the contradictions inherent in life, Volodymyr wonders about the origins of his species and, while stumbling over or upon the power of language, comes to appreciate that bad words, like all words, are above all sounds and nothing else, or almost nothing else

Volodymyr often wondered how his parents met and whether there was ever any love between them. They never talked about their past—indeed, they never talked about the past, thereby effectively asserting that it was dead and gone and unalterable and best forgotten—and, when they hinted at the possibility that the present wasn't quite all there was to the universe, it was invariably in an evasive manner that suggested they had something—perhaps some dark and sinister secret?—to hide. Volodymyr knew that Mamochka had collaborated with the German army; she would occasionally, but only very occasionally, speak with some wistfulness about handling a gun or throwing a grenade or distributing leaflets in the fight for *das neue Europa*. Volodymyr also knew that Papasha had served in the Soviet secret police, the NKVD; he rarely spoke about his exploits in the People's Commissariat of Internal Affairs except to emphasize, usually after having had too much pepper vodka to drink, that someone had to do the hard work of breaking eggs to build socialism.

Volodymyr also knew that, somehow, in a way that remained opaque to all his attempts at understanding, both his parents had ended up in the concentration camp in Auschwitz. How they had met, indeed how they could possibly have met, was a question to which neither had ever even hinted at an answer. For a long time Volodymyr just assumed that they had been inmates and that their paths had crossed—perhaps after traversing some luscious glade?—and they had fallen in love. Perhaps they had met in the canteen? Or in the showers? Or while tending to the sparse lawns that adorned the dull brown barracks? And if their paths had truly crossed, wasn't it the case that—given the way paths are constructed, as the shortest distance between two points—they *had* to cross and that his parents' meeting in Auschwitz was therefore as unavoidable as his being the product of that fateful—yes, alas, *fateful*—encounter?

At some point—Volodymyr couldn't remember the exact second or minute or even hour, but he suspected he might, if pressed, be able to pinpoint the year—he became disabused of the notion that they had fallen in love. They had clearly had sex, at least once, but the intemperate behavior both displayed toward each other, from the earliest time Volodymyr could remember, hardly testified to *le grand amour* and seemed to suggest that love had never been part of the equation. It was possible, he supposed, that what had once been a passionate, all-consuming, and desperate *Liebe* had simply burned out and then, as sometimes happens in such cases, in fiction and films and possibly also in real life, had transmogrified into its opposite—a deep and terrible and unconditional hatred. Perhaps yin had become yang, up had become down, topsy had become turvy, and zig had become zag?

How that transformation could have occurred and when were questions Volodymyr couldn't even begin to answer, except in the most banal sense—that is, sometime after his parents met and sometime before his memory retained the first fleeting images of their incessant brawling. That was the exact word that defined their relationship. They brawled, like two drunken sailors who spoke mutually incomprehensible languages and who, after spending all their money on excessive amounts of cheap rum, lashed out blindly at each other, for no other ostensible reason than that both happened to be in the wrong place at the wrong time. Was there no other way to understand his parents except with recourse to stale metaphors, stale smells, and even staler images? Volodymyr was distressed as much by the banality of how he imagined his parents as by their putatively real behavior.

And could love even be possible between a Nazi anti-Semite and a Stalinist anti-Ukrainian? Could a stupid peasant love a dirty kike? And could a dirty kike love a stupid peasant? Volodymyr knew the conventional wisdom, but that hardly helped. If opposites really attracted, then there was every reason to believe that his parents might have fallen in love precisely because they had hated each other's putative national characters—notwithstanding all the cautionary words that modern experts had to say about the imagined or invented nature of such characters. Perhaps his mother had once said to his father, "I love you, because I hate Jews and you are a Jew." And perhaps his father had then replied, "And I love you, because I despise all Ukrainians and you are a Ukrainian." And perhaps they had then spat at each other, hit each other until their noses and lips bled, and fallen into each other's arms.

It was also possible that their love was so powerful as to overcome all their hatreds. After all, Volodymyr had been told that love conquers all—so why shouldn't it also conquer the passions of a Jew-hater and the passions of a Ukrainian-hater? Although possible, this version struck Volodymyr as rather more implausible than the first. Besides, it seemed too pat, too stereotypical, too much in conformity with the canned expectations of an inauthentic age in which fade-outs and extended embraces were the only appropriate denouements to human dramas. And then, of course, it was also possible that they had no inkling—again that awful word!—of their national backgrounds. One's primary concern in concentration camps was survival. Who cared who was what? But that didn't make sense either. If his father wore a yellow star, his mother couldn't fail to have seen it. And even if she had—perhaps her eyesight was bad or perhaps the midday sun always cast a dark shadow on his father's sunken chest—neither could have failed to notice that they spoke different languages or the same languages with different accents.

And then there was the damned question of language. Volodymyr's mother cast her insults only in Russian and Yiddish, while his father cast his only in German and Ukrainian. Volodymyr knew that they spoke and understood all four languages, as, on those rare occasions that they weren't inebriated and showed some tenderness to the boy, they sometimes betrayed their linguistic versatility and sang songs, told stories, or used expressions in the other parent's preferred tongues. Why a Ukrainian collaborator and anti-Semite should have preferred to speak Russian and not Ukrainian, and why a Jewish secret police officer and anti-Ukrainian should have preferred to speak German and not Russian were questions that mystified Volodymyr. He suspected that some deep secrets, bizarre twists, and incomprehensible post-postmodernist inversions accounted for these curious linguistic turns. When he asked his parents directly, they always replied with silence or laughter or anger, and very quickly he understood that there was no point in probing and that he'd have to discover the truth on his own.

That proved to be a terribly difficult undertaking—partly because the truth was buried under so many layers of meaningless words, evasive behaviors, discursive devices, bad puns, humorless allusions, tasteless analogies, and repressed emotions, but mostly because Volodymyr soon discovered that his own complex personality stood in the way of a single-minded pursuit of the truth. There was, first, that troubling obsession with morality and the moral dimensions of everything, and especially of history. Volodymyr knew that, if the simple life of a soldier only reinforced his moral qualms, the active exploration of the past lives of his parents would be tantamount to running backwards blindfolded through a moral minefield. There was, second, his extreme sensitivity to language, to words and their meanings—a sensitivity that, he suspected, could easily be tested and made raw by repeated confrontations with lies, prevarications, hyperbole, onomatopoeia, metaphors, synecdoches, zeugmas, and awkwardly expressed sentiments. There was, third, his preposterous name, about which more than enough has already been said. And then there was, finally, his divided personality. Volodymyr knew that he was, at the end of the day, when all is said and done, and when the dust settles, the apple that didn't fall far from the tree—in his case, two trees. He was the Jew who was Ukrainian. He was the Ukrainian who was Jewish. He was, in sum, both perfectly symmetrical and perfectly contradictory.

While appreciating the seductiveness and utility of symmetry, Volodymyr had devoted little thought to the dialectic and just a tad more to contradictions. Notwithstanding this gaping lacuna in his knowledge, he was damned sure he had them in spades. As a matter of fact, it initially shocked him to discover that he could actually cheer himself up—especially when he felt tired or depressed or despairing—by engaging in ecstatic bouts of the mutual name-calling that his parents pursued on those exceedingly rare, and with time always rarer, occasions that their paths crossed (whether inevitably or serendipitously or just coincidentally, in the kitchen or living room, of course, and not, obviously, in meadows or valleys or deserts or glens):

"Stupid Ukrainian pig!"
"*Dirty kike!*"
"Killer!"
"*Exploiter!*"
"Pogromchik!"
"*Usurer!*"
"Collaborator!"
"*Boot-licker!*"
"Nazi!"
"*Stalinist!*"
"Peasant!"
"*Banker!*"
"Filthy peasant!"
"*Money-grubbing banker!*"
"Vicious anti-Semite!"
"*Rabid Communist!*"
"Fascist scum!"
"*Socialist scum!*"
"Stupid Ukrainian pig!"
"*Dirty kike!*"

The truly amazing thing was that, as Volodymyr one day realized, if these words were repeated with careful attention to rhythm and cadence and sound, they resembled poetry and their effect approximated a drug-induced trance that transported him to higher levels of reality. And who if not someone with a name such as Volodymyr Frauenzimmer—a name that flowed, like smoothly rounded pebbles that receded pell-mell into the ocean with a gentle wave—could parlay that trance-like state into a deep appreciation of the rhythmic substratum of humanity's existence or the benign indifference of the universe?

Pushed by the force of logic to think the unthinkable, Volodymyr wonders about a family rendezvous that was no picnic in a place that was either hell or a hellhole, but in either case no place for either a rendezvous or a picnic

The question that most perturbed Volodymyr was this: How could his parents have possibly met and procreated in a Nazi death camp? As little as they had told him about their lives before and after their paths crossed and their lives intersected in that godforsaken place, both had, on separate occasions, confirmed that Volodymyr had indeed been conceived in Auschwitz. Once, his mother, losing her temper after Volodymyr committed some indiscretion involving his toy soldiers and her brassiere, threatened to send him back to Oświęcim, "where the devil brought you to life." Little Volodymyr paid scant attention to that particular locution at the time, but it lodged itself in his memory and later, while listening to the Young Yevtushenkos sing of unrequited teenage love in Novgorod, he heard what sounded like—but obviously couldn't have been—the word *devil* and that immediately, and almost magically, brought to mind Mamochka's beet-red face, hot breath, threatening fist, dirty fingernails, and angry words. It was then, as it dawned on him that he must have been conceived among drafty wooden barracks and sturdy brick crematoria, that Volodymyr experienced what may have been his first bolt out of the blue.

On another occasion, as his father sat near the fireplace in a state of almost complete stupefaction, with several bottles of lemon vodka strewn about his unwashed feet, Volodymyr watched him glare in the direction of the kitchen, where his mother was busy drinking scotch, and mutter, "You created a hell worse than Auschwitz." That comment wasn't exactly conclusive proof of anything, but it did place Papasha in the same camp in which, according to Mamochka, he—Volodymyr, that is—had been conceived. Q.E.D., thought Volodymyr: Auschwitz is where they made love and Auschwitz is where they made me.

But how could they have met and made love in a death camp? The women were housed separately from the men, and the Jews were housed separately from the Ukrainians. His parents couldn't have been simple inmates. They had to have performed some functions or played some roles that enabled them to leave their areas of immediate confinement and not only meet, but also have enough time—and privacy?—to engage in the sexual act. Volodymyr knew from personal experience—his girlfriends were always as ready to give as to take—that the act required little time. Some minimal disrobing, some tentative groping, perhaps a kiss or two, and then the inevitable squirts and grunts and sighs, followed by the adjustments in the clothes, the disengagement, the turned-away faces, the backs of hands wiping the sweat from foreheads. One minute seemed too little, but five or six seemed perfectly doable. Presumably, regular inmates wouldn't have had even one minute of privacy. To have had five or six bespoke exalted status in the camp hierarchy.

There was no avoiding it: his parents must have served as cooks or guards or servants or—what did one call those inmates who helped clean the gas chambers and remove the corpses? Did they make love in the kitchen? The latrine? Or did they make love at the foot of the barbed wire fences and guard towers or— Volodymyr had to shudder at the thought—in the shadow of the gas chambers? Considering the venom with which they expressed their hatred of each other, Volodymyr realized that so deep a detestation could be explained only by some especially traumatic event that implicated both to an equal degree. Making love in Auschwitz was arguably just that kind of event. On the other hand, that act also gave life to Volodymyr. That might prove, he concluded, that evil could give rise to good—a small victory, perhaps, for consequentialist morality and its insistence that the road to heaven could be paved with bad intentions—but it didn't get his parents off the intentionalist moral hook. They had collaborated and they had violated the sanctity of a place in which a miserable death and quiet resistance were the only dignified forms of life. Was this the first time that the Moral of the Popcorn had proven true beyond the confines of his claustrophobic existence?

Having come to this sobering conclusion, Volodymyr had no choice but to investigate just how his parents had come to be in Auschwitz. He could guess how they survived it. With their privileged status, they would have been better fed and better housed and less likely to fall victim to execution or extermination or illness. He could also guess why they had decided to stay in each other's presence after being released. His father wouldn't have trusted his mother not to inform on him to the Soviets or to the Allies, and his mother wouldn't have trusted his father not to do the same. As slaves of the symmetry that ruled their lives, they were fated to be together, to live together, and to pretend they had a family together, because the alternative would have spelled death. Volodymyr had to smile when he realized that they had left hell only to reconstruct it at home.

This terrible irony sustained Volodymyr in the many months he devoted to exploring his parents' earthly existence. He rummaged through cardboard suitcases, dented tins, dusty boxes, the backs of drawers; he leafed through every book they possessed; he examined every photograph, every item they kept on mantelpieces and bookshelves, and every souvenir, even the paperweights. He unglued photos from the black pages of their albums and deciphered the scribbles on their backs. He removed the soles and heels from all their shoes and boots and carefully fingered the lining of all their coats. He copied every name in their address books and tracked down and interviewed every person. He read all the books he could find in the libraries. On several occasions he visited archives. At times he felt like a scholar, at other times like an investigative journalist, and still at others like a spy. After several years and some months, he had completed all the research there was to complete. He could think of no other sources, no other libraries, no other archives to examine. He had every relevant and irrelevant fact, he had compiled as complete a picture of his parents' lives as was possible, and he probably knew more about them than they knew themselves. And still the picture remained woefully incomplete. Their history had holes and gaps and lacunae galore and they ranged in size from tiny crevices to grand canyons. Even so, amid all these perforated lines, empty spaces, and fuzzy outlines, they had left a trail, a faint and barely visible trail that was just clear enough to reveal who they had been before their rendezvous in Auschwitz. And what Volodymyr could not learn he could reconstruct or guess at, which, as his research and ruminations had persuaded him, is what respectable historians, cultural critics, book reviewers, gurus, and other truth-seekers did anyway.

Volodymyr retraces his father's rocky road from Odessa to Auschwitz and is amazed to learn that, despite what seems like inevitability in hindsight, it was the product of multiple coincidences, juxtapositions, and serendipities and a variety of portentous moral, personal, and political choices

Solomon Isaakovich Frauenzimmer was born in Odessa a year or two before the Revolution of 1905. His father was a tailor; his mother kept the books, measured the ladies and especially their bosoms and hips, and generally helped run the small shop in a crooked street off one of the leafy boulevards. Solomon was one of five children, three boys and two girls, all raised in line with strict patriarchal traditions and progressive socialist ideals. Solomon's father, Isaak, disliked the Bundists and distrusted the Zionists, and young Solomon appears to have come under his influence rather more than any of his siblings. Sometime after the Revolution of 1917 and the Civil War that followed, the pink-faced Solomon joined the Red Army and took part in military campaigns against the Russian Whites and the Ukrainian nationalists. Had he already joined the Bolsheviks by then or was he only a sympathizer? Did he even shave? Volodymyr liked to think that his father served in the same cavalry unit as Isaac Babel, but he had no way of knowing whether that might be true. In any case, Solomon fought bravely against the Russian generals, Denikin and Wrangel, and he also fought against the Ukrainians, Petliura and Skoropadsky. His unit or units probably crisscrossed Ukraine many times in the course of the war. Volodymyr guessed that he must have witnessed a multitude of pogroms, massacres, murders, shootings, and annihilations. He received three wounds—a bullet in his right shoulder, a whip lash across his back, and a saber cut on his thigh—and emerged from the bloodletting with a position of authority. Did he stay in the army or had he made the move to the Cheka, the secret police?

Once the fighting had ended, Solomon, by then in his early twenties, took a job with the Commissariat of Internal Affairs in Kyiv. Whether he was an analyst, an organizer, or an active agent was unclear. In contrast, his elder brother, Moishe, took advantage of the New Economic Policy to found a profitable business as a Nepman, buying grain from Ukrainian peasants and selling it to Russian and Jewish workers in Odessa. Volodymyr found a yellowing and crumpled letter from some family member hinting at a feud between Moishe and Solomon and implying that Solomon had been wrong to reject his brother. Volodymyr suspected that his father, by then a true believer in communism, must have found his brother's entrepreneurial activities suspiciously akin to a capitalist deviation and had broken all ties with him. It was at about this time as well that both parents passed away, and it was certainly possible that the grief Solomon experienced over their deaths combined with his ideological devotion to Leninism to produce the uncompromising spirit that led him to turn his back on his sibling. Moishe was arrested for commercial crimes in 1934, and Volodymyr had to wonder whether Solomon hadn't denounced him.

By the late twenties and early thirties, Solomon's career in the NKVD had taken off. Exactly why no one knew, but Volodymyr surmised that Solomon had sided with Stalin. Volodymyr failed to uncover just what his father did, but he did succeed in identifying some of the cities, towns, and villages in which he had been stationed, and from the pattern that emerged it seemed clear that he had been assigned to oversee the forced collectivization of the Ukrainian countryside. It was in late 1932 and early 1933, in particular, that Solomon worked in a string of villages in Kharkiv and Poltava provinces—the very areas where a massive famine had convinced millions of peasants to abandon the earthly class struggle and give up the proverbial ghost. Where Solomon was stationed and what he did in the late thirties remained a complete blank spot, but Volodymyr could guess that surviving the purges and the Terror meant that Solomon had sided with the victors in the secret police and, above all, with Stalin. Volodymyr found no evidence of his father's having been arrested, so he concluded that Solomon must have done the arresting. Had his faith in the cause been shaken or strengthened? Did he doubt the wisdom of the great leader or had he sacrificed whatever qualms he might have had to the preparation of communist omelettes? Volodymyr imagined his father taking part in Communist Party congresses and applauding endlessly, the veins on his sweaty forehead pulsating, as the Generalissimo rose to the podium to inspire the masses and their humble servants.

How did Solomon greet the Molotov-Ribbentrop Non-Aggression Pact? Probably in the fashion that the Party demanded—as a strategic masterstroke. Whatever the case, it was in early 1940 that he was transferred to what had formerly been eastern Poland and was now western Ukraine. Volodymyr was able to find several old Jews who testified to his father's having served in Lwów-turned-Lviv, where his job consisted in rooting out anti-Soviet elements from within the Jewish Bund and the Polish intelligentsia. By late 1940, Solomon had been reassigned to a small town, some forty miles south-east of Lwów-turned-Lviv, that was known as a hotbed of the Ukrainian nationalist movement. One Ukrainian living in Detroit, who had sympathized with the Soviets and had served as an informer in his youth, told Volodymyr that Solomon had been his liaison with the secret police. That elderly gentleman, a retired automobile worker who had managed to conceal his collaborationist past by masquerading as a community leader, also said that Solomon had served as an officer in the local prison. Having helped pack off Jews and Poles to Siberia, he supervised the arrests of scores of Ukrainians in 1940 and 1941. They were all massacred immediately after Nazi Germany attacked the Soviet Union on June 22, 1941. Solomon then escaped east with the retreating Soviet forces, eventually joined the partisans, and, sometime in 1943 or 1944, was captured and, as a Jew, shipped off to Auschwitz.

Why did Solomon come to hate Ukrainians? Perhaps because he experienced anti-Semitism as a boy? Perhaps because he saw Ukrainians committing pogroms in 1919 or 1920? Perhaps because Ukrainian peasants resisted communism and had to be starved into submission in the Great Famine of 1933—possibly by Solomon himself? Volodymyr suspected that outrage and guilt could form a powerful combination: the former would justify hating Ukrainians, while the latter would require hating them. Was Solomon's insistence on speaking only German and Ukrainian a symptom of this outrage and a way of expunging his feelings of guilt? Volodymyr saw that his father was a ruthless and bloodthirsty, if also idealistic and dedicated, man who shied away neither from the gratuitous application of violence to his inferiors nor from the slavish pursuit of favor from his superiors. The profile fit perfectly the concentration camp inmate who would have done everything to ingratiate himself with the authorities in order to survive. But Papasha was also a true believer; that much was clear. Whatever his sins, he appeared to be sincere in his commitment to the version of the *Götterdämmerung* composed by Stalin. Volodymyr imagined that his father's life must have been a daily struggle with two irreconcilable tendencies—killing for no reason versus killing for some reason—a struggle that would have worn him down and destroyed him even if he had never met his nemesis, Volodymyr's mother.

Volodymyr retraces his mother's road from Lemberg-not-yet-Lwów to Auschwitz and, unsurprisingly, finds confirmation for his hunch that

inevitability is just another word for retroactively interpreted happenstance
spiced up by a choice or two of little actual consequence
to the narrative explanation

Ivanna Kolomijska was born in Lemberg-not-yet-Lwów in 1909 or 1910. Her father, Ignacy Kolomijskyj, was a distinguished lawyer who specialized in property claims and land rights—two issues that troubled the perpetually quarrelsome peasantry and proved to be the source of a neat annual income—and played a bit role in the movement to establish an independent Western Ukrainian People's Republic, after the Austro-Hungarian Empire fell apart in late 1918. Volodymyr couldn't find Ignacy's name on any official documents, but he did encounter it in some newspaper accounts of the perpetual intra-governmental feuds that plagued the nascent state. How ironic, Volodymyr thought, that Ignacy should have made his money off disputatious peasants and lost his livelihood among disputatious would-be state builders. Ivanna was an only child—Volodymyr could only assume that the marriage was an unhappy one—and her mother, also named Ivanna, devoted much of her free time to teaching teenage peasant girls how to clean house, knit white socks, and avoid pregnancy and venereal disease.

The Republic collapsed ignominiously and, after some impecunious meanderings throughout Poland and Austria, the family finally settled in Paris, where they stayed for over five years. Volodymyr imagined they lived the typical exile's life of penury and politics somewhere on the Left Bank, perhaps even in the Latin Quarter where many Ukrainian émigrés sought refuge in the cheap hotels that, to the delight only of anarchists and Dadaists, smelled of human excrement, sour wine, and unwashed handkerchiefs. Ignacy found employment with a newspaper, *Tryzub*, or Trident, published by the nationalist leader, Simon Petliura, and his supporters. His wife appears to have worked on the Île de la Cité in an *institut de beauté* as a hair stylist—an enormous step down on the social ladder that could only have worsened her relations with her strait-laced husband. Or did she find some comfort in rubbing shoulders with genuine working women, the ones she had championed in her comfortable home in Lwów-not-yet-Lviv? Volodymyr doubted it, but one never could tell.

Their simple world was shattered in 1926, when Sholom Schwartzbard, a Jew from Bessarabia, assassinated Petliura on the corner of the Rue Racine and the Boulevard Saint Michel, shooting five bullets into his torso and crying, *"Canaille!"* Volodymyr's mother would have been old enough to know about the killing and the subsequent trial and exoneration of Schwartzbard in 1927. An impressionable young girl, with a strong-willed father who taught her patriotism, might, Volodymyr surmised, easily have viewed the shooting as an act of violence by Jews against Ukrainians. Her French would have been good enough for her to read the newspaper accounts of the trial and the clever way in which Schwartzbard's quick-footed defense attorney managed to convert the proceedings into a trial *of* Petliura and a condemnation of the pogroms that swept Ukraine under his rule. And she would certainly have been able to read the outraged Ukrainian accounts that denied the imputations of anti-Semitism and claimed that Schwartzbard was really a dupe in the pay of the Kremlin.

Then, for reasons that Volodymyr could not uncover, the family returned to Lwów-not-yet-Lviv, sometime in the late twenties. Ignacy found a job in a distinguished German law firm, his wife resumed her activities on behalf of Ukrainian peasant women, and Ivanna immersed herself in university studies. Volodymyr found records of her courses, almost all in law. She was, apparently, following in her father's footsteps. Then, suddenly, her name appeared on a list of university students protesting the violent Polish "pacification" of Ukrainians in 1930. She appeared again in the memoirs of one of the nationalists involved in the assassination in central Warsaw of the Polish Minister of Interior Bronisław Pieracki in 1934. She had abandoned her studies—Volodymyr could only smile at the consternation with which his grandparents must have greeted that decision—and joined the terrorist wing of the nationalist movement. Volodymyr found his mother's name in one study by an obscure Polish academic, who suggested that she served as liaison between underground cells and devoted herself to organizing patriotic village girls—a nice way, Volodymyr thought, of combining both parents' passions. In 1937, she was captured and sentenced to three years' imprisonment. The fall of Poland in 1939 evidently led to her release, but rather than staying in Soviet-occupied western Ukraine, she found refuge in Berlin and mastered German in a special language school run by the Gestapo.

Another memoirist, this time a former German intelligence officer, mentioned what could have been Ivanna—providing only her first name and an accurate description of her physical appearance—in reference to a training camp for collaborators run by the counterintelligence service, the Abwehr, in Danzig. A Ukrainian socialist claimed that the Germans also trained the Ukrainians in torture, even suggesting they applied their gruesome methods to prisoners, both Communists and Jews. Was *this* what his mother had also learned? After the invasion, Ivanna served briefly as a translator for the Wehrmacht in a small town near Lviv-no-longer-Lvov—until the Gestapo and the SS cracked down on the Ukrainian nationalists who had hoped Germany would give them independence and packed them off to concentration camps. His mother, though innocent of any involvement in the nationalist underground, was caught in the dragnet and, guilty by association if not by intent, was unceremoniously dumped in Auschwitz. Volodymyr imagined that, at that point, her hatred of Jews would have reached its apogee. She must have witnessed the uncovering of the mass graves containing the Ukrainian inmates murdered by the NKVD. And, like so many Ukrainians, she probably concluded that the Jews who welcomed Soviet rule in 1939 by reputedly kissing Russian tanks were at fault—and hence that all Jews were at fault.

Volodymyr could see that Mamochka was just like Papasha—prone both to violence and to idealism. They were birds of a feather. Small wonder that she survived four years in Auschwitz. Volodymyr decided that she must have served as a guard, a position that would have necessitated her being especially coldblooded and unsparing in her ruthlessness. She probably informed on, brutalized, and possibly even killed inmates—Jews, Poles, and her fellow Ukrainians. The source of her own brutalization must have been her hatred of Jews, the product, apparently, of her shock at Petliura's assassination and the massacres of prisoners in 1941. Small wonder as well that her life would have been unlivable, being subject to the same contradictory impulses experienced by his father. Their meeting in Auschwitz may have been a perfect accident of history, but Volodymyr could see that it was also inevitable, a predetermined conclusion to the logic of two separate lives and two existential paths that had to intersect in a Nazi concentration camp. His own birth was, then, just as inevitable. And, he wondered, just as contradictory and just as doomed?

Chapter 3

In what may seem to unimaginative readers like an unjustified departure from the master narrative, Volodymyr meets the lovely, if unfortunately named, Katorga, who seduces him, praises his poetry, and, in a *coup de grâce*, introduces him to her hero, Sholom Schwartzbard

Volodymyr's serendipitous decision to attend a world-class gathering of minds in East Berlin has unexpectedly interesting consequences that, despite some possible pitfalls, point him in a direction that seems right, though, on closer inspection, might actually only be half-right or, for that matter, even quite wrong

It happened this way. One day, mid-way between Passover and Easter, Volodymyr received a thick envelope in the mail. Much to his surprise, it turned out to be an invitation to East Berlin for a conference organized by the Molotov-Ribbentrop League for the Advancement of International Peace. Evidently, someone in Moscow had read his works—Volodymyr's, that is, and not Molotov's or Ribbentrop's, although theirs would surely be worth reading, both as texts *an sich* and as texts in contexts—and decided that he was pro-peace and anti-war. As Volodymyr knew for a fact that he was neither anti-peace nor pro-war, he overcame his reservations about the quality of his thin volume of post-Marxist haikus and decided to accept the League's unusually generous offer of an all-expenses paid junket to the proletarian paradise that surrounded the outpost of imperialism, West Berlin.

The German Democratic Republic had become a shade shabbier than he remembered, but as shabby elegance of the kind he had encountered in the Hotel Metropole in Prague or the old Roosevelt in Manhattan had always struck him as aesthetically pleasing, Volodymyr thoroughly enjoyed the seven days of traipsing up and down the socialist nooks and communist crannies of the workers' state. The League and its fellow travelers finally settled in the Hotel Mauer des Friedens on East Berlin's magnificent main drag, Unter den Galgen. There were seventeen of them, a few genuine peaceniks, a few poets and writers, a few peace researchers from Scandinavia and the other Germany, a few journalists, a few foundation officers, and Volodymyr.

The conference was held in the Palast der Brüderschaft, a glistening brown glass structure that curiously complemented the other buildings, mostly pompous pre-socialist palaces, on the square commemorating the global proletariat's many resounding victories. The tables were arranged in a slightly imperfect square, an embarrassed plant with large drooping leaves occupied the center, bottles of Prague Spring mineral water, Pepsi, and Fanta were grouped every four or five feet, and rows of neon lights were arrayed above like the contending armies in the Battle of Poltava. The chairman greeted them in the name of the people. Someone cheered, the rest applauded, and he then delivered a detailed peroration on the prospects for change, the challenges of peace, the need for new thinking, the continued relevance of old thinking, détente, rapprochement, the horrors of war, the imminence of peace, the correlation of forces, the global class struggle, and the inevitability of socialism. A few more greetings followed his—the League's president sang a glowing encomium to the eternal friendship between the German and Russian peoples—and the participants then broke for what promised to be a lavish lunch at the Pyongyang Delight all-you-can-eat buffet on the top floor of the Palast. Still feeling sated by his unusually large breakfast of lox, pickled herring, black bread, and croissants and strawberry jam, Volodymyr decided to have a Wurst and beer at one of the stands outside and broke away from the group as they headed for the elevator.

An attractive woman of about thirty or forty or fifty approached him with a quizzical expression on her face.

"Do you have the time?" she asked.

"*Ja*," Volodymyr replied, and showed her his watch.

"Swiss," she remarked. "You are not from here. First time?"

They talked of his impressions of East Berlin, and as Volodymyr finished his snack, returned the beer bottle, and was about to say, "*Auf Wiedersehen*," she offered to show him the town.

"Perhaps tonight?" she smiled. "I know these conferences. They will not miss you and you will be glad to get away."

Guided by the knowledgeable Katorga, Volodymyr walks, ambles, and strolls in the forgotten spaces between East and West and discovers by-gone eras covered with a thin film of time and a thick film of grime, which, upon closer inspection, might even have been the very same film

Katorga was waiting at the entrance to the Soviet Embassy wearing a billowing red skirt, a silken black blouse with gold trim, and a broad-rimmed straw hat.

"Have you been to Prenzlauer Berg?" she asked. Volodymyr said no. "Then I will show you the real Berlin," she said.

They walked up Unter den Galgen and across Alexanderplatz and veered left along unevenly paved streets lined with soot-gray buildings with small balconies, satellite dishes, and clothes lines. They passed a Jewish cemetery and then, a few blocks farther, they left East Berlin and, despite the physical impossibility of reversing the arrow of time, entered Weimar Germany. Tucked in some courtyard was a synagogue, not far away stood a tower where SA thugs had pummeled their prisoners, and all around were barren cobblestone streets, pockmarked buildings, and faded print advertising on charred brick walls. Their sense of adventure and romance aroused, they strolled hand in hand to the Spree Canal—closely observing and delighting in the broken windows, empty warehouses, barbed-wire fences, old tires, clumps of weeds, asphalt cracks, variously shaped pieces of metal, chained doors, and rusty locks. They crossed a street that ran parallel to the canal and entered what appeared to be a dead end. A burnt-out chassis sat amid brown and green and white bottles, glistening shards of glass, and charred newspaper fragments. To the left was the black water, beyond it West Berlin. To the right were garbage, thorny bushes and sparse grasses, and the remains of concrete structures—watchtowers or bunkers, perhaps. The canal, a motionless collection of chemicals, effluent, and fetid water, meandered between the two Berlins, keeping each at arm's length from the other by means of the timelessness of decay.

They boarded the S-Bahn at Dimitroff Strasse.

"Now you will see how the working class lives," Katorga said.

They changed trains and finally disembarked somewhere on the Friedenssackgasse—the former Stalinsackgasse. The buildings lining the boulevard looked like balding Soviet youth leaders. The elaborately decorated balconies were crumbling, and the balustrades were rusty. The foyer of Katorga's building, although dark, still betrayed the signs of a portal to the world of the Communist haute bourgeoisie. The marble had been painted olive green, and the staircase was covered with a threadbare red carpet. The chandelier, its crystals shattered or stolen, resembled a spider web. The smell of feces and cooking oil filled the air, growing stronger as they climbed the stairs to the fourth floor.

"This is where I live," Katorga said as she pushed open a solid wood door. "I have no coffee. Do you want tea, or perhaps beer or Schnapps?"

The place had high ceilings and large windows. Thin gas pipes adorned the tiny kitchen, the paint was peeling, and the floors creaked. Katorga opened another door. "This is where I sleep" is all she said as she took Volodymyr's soft hand.

The unusually solicitous and shyly seductive Katorga takes Volodymyr on a romp through the past, when things were things and, despite their awfulness, seemed to make more sense, especially to those with the ideologically inculcated perspicacity to tell right from wrong and left from right

When Volodymyr awoke, the bed was empty and, as he turned toward the door, the springs squeaked and groaned. He could hear Katorga rummaging in the kitchen. The bedroom was just slightly larger than the bed. Faded black and white photographs of some man and woman and of herself covered one wall. There she was, as a young girl, in an embroidered blouse. And there, with friends, walking up a mountain path and looking at the photographer. There was one shot of her in front of a large gray building, another in a parade, waving a flag, and a group photo, of her and three rows of young men and women dressed in some kind of uniform. They were all smiling, but just barely. One of the women was holding a placard with illegible Cyrillic writing. And then there was a photograph—the only one in an expensive mahogany frame—of a man, with a square jaw, bulbous nose, and a white shirt and tie. A chair stood in one corner—her clothes were neatly arranged on it—and a small night table, piled up with his, was squeezed into another corner. Three light bulbs were screwed into the fixture in the center of the ceiling.

"*Kaffee und Kartoffeln?*" she smiled, perching a tray on the side of the bed. "Eat," she ordered.

"So"—Volodymyr tilted his head at the wall—"these are photographs of you?"

Katorga nodded.

"And that"—he pointed at the framed photograph—"is your father?"

"No."

"Your lover?"

She laughed. "Oh, no, not at all."

"Then who is he?"

"He is a great hero," she said. "I knew him. When I was a child."

"A great hero?"

"Have you heard of Sholom Schwartzbard?"

"The Jew who killed the Ukrainian Petliura?"

She smiled. "He avenged his people. He avenged me."

"You are Jewish?" Volodymyr said.

"*Nein,*" Katorga laughed. "My parents were Communists—Ukrainian. They fought with Lenin. In the Cheka." Katorga's smile faded. "The counterrevolutionaries were everywhere, you know—everywhere. They couldn't trust anyone."

"They killed?" Volodymyr poured fresh cream into his coffee.

"Of course—for the cause, for the revolution, for the working class. They were Communists."

"Many?" He added sugar and stirred.

"Thousands," Katorga said proudly, "maybe more. They were all enemies of the people. You cannot, you know, make borscht without peeling beets."

"And they met this man"—Volodymyr nodded at the photograph—"in Ukraine?"

"No, in Paris. They—my parents—were assigned to the Soviet trade mission. They hated Petliura, of course."

"I am," Volodymyr said, "half-Jewish and half-Ukrainian."

Katorga returned to bed. "Then Sholom is both your enemy and your avenger," she said.

"Tell me more about this hero of yours."

"Oh," Katorga gushed, "he was a wonderful man, a kind man, a good man. My father knew him and he would come to visit us, and every time he came he brought me presents. And he would always tell us of the Petliura affair. My father and mother never tired of hearing Sholom retell the story, over and over and over again."

"Didn't the story terrify you?" Volodymyr asked.

"It was heroic, and Sholom told it heroically. We always cried when he described the pogroms and we always shuddered when he told us of the trial."

"I know only that he killed Petliura."

"Sholom was a socialist—they all were—and, after the pogroms of 1905, he left Russia and settled in Paris. He made watches. Did you know that? What a funny occupation for my hero." Katorga raised the cup to her lips and then, without taking a sip, placed it back on the saucer. "In 1917—it was after the Revolution had begun—Sholom joined the Red Guard. In Odessa. He returned to Paris in 1920. That is all. What more do you want to know? He was a good man. My father loved him. All good Communists did."

"When did he die?"

"Sholom? In 1938, in Cape Town."

"In South Africa?" Volodymyr raised his eyebrows. "What was he doing in South Africa?"

"It is almost funny. Here, have this piece of potato. It is my special recipe—fried in animal fat." Katorga watched Volodymyr chew. "My hero was promoting a Yiddish encyclopedia. Together with my father. I think he had a heart attack, or a stroke. He was buried there. Isn't that funny? My hero, the avenger, lies in some cemetery in Cape Town."

"And you"—Volodymyr involuntarily extended his hand for another *Kartoffel*—"you grew up in Paris?"

"We lived there until 1940." Katorga lit a cigarette. "The city of lights was really the city of class conflict. It was full of anti-Soviet émigrés, plotting, scheming—"

"Your parents," Volodymyr interjected, "did they work for the NKVD?"

"Of course," Katorga replied confidently. "My father ran a camp. For political prisoners. Where do you think I got this name?"

Volodymyr sat up in bed. "What did they do in Paris?"

"No more killings, of course. Not in Paris. That wouldn't have worked." Katorga exhaled deeply. "But there were kidnappings. You know, I took part in one. Can you believe it?"

"But you were a child!"

"He was a White Russian, a little man with a cane. I forget his name. He would always take a stroll down Les Grands Boulevards. My mother pretended to be a lost refugee—I was clutching her hand—and she asked him to direct us to some *gare*."

"Which one?" Volodymyr asked. "*Nord? Est?*"

"It doesn't matter." Katorga waved her hand. "As we turned a corner, my father and his comrades stepped out from behind a truck and—boom!—one knock on the head and the enemy of the people was on his way to the *Rodina*."

"How did the Homeland greet him?" Volodymyr suspected he knew the answer.

"Oh"—she took a long drag—"he was shot trying to escape, of course."

"And what have you been doing since?" Volodymyr rose from the bed and grabbed his shirt from the night table. It was time to get back to the conference.

"A little bit of this, a little bit of that. But mostly journalism. And poetry—I also write poems."

"I have a collection of haikus," Volodymyr said timidly.

"I know," Katorga shot back. "I have it. I am your greatest admirer." She lit another cigarette. "It's too bad you never met Sholom. He was also a poet."

"You know my poetry?" Volodymyr cried.

"Of course. You're widely read here. The GDR isn't what it used to be. Our people read more than the other Germans." Katorga thumbed through the thin volume. "Do you know which poem is my favorite?" She adopted a serious expression:

Workers
of all countries
unite, please.
You have nothing
to lose
but your chains.

45

"That *please* is perfect."

"*Danke*," Volodymyr stammered, "but I'm just—"

"—a great Jewish-Ukrainian poet. You know," Katorga said thoughtfully, "We have much in common. Here"—she handed Volodymyr an old magazine—"read this. You will understand me, and yourself, better."

Frankly flattered by Katorga's literary tastes, Volodymyr overcomes oncoming indigestion and flatulence and decides to take a long look at the past, thereby discovering that the temptation to intervene in the flow of time can be irresistible, especially when provoked by courtroom melodrama and a lurid account in a respectable, quotable, and unimpeachable Western source[1]

Court. In the dim court of Assizes, in Paris, during the past fortnight, more than 400 spectators saw the beginning and the end of one of the most gruesome, bloodcurdling, impassioned trials ever to be held in that vaulted hall of justice. Quivering flappers sat to gasp with astonishment beside white & black bearded Jews who exchanged shocked glances with flat-faced Slavic Ukrainians under the noses of red & black-robed judges. Within and without the courtroom was a triple guard of gendarmes to prevent disorder.

Unnerved by the realization that the past appears to have been characterized by an excessive love of maudlin modifiers and bad writing, Volodymyr pauses for a moment's worth of self-reflection and wonders whether such a predilection would enhance or retard his ability to understand just what happened and why

Culprit. The accused man, who not only admitted committing the crime but even boasted of it, was a young Jewish Ukrainian, now a naturalized Frenchman, Sholem (Samuel) Schwartzbard, a watchmaker by profession. Short, ugly, he yet commanded the attention of the whole court, for he told his story, not as do many prisoners, shamefaced and haltingly, forced to reveal their crimes and motives by harassing lawyers—no,

---

[1] "FRANCE: Petlura Trial," *Time*, November 7, 1927. Reprinted with permission of *Time* magazine.
<http://www.time.com/time/printout/0,8816,731176,00.html>

46

Watchmaker Schwartzbard openly confessed with gleaming eyes and hysterical mien, his body trembling with passion, how he slew "General" Simon Petlura to avenge the deaths of thousands of Jews slain in pogroms, which he charged "General" Petlura instigated.

Volodymyr wonders whether shortness, ugliness, hysteria, and gleaming eyes promote truth-telling or obstruct it—or whether all or some of these physical characteristics have a stronger causal relationship as necessary or sufficient conditions or, finally, whether they're completely irrelevant to the question at hand

Victim. Simon Petlura, in the opinion of many, was an adventurer. The son of a Russian cabman, he is said to have been active in plotting against the Tsar. In 1918 he entered Kiev, capital of the Ukraine, with the Austrian and German armies, under whose auspices he took the lead in trying to separate that province from the rest of Russia. He not only promoted himself a general but also declared himself ruler of the Ukraine. He failed and was obliged to flee. Two years later he reappeared, this time under the Poles, becoming president of a short-lived Ukrainian republic. He played off the Poles against the Bolsheviki and the Bolsheviki against the Poles and, eventually, again fell from power, this time to flee to France, where he lived in Paris until slain there by M. Schwartzbard. Under his regime, it is charged, more than 50,000 Jews were killed.

Suppressing a chuckle, Volodymyr realizes that the passive voice, although scorned by stylists, journalists, and language teachers, can have great advantages over the active voice—especially when it comes to obscuring responsibility and implying more or less than is indeed the case, as might be necessary or desirable during courtroom melodramas

Lawyers. Henri Torres, chief counsel for the defense, florid, bloated, dynamic, put his histrionic abilities to the test when, leaping past his colleagues into the middle of the courtroom, he brandished a revolver, produced from under his voluminous black gown. Shrieks of terror mingled with gasps met this display.

Flappers sat with blanched faces; bewhiskered Hebrews rocked back and forth with suppressed excitement; Ukrainians, more pallid than ever, glanced nervously through their narrow eyes. Maitre Torres, aiming at a chair, pulled the trigger—there was a dull click, followed by sighs of relief. He was attempting to prove that M. Schwartzbard could not have shot Simon Petlura as he lay, prone on the ground.

Cesare Campinchi, flaccid, verbose, excitable, chief prosecution lawyer representing the Petlura family, particularly Widow Petlura, who was in court, proved himself the equal of Maitre Torres in oratorical and theatrical ability. Accused of suppressing evidence by M. Torres, he roared: "Don't accuse me of suppressing evidence, Torres!" "Don't force me to place in evidence your personal pedigree!" yelled Torres. And thus they continued.

Provoked to an extreme degree of excitability by both lawyers' unseemly antics, Volodymyr overcomes his self-restraint and joins the fray, injecting himself into the text and into history, and thereby proving, among other things, that texts and history are mere constructions that, as some insist, may be invented, imagined, reinvented, and reimagined more or less at will, or, as others say, may not

Volodymyr's 1st Antihistorical Intervention. And thus they continued until the defiant Frauenzimmer rose from his seat and turned to the blanched flappers, bewhiskered Hebrews, and pallid Ukrainians and, pointing accusingly at both lawyers, screamed, his eyes glistening with hysteria and fanatical exultation: "You are buffoons! You are distorting the truth! You are doing a great disservice to all later generations! Stop! I order you to stop!" Then, dropping limp, he fell into his seat.

*

Crime. Simon Petlura was shot at the corner of the Rue Racine, and the Boulevard St. Michel, on May 25, 1926. As M. Schwartzbard described the murder to the court:

"Here's my chance, I thought. 'Are you Petlura?' I asked him. He did not answer, simply lifting his heavy cane. I knew it was he.

"I shot him five times. I shot him like a soldier who knows how to shoot, and I shot straight so as not to hit any innocent passerby. At the fifth shot he fell. He didn't say a word. There were only cries and convulsions.

"When I saw him fall I knew he had received five bullets. Then I emptied my revolver. The crowd had scattered. A policeman came up quietly and said: 'Is that enough?' I answered: 'Yes.' He said: 'Then give me your revolver.' I gave him the revolver, saying: 'I have killed a great assassin.'

"When the policeman told me Petlura was dead I could not hide my joy. I leaped forward and threw my arms about his neck."

"Then you admit premeditation?" asked the judge.

"Yes, yes!" replied M. Schwartzbard, his face lit with fanatical exultation.

His opinion of the presiding judge greatly diminished by his having asked the obvious of the defendant, Volodymyr decides to roar in the hope that roaring may change the course of history or, at the very least, that it may demonstrate to the histrionic attorneys and assembled journalists just how bold stands are taken and vigorous points are made

Volodymyr's 2nd Antihistorical Intervention. And thus they continued until the defiant Frauenzimmer again rose from his seat and turned to the blanched flappers, bewhiskered Hebrews, and pallid Ukrainians and, pointing accusingly at both lawyers, screamed, his eyes glistening with hysteria and fanatical exultation: "Of course there was premeditation! The real question, M. Schwartzbard, is just why you were fixated on exactly five shots, when a soldier who knows how to shoot could have easily done the job at that range with one bullet. You wanted to kill Petlura five times, M. Schwartzbard! That's how great your hatred of him must have been! That's why you used five bullets!" Then, dropping limp, he fell into his seat.

*

Trial. The case opened with M. Schwartzbard telling the court in a high pitched voice and halting French, his beady eyes gleaming, his face suffused with joy, how he had tracked Petlura down. With a photograph of his intended victim in his pocket and a loaded pistol in another, he was wont to roam the street peering into the faces of passers-by to see if they were Petlura. All this, he said, he did to avenge the assassinations of his coreligionists. Finally, he found and killed him.

One Reginald Smith, an Englishman, a reputed eye-witness of the crime, was called to describe the crime. Quoting Shakespeare, he ended his testimony by referring to Schwartzbard's expression as Petlura fell: "He wore an expression of exaltation mixed with anguish."

Many witnesses called by the prosecution declared that Petlura was not an enemy of the Jews, but Maitre Torres insisted that "Petlura's proclamations expressing indignation over the pogroms were mere blinds. While murdering Jewish men, women & children, he had to maintain a straight face before the opinion of the world. He also wanted money from Jewish bankers."

"No," said a massive Slav, "Petlura was not anti-Semitic. He was a humanitarian—a friend of the Jews."

"No, no, no, he lies!" chorused a dozen people in the court in as many languages.

Disconcerted by the dozen or more languages resounding in the chamber, but struck by the cultural elitism of the implied comparison with a Shakespearean tragedy, Volodymyr overcomes his hesitation and his naturally reclusive character and again places his money on roaring, on the assumption that, while it may fail to sway the jury, it just might succeed in impressing the massive Slavs

Volodymyr's 3rd Antihistorical Intervention. And thus they continued until the defiant Frauenzimmer again rose from his seat and turned to the blanched flappers, bewhiskered Hebrews, and pallid Ukrainians and, pointing accusingly at both lawyers, screamed, his eyes glistening with hysteria and fanatical exultation: "How, ladies and gentlemen of the jury, are we to resolve this contradiction? Maitre Torres asserts that Petlura's proclamations were insincere. The massive Slav asserts they were sincere.

Neither provides us with any evidence, and both cannot be right. So whom do we believe? A fanatic? A lawyer? Or a fat man? And what difference does our belief make to the question of whether the 'General' was or was not an anti-Semite?" Then, dropping limp, he fell into his seat.

*

"They cut them down with naked blades," screamed M. Schwartzbard.

"I accuse that man of being an agent of Moscow. I swear it a thousand times!" roared another witness for the prosecution, pointing an accusatory forefinger at M. Schwartzbard.

"You—! You—!" yelled Schwartzbard, jumping to his, feet, incoherent with rage, his shoulders quivering in spasmodic jerks. Recovering his power of speech, he continued:

"Do you remember the terrible days of 1910 and 1911 at Kiev? Do you remember the accusations that Jews were using Christian blood for Easter ceremonies? You hate me because I am a Jew!"

"No," screamed the other in a high falsetto, "because you are a Bolshevik!"

"Prove it! Prove it, then!" flung back the defiant Schwartzbard, dropping limp, into his seat.

Equally determined both to avoid quivering and spasmodic jerking and to prevent history from dropping limply into its metaphorical seat, Volodymyr again goes on the offensive and roars, like a lion roaming the savannah for gazelles, antelopes, camels, and other noble beasts, while secretly wondering whether all his roaring might be for naught

Volodymyr's 4th Antihistorical Intervention. And thus they continued until the defiant Frauenzimmer again rose from his seat and turned to the blanched flappers, bewhiskered Hebrews, and pallid Ukrainians and, pointing accusingly at both lawyers, screamed, his eyes glistening with hysteria and fanatical exultation: "Ladies and gentlemen of the jury, we have here another instance of unsupported charges and counter-charges that belie easy resolution and reflect the hysterical mien of this trial. Could M.

Schwartzbard be a Soviet agent? Of course he could and he wouldn't be the first. Could he be an avenger of his people? Of course he could and, once again, he wouldn't be the first. So whom do we believe? The spasmodic defendant or his falsetto-voiced accuser?" Then, dropping limp, he fell into his seat.

*

A squat Slav, called by the prosecution, who described himself as an "historian, a man of letters and at present an assistant to a stone-mason," gave evidence in Petlura's philo-Semiticism, denying with a grief-contorted face that the "General" had ever killed Jews or caused them to be massacred.

"Yes! Yes! He massacred them!" shouted Schwartzbard, unnerved.

The most notable witness called, however, was Mlle. Haia Greenberg, 29, a curly bobbed-haired nurse. In a soft, low voice, she told of the carnage and rapine ordered by Simon Petlura and of the blood-bathed home of her grandparents. Murmured she:

"I shall never forget the reddened snow sleds, filled with the hacked bodies, going to the cemetery to deposit their sad burden, in a common pit. They brought the wounded to the hospital—armless and legless men, mutilated babies and young women whose screams became faint as their wounds overcame them."

Then breaking down and sobbing convulsively she screamed: "Oh, no, no! I cannot go on! They are before my eyes!

"Petlura was responsible. Even Ukrainian officers said so. His soldiers killed our people, shouting his name. One regiment had a band and it played while knives fell on the heads of innocent babies. Petlura could have stopped it, but he wouldn't listen to our pleas."

Deeply shocked by the image of red snow and completely aghast at the awful sound of a band playing while knives are falling, Volodymyr musters up just enough strength for one last roar, while secretly suspecting that gasping a last roar is almost as pathetic as grasping for a last straw

Volodymyr's 5th Antihistorical Intervention. And thus they continued until the defiant Frauenzimmer again rose from his seat and turned to the blanched flappers, bewhiskered Hebrews, and pallid Ukrainians and, pointing accusingly at both lawyers, screamed, his eyes glistening with hysteria and fanatical exultation: "Ladies and gentlemen of the jury, we appear, finally, to have touched the most important, and perhaps the only important, question of this trial. Was Petlura responsible for the pogroms? Could he have stopped them? I think you will agree that whether or not he was anti-Semitic and whether or not M. Schwartzbard was a Soviet agent is quite secondary to this—the only question that matters. I think you will also agree that this trial has provided no answer whatsoever to this question." Then, dropping limp, he fell into his seat.

*

Verdict. Amid tense excitement, after an absence of 35 minutes, the jury returned a verdict for the young, pale faced Jew's acquittal. Frenzied cheering greeted the decision. M. Schwartzbard, calm, kissed his lawyer, Maitre Henri Torres. "Vive la France!" shouted somebody. "Vive la France!" echoed some 500 voices.

In addition to setting M. Schwartzbard free, the verdict ordered the Petlura family, represented by Maitre Caesare Campinchi, to pay the costs of the trial, but awarded damages of one franc each to Mme. Petlura, widow of the slain "General," and to M. Petlura, his brother.

The outcome of the trial, which gripped all Europe, was regarded by the Jews as establishing proof of the horrors perpetrated against their co-religionists in the Ukraine under the dictatorship of Simon Petlura; radical opinion rejoiced, but the conservatives saw justice flouted and the decorum of the French courts immeasurably impaired.

Schwartzbard, free, went into hiding, fearing assassination at the hands of anti-Semites.

Realizing that his interventions at the trial have come to naught and suspecting that history may not be open to easy intervention, Volodymyr abandons roaring and decides to try reason and discourse, while strongly suspecting, of course, that the ex post facto application of reason and discourse to historical facts can probably change nothing

Volodymyr's 6th Antihistorical Intervention. And thus they continued until the defiant Frauenzimmer again rose from his seat and turned to the blanched flappers, bewhiskered Hebrews, and pallid Ukrainians and, pointing accusingly at both lawyers, whispered, his eyes glistening with hysteria and fanatical exultation: "Ladies and gentlemen of the jury, should M. Schwartzbard have been set free? Was the verdict just? On the one hand, I am delighted that an idealist was not punished for attempting to right a perceived wrong. On the other hand, I confess to being fearful of the consequences of letting any idealist, however just his cause and however sympathetic his character, mete out justice on his own. This linguistic travesty has brought us no nearer the truth. You leave me no choice but to cross-examine Sholom Schwartzbard and Simon Petlura on my own." Then, dropping limp, he fell into his seat.

Chapter 4

Emboldened by his new-found knowledge of human nature and feeling privileged, and perhaps a bit cocky, at having witnessed a turning point in history, Volodymyr embarks on his first premeditated attempt to change the past, only to be, unsurprisingly, demoralized by its uncertain results

Fearful of succumbing to the seductiveness of moral symmetry, but fully determined to get to the bottom of things that elude easy understanding, Volodymyr cross-examines the defendant Sholom Schwartzbard in the hope of discovering what made him tick, both literally and figuratively, and, thus, of determining just how the five bullets he fired interacted with the arrow of time

Frauenzimmer: Your name?

Schwartzbard: Sholom Schwartzbard.

Frauenzimmer: Your occupation?

Schwartzbard: Avenger.

Frauenzimmer: And a watchmaker, *n'est-ce pas?* In any case, whom did you avenge?

Schwartzbard: My people—the Jews.

Frauenzimmer: And *my* people. Please do not forget that. Please do not forget that I, too, am a Jew. And how did you avenge them—*us, me?*

Schwartzbard: By shooting Petliura.

Frauenzimmer: So you admit to killing him?

Schwartzbard: Of course, I admitted to it in the Rue Racine and at the trial. It's no secret.

Frauenzimmer: You should know that I am also Ukrainian.

Schwartzbard: Ah, so I avenged you *and*—

Frauenzimmer: —inflicted harm on me? Yes.

Schwartzbard: But not on you personally.

Frauenzimmer: Yes and no. If you avenged me, then you also harmed me.

Schwartzbard: You talk like a Jesuit.

Frauenzimmer: I've been called that before. But let us return to you—to your assassination of Petliura.

Schwartzbard: *Bon.*

Frauenzimmer: You had lived in Paris since 1910. Is that right?

Schwartzbard: Correct.

Frauenzimmer: And you worked as a watchmaker.

Schwartzbard: Also correct.

Frauenzimmer: But then, when revolution broke out in Russia, you went there.

Schwartzbard: Yes.

Frauenzimmer: Why would a watchmaker from Paris go to Russia?

Schwartzbard: I was a socialist and an anarchist, and Russia had just experienced a revolution.

Frauenzimmer: And there you joined the Bolshevik Red Guard.

Schwartzbard: Yes.

Frauenzimmer: Why?

Schwartzbard: I was a Marxist. And to defend Jews.

Frauenzimmer: But only briefly.

Schwartzbard: Yes, I returned to Paris in 1920.

Frauenzimmer: To resume your work as a watchmaker?

Schwartzbard: *Oui.*

Frauenzimmer: Were you still associated with the Bolsheviks?

Schwartzbard: That's what they said at the trial. Of course not.

Frauenzimmer: It would be a reasonable inference, wouldn't it? After all, why would a watchmaker go to Russia to be a revolutionary and why would a revolutionary return to Paris to be a watchmaker?

Schwartzbard: Ah, you are suggesting I was a Soviet agent!

Frauenzimmer: Were you?

Schwartzbard: Of course not.

Frauenzimmer: So you decided to kill Petliura on your own, without any prompting, without any instructions from your Soviet friends?

Schwartzbard: I am an idealist, and I killed Petliura because he was a pogromchik.

Frauenzimmer: Did you see him kill Jews?

Schwartzbard: He was responsible.

Frauenzimmer: But did you actually see him?

Schwartzbard: I told you: he was responsible. That is the same thing.

Frauenzimmer: Well, not quite. You actually killed him, didn't you? You weren't just responsible.

Schwartzbard: You are being Jesuitical again.

Frauenzimmer: Perhaps, but let's return to your political sympathies. You were an anarchist, a socialist, a Bolshevik, a member of the Red Guard?

Schwartzbard: That is what they say.

Frauenzimmer: So which of your many personalities pulled the trigger?

Schwartzbard: I did—Sholom Schwartzbard, the avenger of dead Jews.

Frauenzimmer: You are being evasive again.

Schwartzbard: If that is what you say.

Frauenzimmer: But why kill Petliura?

Schwartzbard: I told you: because he was a pogromchik.

Frauenzimmer: That's what I don't understand. You were in Ukraine during the Civil War; you witnessed the carnage; you saw the Bolsheviks kill their enemies mercilessly. You saw the Whites attack Jews. And yet, only Petliura haunts you.

Schwartzbard: The Bolsheviks were promoting revolution; they had no choice but to kill their enemies. And the Whites were anti-Semites. I expected nothing less from them.

Frauenzimmer: Wasn't Petliura a philo-Semite?

Schwartzbard: The soldiers killed Jews in his name, and he did nothing to stop the massacres.

Frauenzimmer: Neither did the Whites. And the Bolsheviks never even had pangs of conscience.

Schwartzbard: That is irrelevant.

Frauenzimmer: And how many people did *you* kill in Russia?

Schwartzbard: That, too, is irrelevant.

Frauenzimmer: It's not. It can't be. You were in the Red Guard. You must have killed Ukrainian nationalists and Russian Whites. How many peasants did you kill?

Schwartzbard: That is irrelevant. I killed Petliura. That is all that matters.

Frauenzimmer: Here's what you wrote in one of your books:

I need only recall the dreadful time for a shudder to pass over my body. The hideous visions pursue me always, though I strive to ward them off. Though I seek to expunge them from my memory, they remain always fresh and fearful. Pogrom scenes I witnessed float before my eyes and at night keep me awake. I jump up from my sleep and cannot shake off the bloody nightmares. All the remembrances of my life are gruesome, as is our whole history of martyrdom. My anguish grows greater when I cannot aid my suffering brothers and sisters. There are times when private sorrows disappear in public woe, like a drop of water in the sea. But as for him who suffers for humanity, his sorrows continue and are vast as the world. These sensitive souls suffer every injustice done on earth, on their bodies they feel whiplash, they cannot endure the oppressor's arrogance and the slow pace of justice. They must act. The blood of the innocent and of the martyrs demands justice and vengeance.[2]

Frauenzimmer: Why did you wait until 1926? Petliura left Ukraine in 1920, and he came to Paris in 1924. You could have shot him earlier. Why wait six years if your heart was so full of anguish and rage?

Schwartzbard: I was a poor watchmaker. How was I to know where he was?

Frauenzimmer: And yet you found out.

Schwartzbard: Everybody in Paris eventually knew. It was in the air.

Frauenzimmer: Even so, why wait until May 25, 1926? You see, it's the timing that puzzles me.

Schwartzbard: I did not, as you put it, wait until then. I waited for an opportune moment, and that moment happened to be that day. That is all.

Frauenzimmer: Very well then. Tell me how you prepared to kill Petliura. The killing was premeditated. You said as much.

---

[2] *Inem loif fun yorem*, <http://asimplejew.blogspot.com/2006/03/ukrainian-jews-remember.html>

Schwartzbard: Of course it was premeditated. As soon as I learned that he was in Paris, I knew I had to destroy him—just as he destroyed my people.

Frauenzimmer: So what did you do?

Schwartzbard: First, I had to find out where he lived. That took some time. Eventually, I determined that he resided in a cheap hotel in the Rue des Écoles. Many Ukrainian émigrés lived in that area. Then I followed him—to determine what his routines were. He liked to dine in a small restaurant in the Rue Racine, the Chartier, just beyond the Boulevard Saint Michel. Then I had to find a gun. The rest was easy.

Frauenzimmer: Where did you get a gun?

Schwartzbard: In Paris in 1926 anyone could buy a gun.

Frauenzimmer: And you waited for him as he left the restaurant?

Schwartzbard: Yes. He strolled down the street with his cane, his belly full, as if he hadn't a worry in the world.

Frauenzimmer: Why didn't you kill him before he ate?

Schwartzbard: I wanted him to be sluggish. Hungry men are nervous, suspicious.

Frauenzimmer: What did you think when you saw him?

Schwartzbard: My blood boiled. And then I thought, "You have no idea that your fate awaits you, that in a few seconds you will be dead." That eased my anguish.

Frauenzimmer: You knew it was him. Why didn't you just shoot? Why did you first ask, "Are you Petliura?"

Schwartzbard: I wanted him to see the face of his killer.

Frauenzimmer: And what did you see on his face?

Schwartzbard: Surprise, anger—and fear.

Frauenzimmer: And then you shot him.

Schwartzbard: And then I shot him: five times. Five bullets entered his body.

Frauenzimmer: Why so many?

Schwartzbard: I wanted to make sure the dog died.

Frauenzimmer: But you said you shot like a soldier, and a soldier needs only one bullet.

Schwartzbard: That was a figure of speech.

Frauenzimmer: You were standing very close to Petliura. Why not just aim at his heart or his face?

Schwartzbard: He had a cane. I was agitated.

Frauenzimmer: Still, why so many bullets, when one or two would have sufficed?

Schwartzbard: I wasn't counting.

Frauenzimmer: Yes you were. You just said so.

Schwartzbard: I don't know. How can you expect me to know?

Frauenzimmer: You didn't just want to kill Petliura. I think you wanted to obliterate him—to kill him five times.

Schwartzbard: I hated the dog. I told you: my blood boiled.

Frauenzimmer: And why didn't you run afterwards?

Schwartzbard: Only criminals run. I was no criminal. I was an avenger. I had done nothing wrong.

Frauenzimmer: Are you still proud of what you did?

Schwartzbard: I would do it again, a million times, if necessary.

Frauenzimmer: Your trial, in 1927, exonerated you.

Schwartzbard: Naturally. I was innocent of any wrong-doing.

Frauenzimmer: But you killed a man. Isn't that wrong?

Schwartzbard: I killed scum—a *canaille*.

Frauenzimmer: Are you saying that you don't consider Petliura to have been human?

Schwartzbard: A human being wouldn't have killed Jews.

Frauenzimmer: So you had the right to execute him because he was less than fully human?

Schwartzbard: *Exactement.*

Frauenzimmer: That is a terrible right. Who gave it to you?

Schwartzbard: The suffering of my people.

Frauenzimmer: Now I must ask you a moral question. You say you were justified in killing a man you held responsible for your people's suffering. Would Petliura's supporters be right in wanting to avenge *their* people's suffering?

Schwartzbard: They killed Jews first.

Frauenzimmer: But they'd say Jews exploited them first. Who is right?

Schwartzbard: You are being Jesuitical again.

Frauenzimmer: If every eye must be avenged with an eye, eventually everyone will be blind. And then what?

Schwartzbard: Then we will all be blind. But we will see justice.

Volodymyr interrogates the watchmaker's victim, Simon Petliura, in the hope of discovering whether the question of responsibility can ever be answered to the satisfaction of history and, in particular, to the satisfaction of those who must live with history, especially after their deaths

Frauenzimmer: Your name?
Petliura: Simon Petliura.
Frauenzimmer: Your occupation?
Petliura: Revolutionary.
Frauenzimmer: What kind of revolution did you pursue?
Petliura: The Ukrainian revolution. I wanted to build a free and independent Ukrainian state.
Frauenzimmer: Did you?
Petliura: No, I failed.
Frauenzimmer: Why?
Petliura: It was impossible. The conditions were impossible.
Frauenzimmer: You made no mistakes?
Petliura: I made many mistakes. But we wouldn't have succeeded even if I had made no mistakes.
Frauenzimmer: Please explain.
Petliura: Ukraine was in flames. The Germans had just withdrawn. The Bolsheviks and Whites were advancing. They had real armies. And we? What did we have? A ragtag government, a rabble army, and the ground on which we stood.
Frauenzimmer: So your revolution was doomed from the start.
Petliura: I fear so.
Frauenzimmer: Did you know, or suspect, that then?
Petliura: All of us—we saw only the opportunity before us. Our enemies had been defeated, and we hoped that a mass mobilization of the nation might lead to success. We were wrong.
Frauenzimmer: So you are a failed revolutionary and a failed state builder!
Petliura: *Hélas.*

Frauenzimmer: And yet you continued your struggle—even from Paris.

Petliura: Old revolutionaries never die.

Frauenzimmer: You did. To be precise, you were killed.

Petliura: A pity for me. But the struggle continued.

Frauenzimmer: And you became a hero for all Ukrainians, a symbol of the cause.

Petliura: What an irony! Most of them hated me before I died.

Frauenzimmer: Why?

Petliura: No one likes a loser.

Frauenzimmer: You know why Sholom Schwartzbard killed you, don't you?

Petliura: Yes, yes, I have been through all this thousands of times. He says I was an anti-Semite and that I killed Jews.

Frauenzimmer: Were you? Did you?

Petliura: Of course not. Schwartzbard was wrong on both counts. Alas, I paid the price for his error.

Frauenzimmer: Are you saying you weren't anti-Semitic?

Petliura: That's exactly what I'm saying. I've always supported the rights of Jews. Never, not in a single written or spoken line did I ever express anti-Semitic sentiments. Read what I wrote.

Frauenzimmer: Actions speak louder than words. Schwartzbard insists you killed Jews.

Petliura: *I* never killed a single Jew. He means the pogroms, of course, the ones perpetrated by the soldiers and peasants.

Frauenzimmer: Yes, he says you instructed them to kill Jews and did nothing to stop them from killing Jews.

Petliura: That's absurd. Why would I tell my soldiers to engage in pogroms? That would've been senseless with the Bolsheviks breathing down our necks. As a matter of fact, I issued decrees condemning the pogroms.

Frauenzimmer: And yet the pogroms did take place. Are you denying that?

Petliura: Of course they did. They were a tragedy and a black mark on our revolution.

Frauenzimmer: But you were the commander-in-chief, and the pogromchiks were under your command.

Petliura: You must understand the circumstances. I barely controlled my ministers, and our government had no control over the armed forces. And Ukraine, as I said, was engulfed in chaos. It was a terrible time.

Frauenzimmer: So why did the pogroms take place?

Petliura: Have you ever lived through war and revolution? The Germans had been slaughtering the Russian army for four years. They took everything from the peasants. And when they withdrew at the end of 1918, everybody—the peasants, the workers, the Bolsheviks, the anarchists, the Whites, the nationalists—began settling old scores, stealing, burning, looting, raping. Ukrainians and Russians were dying en masse. And so were Jews. Everyone was killing, and everyone was being killed. Everyone was a victim and everyone was an assassin.

Frauenzimmer: Perhaps, but it was *your* soldiers who killed the Jews.

Petliura: I know, but there was nothing I could do to stop it. Just as there was nothing I could do to stop the war or the revolution or the chaos.

Frauenzimmer: You could have issued a decree.

Petliura: I did. You can read them. I suppose I could have issued more decrees. Historians might have vindicated me, but it wouldn't have made the slightest difference for the poor Jews. Or the poor Ukrainians. Or the poor Russians.

Frauenzimmer: You could have arrested the leaders of the violence.

Petliura: The pogromchiks made their own decisions, and they were beyond my control. Even if I had arrested all of them, what difference would it have made? I'd have had to arrest the entire peasantry! What would *you* have done?

Frauenzimmer: I don't know—

Petliura: Ah!

Frauenzimmer: —but I still have the feeling that you could have done something.

Petliura: Possibly. Maybe. Who knows? Why don't you accuse me of failing to stop the killing of Ukrainians and Russians, of peasants and workers? Millions of them died.

Frauenzimmer: Well, why didn't you?

Petliura: I was a figurehead, the president of a fictitious country, the commander-in-chief of a fictitious army. Survival was our only goal, and it was threatened every single minute of every day.

Frauenzimmer: And yet Schwartzbard held _you_ responsible for the killings!

Petliura: He was tragically mistaken.

Frauenzimmer: But he was right about the pogroms.

Petliura: That they took place? Of course they did. I already said so. But he's wrong to say that they were the only atrocities, or even the worst atrocities. You know, I _do_ understand Schwartzbard. Ukrainian nationalists can be just like him, seeing nothing beyond the suffering of their own nation.

Frauenzimmer: Does that get you off the hook?

Petliura: My point is that I wasn't a primitive anti-Semite who wanted only to kill Jews. That's what Torrès said. That's what Schwartzbard said. But they're wrong. They're distorting history. It's as simple as that.

Frauenzimmer: What did you think when he approached you on the Rue Racine?

Petliura: At first, I thought nothing. Here comes some man who wants to know if I am Petliura.

Frauenzimmer: But surely you saw that he was agitated.

Petliura: Not at first. But I obviously became alarmed when he pointed the pistol at me and began firing.

Frauenzimmer: Did you suspect you might die?

Petliura: Yes, especially after he wouldn't stop shooting.

Frauenzimmer: Did you know why Schwartzbard was shooting at you?

Petliura: No, he never identified himself, and he never said anything. I assumed he was one of my many enemies—a Bolshevik perhaps, or even some Ukrainian.

Frauenzimmer: You didn't think a Jew might want to kill you?

Petliura: No. As I said, I committed no crimes against the Jews.

Frauenzimmer: And yet you are not blameless. You were the commander-in-chief, even if the army was not, as you insist, fully under your control.

Petliura: I may be guilty of a crime of omission, not of commission. Should we be executed for things we did not do, for our failings?

Frauenzimmer: But shouldn't crimes of omission still be treated as crimes? Shouldn't their perpetrators be punished?

Petliura: With death? You'd have to guillotine the entire human race!

Frauenzimmer: But there are degrees of responsibility, aren't there? And Schwartzbard claims that you bore more responsibility than some illiterate peasant.

Petliura: That's just what I dispute. The peasant who killed Jews deserves to be punished—but he's too insignificant, so he isn't. My crime is surely less than the peasant's, but Schwartzbard metes out the ultimate punishment on me—not because I ever killed anyone, but because I was commander-in-chief. And I've already admitted to you that I commanded very little.

Frauenzimmer: So you were a poor commander-in-chief!

Petliura: *Hélas!*

Frauenzimmer: Then perhaps you should have acknowledged your failings and apologized.

Petliura: Have the French or the British apologized for their colonial massacres? Have the Bolsheviks? Why single me out?

Frauenzimmer: And yet…

Petliura: And yet, I could have—I know.

Frauenzimmer: Nothing might have changed, but history would have judged you differently.

Petliura: History? No, not history. There is no history. There are only historians.

Chapter 5

Much to the relief of unimaginative readers, the logic of the master narrative roaringly reasserts itself and Volodymyr's quest for self-knowledge culminates in the discovery of the terrible truth about the past, his parents' past, and of course his own past

Volodymyr wonders whether using force and deceit to extract confessions is permissible, especially if the objects of force and deceit are closely, indeed very, very closely, related to him, as indeed his parents were, necessarily and by definition, even if not by choice and even if as a result of an accidental crossing of paths and loins

Amid this overflowing cornucopia of confusing facts, inconsistent claims, incomplete narratives, loose ends, lurid adjectives, tasteless humor, and frustrating forays into a past that stubbornly resisted being changed or even understood, there was one picayune detail that gave Volodymyr no rest. Given the story-like quality of his parents' lives, wasn't it just possible that their lives had intersected before they had met in Auschwitz? Wasn't it possible that his father had supervised the prison in the very town his mother entered in 1941? Wasn't it possible that they had met, perhaps at the very moment when he was sheathing his knife and she was brandishing hers? Such a meeting seemed far-fetched, even to a man who, like Volodymyr, was inured to the ubiquity of the preposterous, but his parents' lives were already so preposterous—even more preposterous than my name, he thought—that there was no reason to think that the preposterously preposterous couldn't be more likely than the preposterously quotidian. After all, Volodymyr concluded, if my life were normal, I shouldn't be here, I should never have been born. But I am here, and I was born. It seemed to follow, albeit with admittedly less than ironclad logic, that this hypothesized meeting must have taken place.

Volodymyr resolved to interrogate his parents on this point. They would resist. As we know, they never spoke of their past or, indeed, of the past, and they'd be suspicious if he began poking around too closely. Encouraged by the nuggets of truth he extracted from Schwartzbard and Petliura, however, Volodymyr felt confident of his ability to crack the parental nut. Volodymyr knew he'd have to interrogate Mamochka and Papasha. He'd have to get them to spill the beans, to divulge the one bit of information each kept in reserve in order to blackmail the other into silence and submission. They'd never willingly surrender that weapon unless and until they could be assured that the balance of terror with which each kept the other in the hopeless relationship they called their marriage would continue to be maintained—even after they talked. It dawned on Volodymyr that he could maintain that balance of terror only by humiliating them, weakening them, grinding them down, and forcing them to empower him as their guardian. Reason wouldn't achieve that goal, if only because it was unreasonable and irrational for them to surrender their power to him. Trickery and force were imperative.

It became obvious to Volodymyr that he had to exploit their weaknesses. Both could not live without the daily consumption of vast amounts of alcohol. He would deprive them of drink and then, at the point that they turned desperate and, like Oriental junkies starved of opium, would be ready to do anything for a sip or a shot or a snort, he would ply them with excessive amounts of their favorite firewater. They were elderly, they were sickly, and they preferred not to leave the house, each inhabiting a room that was off limits to the other. Once they were slobbering over their drinks, once they focused exclusively on the bottles that promised release from their torments, he would strike. They understood force and they understood violence, and he would be forceful and violent with them. He had never raised a hand against either, but he knew that there was no alternative to using the only language they understood. He would bind them to their chairs, he would tie their legs and cover their eyes, and he would smack them across their faces with the back of his hand. Who knows, Volodymyr thought, they might even welcome such behavior. Perhaps their souls had become so contorted by the many years of mendacity and silence that a touch of violence would have an immediately cathartic effect? Perhaps he would be doing them good?

The only question that remained was the obvious one: Could *he* pull it off? Could *he* engage in violence—against his parents? After all, they were who they were—his mother and father. They had given him life, or what passed for life. And violence repelled the naturally pacific Volodymyr, especially after his experience in the Russian *Heer*. He had learned to fight, to jab straw revisionists with bayonets, to pull triggers at Mother Russia's black-ass enemies, and to hurl bombs with both long and short fuses, but at no time did he contemplate—or even need to contemplate—the necessity of torture. Volodymyr's devotion to essentialism and consequentialism gave him no answers to these questions, and, despite being set on the course he had adopted, philosophy offered no consolation. Only the Moral of the Popcorn offered some guidance, seeming to imply that he lacked the will-power to stay on this course to the required logical end.

As happens so often in life, and as had happened so often in Volodymyr's life, all his anguished considerations turned out to be pointless. In a bizarre twist of fate, Volodymyr came upon the solution to his conundrum—one that promised success while enabling him to pry the truth from his parents without recourse to violence or force. The approach he adopted wasn't completely benign. It did involve the use of deceit and manipulation—which could, especially in light of the Fifth Commandment, be regarded as sinful and wrong and immoral—but deceit and manipulation were, despite their faults, surely preferable to violence—well, some of the time if not most of the time or, depending on circumstances, most of the time if not some of the time.

Applying the Moral of the Popcorn and cleverly drawing on a form of sophisticated social-scientific enquiry that combined critical theory with critical praxis, Volodymyr outwits his parents, while retaining his sense of moral superiority more or less unblemished, untarnished, and untouched

It happened this way. One day, sometime in the late fall, when the leaves were turning the bright gold he loved so much, Volodymyr dropped by his Transsiberian ex-girlfriend Baba's flat (both *a*'s, curiously, were pronounced as *o*'s) to return the eighth volume of *Mother Russia's Favorite Russian Memoirs*. They were drinking beer and wine and vodka and working on a foolproof proof—neither circular, nor tautological—of the existence of God, and, after having imbibed more logic and alcohol than their fair share, Volodymyr rose from the sofa to go to the bathroom. As he did, he inadvertently knocked over a beer bottle that just happened to be standing on the floor next to an open hardcover book. The bottle fell on the inside of the volume and the tepid beer splashed out, spreading relentlessly across the pages. The hyperintellectual Baba, preoccupied with a self-absorbed soliloquy on the end of history, pretended to be unconcerned, but Volodymyr, his sense of moral acuity undulled by the overabundance of spirits, immediately insisted on buying her a new copy.

And he did. It was an overpriced book on something Volodymyr had never heard of before—the prisoner's dilemma. As a self-styled prisoner of his parents, indeed of life, Volodymyr sensed that he may have stumbled onto an oracular text of enormous potential significance to his own life and its dilemmas and, indeed, to the Moral of the Popcorn. Volodymyr could never have imagined that such a dense text would speak to him, especially out of context, but as he flipped through the pages and then, at some point, actually began reading, he knew that he had found the solution to his problems and even came within a hair of crying, "Eureka!"—not once, but twice. The author, a Teutonic theorist with roots in Königsberg and a childhood in Kaliningrad, insisted that the prisoner's dilemma could explain everything in life. If so, thought Volodymyr, then it can surely tell me what to do about my parents and their reluctance to tell me the truth.

According to this dilemma, two prisoners—when confronted with the choice of betraying the other and getting a lighter sentence or not saying a word and being released—will, due to their lack of trust, betray each other and therefore be worse off than the alternative: trust and silence and freedom. Wasn't this dilemma an exact description of his parents' condition? Both refused to speak, because their own silence was the best way of guaranteeing the other's silence. Like the prisoners in the Kaliningrader's dilemma, Volodymyr's parents were acting rationally by saying nothing. But, like the prisoners in the dilemma, they could be made to act rationally and spill all the beans—if each came to believe that the other was ratting on him. Years of silence had inured them to assuming that silence was the norm and that they could count on the other to remain mum. But what if they came to the opposite conclusion? What if he could make them believe that they *had* to sing in order to save themselves from the confession of the other?

Volodymyr knew that enhancing each parent's mistrust of the other was a piece of matzo. They never spoke, they always occupied different parts of the house, and they never communicated—except, perhaps, through him. He, Volodymyr, was the only point of contact between them. Whatever he said would have to be believed, because there was no alternative source of information. Indeed, the condition was perfectly, and deliciously, asymmetrical! Up to this moment, Volodymyr had always been truthful with Mamochka and Papasha. It now dawned upon him that carefully laid lies could easily disrupt this equilibrium and induce both to believe that telling him the truth was necessary for their self-preservation. How odd, he thought, that his parents should have spent the greater part of their lives thinking that mendacity promised greater utility than veracity. To be sure, such a course of action was, arguably, inconsistent with essentialist morality; on the other hand, thought Volodymyr, it sure as hell promised to deliver a consequentialist bang for the buck.

His manipulation was, as he came to realize in retrospect, as masterful as Iago's. He began dropping little hints or making casual remarks that, upon closer inspection, appeared to have double meanings. At first, his parents didn't respond, but after several such attempts one or the other or both would raise an eyebrow, grunt unexpectedly, stare at Volodymyr a bit longer than usual, or lean back in the chair. Volodymyr knew that these were all signs of agitation, but, in contrast to the past, when he would've asked what troubled them, now he kept silent, enhancing their sense of unease. Then, when he saw that their usually calm demeanor had been sufficiently disturbed—it was as if he were casting smoothly shaped pebbles into a serene swimming pool—Volodymyr proceeded with the second part of his plan.

One day, while dropping the second olive into his mother's vodka martini, he peered intently into her brown eyes and said, very, very quietly, "I know, you know. He told me." Before she could respond, he placed the jar on the table and quickly excused himself, claiming to have developed a sudden migraine. That same day, while raising a glass of buffalo-grass vodka with his father, he repeated the same words—"I know, you know. She told me."—and quickly departed. Both cried for him to return, but he steadfastly refused and stayed in his room, giggling uncontrollably and barely suppressing his glee, knowing full well that neither would dare venture into the no-man's land between their chambers. The next day's events also went according to plan. Both asked him what he meant by saying what he said, and Volodymyr only smiled mysteriously and mumbled, "You know what I meant."

On the third day, he knew he had to strike. Both were unnerved, both were eager to be reassured, and, if he waited any longer, both might begin to imagine that their fears were exaggerated or that he was just joking or that the other would never turn canary. It turned out to be an exceedingly long and tiring day, but, after plying first his mother and then his father with excessive amounts of their favorite booze, he was finally able to learn the unvarnished truth about their first meeting in that fateful town and about their second in that fateful camp. The prisoners finally talked, and Volodymyr's dilemma was finally overcome— well, almost, but even almost can be pretty good, especially if one considers the alternatives, which can range from not at all to quite a lot to someplace in between.

Impressed by the unexpected turns that history can take, Volodymyr learns just how Ivanna and Solomon met and what she did afterwards, and how Solomon repaid the favor, possibly to Volodymyr's consternation, or possibly not, possibly in furtherance of historical progress, or possibly not

The story, as Volodymyr was able to piece it together from their somewhat hysterical and frequently incoherent and possibly mendacious accounts, came down to this. The most important part of the puzzle was that both Solomon and Ivanna had indeed been in the same western Ukrainian town in June 1941. She had arrived on June 25 with several other translators in the wake of the German attack three days earlier; he had left on June 26, two days after the prisoners had been massacred in the local prison in the night of June 24.

The shooting had started just after news of the Blitzkrieg had reached the Soviet authorities in the town. The Communist leaders and military commanders were dumbstruck, unwilling to countenance the possibility that Hitler could have betrayed *Genosse* Stalin in so underhanded a fashion. Despite their immobility— they immediately called Moscow, but the comrades there were in no less a state of shock—the secret police cadres knew better than to panic and concluded that preventive measures should be adopted to minimize the harm to Mother Russia's soft underbelly. The NKVD officers who ran the prison—and Solomon was among them—secretly conferred in a side room of the former town hall and decided to eliminate the nationalist threat once and for all. There were seventy-four prisoners (sixty Ukrainians, eight Jews, and six Poles) and there were eleven NKVD agents. Four local Ukrainian collaborators were given picks and shovels and instructed to dig a mass grave. When they finished, they received shots to their heads and were dumped at the bottom of the ditch.

The NKVD agents disagreed on how to proceed next. Some argued that the prisoners should be killed in their cells and then carried to the pit. That would prevent flight, but it also meant that more locals would have to be included in the operation and, the agents realized, it would be difficult to recruit collaborators as the Germans advanced and news of the disappearance of the four grave-diggers spread through town. Others suggested that the prisoners be escorted to the hole, shot, and thrown in—but, given the logistical complexity of such an operation, some might be tempted to run, some might succeed, and the whole undertaking might then be placed in jeopardy. Finally, one inventive agent provided a Solomonic solution to this awful conundrum. He suggested that the prisoners first be tortured in their cells—that would disable them and prevent escape—and then be dragged to the pit. The comrades breathed a collective sigh of relief and agreed that his solution was excellent, especially as it also afforded them an unparalleled opportunity to vent ideological anger at their class enemies. Some expressed that anger by beating the prisoners across their faces and feet; some tore out fingernails, poked out eyeballs, or cut off tongues, testicles, or penises; some just confined themselves to severing hamstring muscles and tendons that made walking, and of course running, quite impossible. It took a few hours, rather more than expected, to disable all seventy-four enemies of the people, but when the process was over, the NKVD agents agreed that the prisoners had become docile, even friendly, and that leading them to the ditch required at most a few pokes in the back and a curt remark or two.

The inmates were lined up at the edge of the hole, fifteen at a time, and told to wait patiently until the agents cocked their guns and raised their muzzles to their shaven heads. A few managed to stand and acknowledge the bullets with slight nods; others fainted or fell or stumbled, thereby necessitating two and sometimes even three shots. It took about ten minutes for each group of fifteen to be dispatched to Kingdom come, so that all seventy-four were comfortably ensconced in the pit in just under an hour. Filling it in with earth took another hour. After each layer of soil was deposited on the corpses, the agents stomped about, packing the bodies and dirt as tightly as possible. Some seven layers later—with two or three carefully deposited on the very top—the earth seemed firm and the top of the grave was level with the surrounding ground. The agents assembled bricks and boards and branches and other debris and scattered it over the grave. They then boarded their cars and drove east. Only Solomon and two other agents, one Russian and one Ukrainian, were left behind, with the task of waiting for the Germans, organizing a resistance, and informing headquarters of enemy troop strength. They hid in a small house off the main street, after first killing the owners and informing their daughter that a similar fate would befall her if she failed to cooperate.

The day before the Wehrmacht marched into town—their black helmets, black rifles, and black boots glistening in the sun— the Ukrainian reconnaissance teams and translators arrived. They came in three olive-green vehicles, some fourteen young men and women dressed in civilian clothes. Ivanna sat in the front seat of the lead car, a Luger pistol in her hand. The local population stayed indoors as they sped down the streets, directly to the town hall, where they found broken furniture and documents scattered about the rooms and corridors and stairwells. In the backyard, piles of documents had been set on fire; pieces of charred paper had been lifted by the hot air and deposited among bushes and in the branches of trees. It was then that the locals who lived near the prison informed Ivanna's comrades of the inhuman cries they had heard two nights before, and of the volleys of shots that followed soon thereafter. They rushed to the prison and found it empty— except for the trails of blood, the broken teeth, the clumps of hair, the thin traces of excrement, and the bits of human entrails. The clues pointed to the yard, which was also empty except for piles of bricks and boards and branches and other debris. But the earth beneath the piles seemed a different consistency and color—

auburn instead of burnt sienna, to be exact—and everyone immediately guessed what lay beneath. The digging that followed quickly revealed the layers of contorted bodies. Someone said the murderers were Jews, and everyone agreed that they would be made to pay. Ivanna raised her fist to the heavens and vowed to avenge her brethren.

That evening, Ivanna and two of her male colleagues were billeted at the home of a school teacher near the center of town. As luck would have it, the house was next door to the one in which Solomon and his two comrades had found refuge. When Volodymyr learned of this remarkable coincidence he could but marvel at how, once again, fate or God or history was playing with him. The coincidence was remarkable, so much so that it even seemed preposterous. To think that his life might have been different—or, rather, that he might not even have been alive—had Ivanna found an abode two or three houses away from Solomon's made his head spin. I am, he thought, the logical consequence of an accident of fate, the physical embodiment of two contradictory principles, two contradictory lives, two contradictory histories, two contradictory worlds. Was that what psychiatrists called schizophrenia? Was that what philosophers called overdetermination? Or was that what historians called contingency?

The teacher noticed that something was amiss when he visited the outhouse and saw that the familiar glow of dancing candles was absent from his neighbors' curtains. He couldn't imagine that they wouldn't be reading at night or, even more improbably, that they had left with the retreating Soviets. He then called on Ivanna and the two men to take their guns and join him in taking a closer look at the suspicious house. As they positioned themselves near the dark windows, the teacher knocked on the front door. Solomon and his comrades sensed that trouble was afoot and, as the girl opened the door, they began firing their semiautomatic weapons, killing her and the unfortunate pedagogue instantly. In the resulting firefight, Solomon's and Ivanna's comrades also died and Solomon received a shoulder wound. As he lay on the floor, struggling to get to his feet, Ivanna calmly approached him, pointed her Luger at his head, and hissed, "You dirty Communist Jew, get ready to die." But the gun—amazingly for a German product known for its reliability—misfired and she missed, grazing his right ear instead. Solomon then gave her a quick kick and she fell to the ground. He jumped on her and, as they struggled in a fashion that, Volodymyr thought, must have resembled love making, they came face to face. She spat in Solomon's eyes, and Solomon responded by bringing his fist down against her temple. She passed out and, with reinforcements sure to arrive any second, he ran out of the house, climbed over the back fence, wended his way through the cherry orchards, and escaped. That non-decision to kill her, thought Volodymyr, that one moment of hesitation is, *mirabile dictu*, why I am here—why I am alive.

As to his parents, those two or three seconds in which they looked each other in the eyes created an indelible impression that obviously stayed with them. Ivanna resolved to hunt down the dirty Jew who killed her comrades; Solomon resolved to hunt down the dirty Ukrainian who killed his comrades. Once again, Volodymyr was struck by the slight coincidence that would have such baleful, and such symmetrically baleful, consequences. Would he never escape the clutches of moral symmetry? Did his parents have to struggle in a manner that even they must have realized, at least in retrospect, resembled love making? Did their faces have to come up against each other for those fateful seconds, giving them just enough time to memorize each other's features? Did there have to be just enough light in the house for them to see and remember each other's faces? How little it took, Volodymyr marveled, for fates to be altered and lives to be ruined—or begotten, as in his case. And what awful circumstances molded people's lives. We are, he concluded a tad lugubriously, the products of death and destruction—all of us. Small wonder that we take so naturally to killing.

When Ivanna arrived at Auschwitz, she volunteered to be a guard, just as Volodymyr had surmised. She carried a whip and a pistol and wore high black boots that she gleefully used to kick Jewish slackers, malingerers, and other doubters of *Arbeit*'s capacity to make them existentially *frei*. Rumor had it that her predilection for whipping and pistol-whipping prisoners as they were being marched to the gas chambers won her the moniker, Ivanna the Terrible. When Solomon's turn came to be incarcerated, he volunteered to remove gold teeth from corpses in the hope, quite possibly, of saving a few nuggets for a rainy day. They must have

76

passed each other on many occasions, but they only recognized each other in the fall of 1944. Neither knew what to do at first, but each resolved to kill the other. The memory of their desperate eyes and intertwined limbs had stayed with them. One day, a few weeks before liberation, as Solomon was returning from the gas chambers, Ivanna crossed his path, whip in hand and ready to strike. He caught the whip and jerked it, dragging her to the ground. Once again, their bodies became entangled in what must have appeared like love making until Solomon, his hatred approaching boiling point, tied her hands with the whip, lifted her skirt, and penetrated her.

Chapter 6

As cynics, frustrated idealists, corrupt politicians, and saints might have predicted, Volodymyr's encounter with the truth has less than salutary consequences for his well-being and sense of humor and leaves him wondering whether truth is all that it's cracked out to be

Puzzled, confused, and even exasperated, Volodymyr ponders the nature of the straw that broke the camel's back and other savage conundrums of direct, indirect, and possibly no relevance to the tortured condition of his poor and progressively poorer soul

Having learned what he had learned about his parents, Volodymyr was, truth to tell, of at least two minds about the old dictum that the truth shall set ye free. He now knew the truth, all of it, but didn't feel a bit freer. Indeed, he arguably felt less free, if freedom had anything to do with peace of mind, tranquility, and inner harmony. Ignorance was indeed bliss, he reluctantly concluded, and the truth may just as easily *not* set you free as set you free—a proposition that, he sensed only vaguely, had portentous implications for his life, for life, and for the universe. After all, if ignorance really were preferable to knowledge, then neither essentialism nor consequentialism had a leg to stand on, and only the Moral of the Popcorn, which presupposed neither knowledge nor ignorance, retained any validity. But who would ever believe that popcorn could have more to say about life than philosophy in general or pipe-smoking philosophers in particular?

In any case, it was indisputably true that, in his case, the truth had none of its reputed favorable effects. It was bad enough to be the progeny of an anti-Semite and a Jew, of an anti-Ukrainian and a Ukrainian, of two people who faced each other in a personalized equivalent of a Hobbesian state of nature for all their lives together. But to learn that his mother had tried to shoot his father and that his father had violated his mother—and that he, Volodymyr, was the product of that unsuccessful killing and that successful rape—was simply intolerable. But how exactly was Volodymyr *not* to tolerate this intolerable thing? Was pulling the trigger in war really an attempted murder? Wasn't the rape really just a personalized form of self-defense? And weren't both actions really ways of negotiating, interrogating, and exploring reality, which, as everyone with half a brain and an advanced degree knew, was at best unknowable and at worst opaque? Alas, after failing miserably to contextualize his parents' actions, Volodymyr knew that the problem was beyond solution.

That, evidently, was that. And when things got to the point that all one could say was, "That was that," and shrug, then that was indeed that. Sometimes Volodymyr even regretted his curiosity—which, he recalled ruefully, was known to kill cats—and wondered what his life would be like if he had never decided to discover the truth about his parents and himself and the past. It would still have been intolerable—and that distressed him—but it would also have been slightly less intolerable—and that distressed him even more. But there was no going back. Having bitten from the apple of the Tree of Knowledge, he could no longer get the toothpaste back into the tube. If you break it, you own it, a jealous Indo-European girlfriend named Dodo (the *d*'s, oddly, were pronounced as *b*'s), who was trying to extricate a marriage proposal from him, once said, in reference, presumably, to her heart and not her hymen.

But perhaps all was not lost. Perhaps that was not quite that. After all, getting the toothpaste back into the tube had always struck Volodymyr as a difficult, but not intrinsically impossible task. One obviously couldn't un-squeeze the tube—Volodymyr knew enough about physics and metaphors to know that one couldn't reverse the arrow of time, at least not without breaking it or puncturing the palm of one's hand—but there was no reason that he couldn't procure or construct a device that would pump the paste back into the tube. It might be easier still to open the tube and scoop up the toothpaste with a spatula and slap it back in. Some of the toothpaste would be irretrievably lost, but a healthy amount could probably be saved, and that sure as hell was pretty darned good, enough to warrant hoping that he *just might* get the toothpaste back into the tube and that that was *not* that.

No, far more worrisome was the possibility that biting from the apple of the Tree of Knowledge amounted to the straw that broke the camel's back. Were that to be the case, then that really would be that. Volodymyr had always wondered just how one could determine which particular straw would have such a tragic effect on a poor camel, but, as with the puzzle of the toothpaste, he knew that creative thinking could go a long way toward clarifying such moral dilemmas. Why not do an experiment? He'd need a typical camel—not too big, not too small, not too weak, not too strong. He could canvas a statistically significant number of camel owners or just average the weight of every existing camel and then pick one that most closely approximated that number. Once the camel was on hand, the rest would be a bowl of borscht. He'd construct a box made of some light but sturdy new-age material that would fit snugly above the hump; it could be suspended from the ceiling with ropes and pulleys and the average camel wouldn't feel its weight at all. And then he'd take average pieces of straw—each of the same weight— and drop them into the box one by one. At some point, the weight would become so great that the camel's back would approach breaking. At some subsequent point, a telltale straw would actually break the camel's back. The world would have one less camel— and the noble beast would surely be missed, especially by lovers of animals, lovers of the desert, and lovers of scientific progress—but the world, through Volodymyr's wise intercession, would also acquire genuine knowledge and finally be able to say with complete confidence that the straw that indisputably breaks the average camel's back is always and everywhere the Nth, and not, as some contrarians might claim, the Xth or the Yth or even the Zth. The result would be the transformation of a metaphor into a real claim about the nature of reality and the relationship between means and ends and straws and camels—and by extension between straws and camels and human beings.

That was a project for the future. In the meantime, Volodymyr knew that the knowledge he had acquired about his parents could very well be the straw that threatened to break the camel's back. The good news was that the camel's back was still intact; the bad news was that it was arguably only a few straws from breaking. Volodymyr knew that his life was in just such a precarious position. He was approaching a precipice. He was almost at the edge of a chasm. One more straw, one little push— and he might be plunged to his doom. It dawned upon Volodymyr that time was running out—though where exactly he couldn't say—and that he had to do something quick in order to fix things, if only to avoid the pitfalls of mixed and mixed-up metaphors.

Confronted with the undeniable fact that things had become a big mess, Volodymyr wonders about the nature of mess-becoming things, humanity's ability, or inability, to grasp this nature fully, and his own inability to express himself in ways that even he could understand

It was well and good for Volodymyr to have resolved to fix things, but he soon discovered—or, more precisely, rediscovered, as it was hardly the case that he had no inkling (oh, that damned word again!) of what he was about to rediscover— that it was one thing to realize that things were a complete mess and quite another thing to figure out just what the alternative was and just what one could possibly do, or say, or for that matter even think to change things. As Volodymyr contemplated the pickle he was in, he came to appreciate that the core of the problem lay in those damned things that amounted to a mess and that were so slippery as to elide any possible, or any possibly obvious or obviously possible, resolution. What exactly were these devilishly vexing things? Were these things *real* things—*real* objects of the kind one could touch and feel and sense? Or were these things just metaphors for something else, for something that truly was in and of itself—Volodymyr had picked up that phrase, *an und für sich*, while chatting with an existentialist over a plate of chow mein and marveling at the food's incongruity with the Shanghai Garden's elegant decor—elusive and slippery?

That slight distinction masked an enormous difference. Thing-like things that amounted to a mess could presumably be fixed with relative ease. Perhaps not quite with scissors and glue or with screwdrivers and hammers and screws and nails, but surely a touch of dexterity would suffice to make whole what had fallen apart. If those elusive things were like a vase or a shoe or even a shirt, and if the mess these things made was like a crack or a worn out sole or a missing button, then fixing that crack or sole or button didn't require too much skill or imagination. But if those elusive things were notions or emotions or conditions of the soul or some such stuff, then Volodymyr knew he was pretty much a dead duck trapped in a dead end of his own making. After all, how was he to go about fixing a crack in his soul (to use a terribly hackneyed phrase that had only one virtue—namely, that it just might be preferable to the notion of a crack in his heart)? Now *that*—a crack in his heart—was an image that Volodymyr simply refused to countenance and, even if the crack he confronted truly concerned his heart, he was determined to leave it untouched and unsolved and unfixed. That was, after all, the least he could do or, to be more exact, *not* do to maintain the purity of language and whatever moral acuity or personal integrity such purity implied.

But this is where the going really got rough. His ruminations about those damned elusive things—which reminded him, unsurprisingly, of that damned elusive Pimpernel—pointed to no obvious solution. The more he thought about these things, the more elusive and slippery and unapproachable and, indeed, incomprehensible they became. It was almost as if he were meditating and focusing on the light, the truth, the reality, the godhead—and then finding that, the more successfully he focused, the less accessible that light, that truth, that reality, that godhead became. *Veni* and *vidi* just didn't culminate in *vici*. Indeed, the closer he came, the more they receded into the mists of—of what? Time? No, it wasn't time that they were receding into. The future? But the future was just time. As was the past. And just what kind of mists were they, to be able to *swallow*—yes, *that*, Volodymyr decided, was just the word he was looking for—his attempts at comprehension?

Besides, could a mist really swallow something? Of course not. Mists were droplets of water and had no organs capable of producing swallowing-like behavior. That Volodymyr knew for a fact. Did he simply mean that the things to which he aspired—the light and the truth and the reality and the godhead—were simply unattainable? That could very well be the case, but then why not come right out and say it? Why beat around the bush with silly metaphors and talk about mists and swallowing, when all he really meant was that these metaphors and images were as preposterous as his name and that, instead of fretting about them and their appropriateness, all he had to do was hit the nail on the head and get to the point? Or, indeed, simply *get* the point? Why employ the preposition, *to*, when it added nothing to the meaning of the sentence and the complex thought and moral anguish he was trying to express?

And just as Volodymyr was thinking these thoughts and suspecting that he might be on the verge of understanding the nature of reality—or at least of time or of language—it suddenly struck him, like a bolt out of the blue, that his supposed triumph over obscurity and obscurantist language was taking place in terms of obscure and obscurantist language! *Sacré bleu*, he cried, I am trapped in a vicious circle. I am walking along an endlessly long, and closed, path. I can never get from here to there, because there is no distinct *here* and no distinct *there*. In a world such as this there could be, Volodymyr sadly realized, no hard and fast truth. Indeed, there couldn't even be a soft and slow truth. In a world such as this, truth was dead, period.

Did that mean that what he had learned about Mamochka and Papasha was not true? That conclusion seemed to follow, but it couldn't be right. *That* truth was the truth that had started the whole mess in the first place. *That* truth had to be true, or else nothing else would matter. Of course, if by some happy coincidence he could come to believe that that first truth was untrue, then all his troubles with things, both thing-like and non-thing-like, would vanish and everything would be fine once again. The logic seemed impeccable, but Volodymyr knew enough about the incestuous relationship between *modus ponens* and *modus tollens* to appreciate that he couldn't just revise his premises if the conclusions were not to his liking. He was stuck, he was trapped— and he knew that the Moral of the Popcorn had proven correct— alas, again.

Beset by doubts about reality's reality and increasingly incapable of speech acts, Volodymyr grasps at Cartesian straws and wonders whether being a thing that thinks but does not talk is possible or whether being a thing that thinks but does not talk is quite impossible

Although most truth might therefore be as dead as a doornail, the fact that the one truth about his parents was actually true was a relief of sorts. For an all too brief moment, Volodymyr delighted at the thought that he was retracing Descartes' bold steps and even toyed with the possibility of developing a modern-day variant of *Cogito, ergo sum*—until he realized that he had lost all ability to express himself clearly, concisely, and without constant recourse to colorful metaphors, unpersuasive images, hackneyed phrases, and trite sayings. The temptation to descend to triviality had always tormented Volodymyr—not unlike the way the demon had tempted St. Antony—but it was only now that he came to appreciate that he had fallen like a rotting log to the bottom of a filthy pond. And there he lay, mired in the mud and muck of linguistic decay, powerless to extricate himself from, or even correctly diagnose, his unenviable and unviable condition.

Volodymyr saw that he retained his capacity to speak. His tongue was healthy and he still remembered the sounds that words were supposed to make, but he was quite incapable of expressing any words. This is not to say—this is *decidedly* not to say—that Volodymyr became incapable of thought. He remained, much to his relief, a *res cogitans* perfectly able to point to some object, raise his eyebrows quizzically, take the money from his wallet, and pay for it. And he could hold elaborate conversations about any topic under the sun with deaf mutes. Notwithstanding these small triumphs of mind over matter, however, Volodymyr felt like a fish without fins or a crab without claws. He could, *mirabile dictu*, still whisper his own name, and the sound of smoothly rounded pebbles receding pell-mell into the ocean with a gentle wave still proved to be a source of intense pleasure and great consolation. I may no longer amount to much, he thought, but I am, still, who I am. I am still Volodymyr Frauenzimmer—just as a fish without fins is still a fish and a crab without claws is still a crab. And, he added, lest the point be unclear, an octopus without tentacles is still an octopus.

But then something happened—something quite surprising and utterly unexpected. When Volodymyr tried to recite, in the lyrical manner that always gave him such solace, the words that, like a mantra, could transpose him into higher realms of reality—

"Stupid Ukrainian pig!"
"*Dirty kike!*"
"Killer!"
"*Exploiter!*"
"Pogromchik!"
"*Usurer!*"
"Collaborator!"
"*Boot-licker!*"
"Nazi!"
"*Stalinist!*"
"Peasant!"
"*Banker!*"

85

"Filthy peasant!"

"Money-grubbing banker!"

"Vicious anti-Semite!"

"Rabid Communist!"

"Fascist scum!"

"Socialist scum!"

"Stupid Ukrainian pig!"

"Dirty kike!"

—he found that his tongue remained tied and he could not. This, he knew, was the veritable last straw. The camel's back may have remained intact, but his own moral backbone had been broken.

Volodymyr comes face to face with nothing less than ontological evaporation, an intrinsically disturbing phenomenon if there ever was one, which rears its ugly head and assumes alarming and puzzling and mysterious proportions of a kind rarely encountered in all of history, whether real or constructed or merely imagined

Volodymyr was savvy enough to know that language obviously constructed reality, and his first reaction to the realization that he had lost his ability to speak was to think, Egad! Is my reality going out the window as well? But then, upon deeper reflection, he saw that, in his case in any case, the causal arrow seemed to go the other way. As a matter of fact, the more he thought about it, the more he saw that it wasn't language that had sabotaged his reality, but that the reality he had learned about Ivanna and Solomon had sabotaged language. That, Volodymyr concluded with no small pride, was quite a discovery. Indeed, it was more than a discovery. It was actually proof positive that language was irrelevant. All that mattered was the stuff around us—the things.

But then these very things got worse, much, much worse. Volodymyr came to understand this while traveling by train to Moscow, where he planned to spend three restful weeks at the Serbsky Institute for Discursive Wellness. He was alone in the sleeping compartment. The bed sheets were badly ironed, the mattress was lumpy and thin, and breakfast consisted of a glass of dark tea, two cubes of brown sugar, and a small spoon, all precariously balanced on a wet saucer. When he awoke he noticed that the water in his glass had, apparently, evaporated. He had left the glass on the little table next to his bed. As Volodymyr turned off the light at night, he distinctly remembered that there was water in the glass, if only because he distinctly remembered thinking that he might enjoy a short tepid sip first thing in the morning. He decidedly did not remember waking up in the middle of the night and drinking from the glass. There was no one else in the compartment, so the water must have evaporated. This thought— or was it this fact?—made Volodymyr profoundly anxious. Worse, he couldn't figure out why it made him anxious. And that also made him anxious.

As the train approached the border Volodymyr realized that something else gave him sleepless nights. Things break. He knew they should and would, but he suddenly understood that he couldn't understand their breaking. Or perhaps the problem was that he did understand why they broke. For instance, his glasses. Several weeks before Volodymyr had boarded that train, just as he was preparing to leave for the airport, the frame of his glasses had snapped in two. He'd had these glasses and that frame for six years and there had never been any hint of trouble. Volodymyr understood that the metal was wearing thin from use, from constant bending and flexing. Sooner or later, it had to snap. But that was just a generalization, like saying that things fall or that causes always have effects. Yes, yes, he knew, this was all quite true, in the abstract, as a rule, even as a natural law. What worried him was that this particular frame should have snapped at this particular time. Or that the water in this particular glass should have evaporated during this particular night. No general causes could account for these particular effects. And yet, the effects happened, and he knew they did, because he happened to witness them with his own eyes.

The train stopped at the border and Volodymyr realized that other things also worried him. For instance, his shirt buttons fell off, always, it seems, at the worst possible time—when he'd be rushing somewhere, when he had to make a good impression and buy high and sell low, when this was the only shirt that went with those pants, when this was the only shirt that made just the semiotic statement he wanted to make. And then off went the button—never an inconspicuously placed or irrelevant button. No, it was always the top button, or the button located in the middle of his chest, or the button holding down his collar. Clearly, it wasn't just the question of causes and effects that worried Volodymyr. It was above all the question of important effects that gave him no peace.

Or take another example from a weekend trip to the races in Perm, when the ink in Volodymyr's ballpoint pen ran out. He knew it had to. After all, the cartridge was of limited size, only a certain amount of ink could be stored inside, and, sooner or later, especially if he actually used the pen, the ink simply had to run out. One could probably calculate the exact time mathematically, dividing the total amount of ink in the cartridge by the amount expended per minute of writing. Volodymyr understood the laws of nature, having employed them to good effect in determining which straw would break the average camel's back. He understood that finite amounts were finite and, thus, could not be infinite. He understood that the ink in pens could not last forever. But he couldn't understand why the ink in this particular pen, the one he might be writing with, should run out. And, especially, why it should run out just *now*—say, at the very moment he'd be signing an important document, so that one third of his name would appear in bold ink and the second third in increasingly faint ink, and he'd be forced either to write over his entire name—thereby producing an oddly shaped signature, fat in front and thin at the end—or to continue at the point where the first pen's ink began running out, which invariably meant that the flow of his handwriting would be interrupted in mid-signature—thereby creating the impression that he had a hiccup while signing the important document. Either way, it looked as if he were unable to appreciate the seriousness of the document and, by extension, the seriousness of life and existence and all that jazz.

Beset with linguistic decay and ontological evaporation, Volodymyr resolves to fix this existential crack by searching for epistemological solutions—a move that some might endorse, some might reject, and few could comprehend, especially outside the withered groves of academe

Although he had every reason to descend into the depths of depression, Volodymyr did not. Nor did he just accept his fate passively. Quite the contrary, he resolved to seize the bull of perplexity by the horns and force it to his will. First, he did what any educated person would do when confronted with complexity and began reading poetry, which, as a Turco-Iranian girlfriend named Q'Bobo (the *q*, apparently, was silent) had once told him, held the answers to all of life's questions. But Homer seemed of more relevance to Aegean tourists, Catullus to Latin lovers, Vergil to urban planners, and Ovid—well what could one possible say about Ovid?—and Volodymyr concluded, perhaps a tad too hastily, that if the classics had nothing to say to him, neither would the moderns. Volodymyr then turned to prose, while resolving to start with the moderns and work his way back to the ancients. Alas, as he soon learned, the novel, like the truth and the author, was as dead as a doornail, and there seemed no point to working his way through a graveyard genre that might have had a past, but obviously had no future or present, except perhaps on the paperback stands of small-town drugstores and provincial airports of emerging-market countries.

Volodymyr then sought solace amidst the shady groves of academe. But no one, he quickly determined, had quite experienced what he had experienced and all the psychological, theological, sociological, criminological, Kremlinological, anthropological, anthroposophical, scatological, eschatological, metaphysical, philosophical, or self-help books promising instant self-esteem had anything to say to him. Volodymyr then went to specialists. The psychoanalysts told him that he should investigate his childhood traumas, but that was obvious and unhelpful. The psychiatrists prescribed powerful drugs, but none could tell him what to do after the effects wore off. The priests and rabbis told him to pray, but his inability to decide on the language and the prayer only discouraged the chickens from coming home to roost. Healers recommended that he practice yoga, improve his posture, find his inner child, and center himself, but once he moved past the physical movements, words failed him and the whole production turned into a major-league flop. A historian told him that his case proved that individuals were the product of the *longue durée*, a sociologist informed him that individuals were the products of social anomie, while a Slovenian culturologist named Zigzag said that it was all discourse anyway. Some friends suggested that he drink more, others that he drink less. An Argentinean toreador suggested he have a torrid affair; a Moroccan dentist—that he practice self-restraint and have a root canal. And to what end? thought Volodymyr. Whether or not these learned folk are right or wrong or right and wrong, my whole goddam *Lebenswelt* is going to pot. It was all very confusing and very disturbing and very, very inconclusive, even damnably so.

Chapter 7

In what surely seems to unimaginative readers like yet another unjustified departure from the master narrative and its iron-clad logic, Volodymyr meets the tortured Putschkin who impresses him with his truthfulness and introduces him to his villain, Bohdan Stashinsky

Volodymyr's above-mentioned visit to a gathering of pacifically inclined intellects in East Berlin turns out to have unexpectedly interesting consequences in, of all places, Moscow, proof positive, perhaps, either of Heisenberg's Uncertainty Principle or of the ability of quantum physics to produce effects at a distance

It happened this way. Volodymyr was in Moscow visiting Putschkin, a frail poet he had first met at the peace conference in East Berlin. Understandably distracted at that time by the unexpectedly lascivious lover of his haikus, Katorga, Volodymyr had exchanged few words with the verse-smith and would have forgotten the badly dressed Russian-speaking German Jew, had Putschkin not written to him several months later and asked if it wouldn't be too much trouble for Volodymyr to send him the abridged English-language edition of the *Compleat Mother Russia's Favorite Russian Memoirs.* Volodymyr gladly, and unthinkingly, agreed, believing that this was both the right thing to do (thereby paying service to his essentialist moral streak) and the best way to promote human rights and democracy (thereby paying service to his consequentialist moral streak). A few months later, Putschkin invited him to Moscow and assured him that he needn't worry about visas, invitations, and other irksome formalities that his good friends in the corridors, chambers, and antechambers of power would be happy to expedite.

The poet owned few things, because, as he insisted, he disdained the things of this world. Books lay scattered about his apartment, a dusty cactus stood silently in a corner of the living room that, equipped with a small fold-out sofa, also served as his bedroom, and clothes were draped over the backs of two fold-out chairs. Putschkin also possessed one table, several lacquered pine bookshelves, and a cornucopia of dirty bottles arrayed along ledges and windowsills, presumably as weak stabs at decoration. The yellow walls were bare, except for the outlines of prints or paintings that were no longer there.

Volodymyr slept on the sofa, while Putschkin, claiming that the hardwood floors were good for his moral backbone, retired to a sleeping bag between the chairs. At night, after consuming several bottles of semi-dry Siberian champagne, the two would hold extended conversations in the darkness, until the drone of their voices lulled them to sleep. After four such sessions, the outwardly reserved Putschkin had managed to spill enough beans to permit Volodymyr to reconstruct his incredible life.

Putschkin's father had been born and raised in Potsdam, as a thoroughly assimilated Russian with little sense of his origins, identity, or religion. A grandfather or great grandfather named Puschkin (without a *t*) had accompanied the tsar to the great palace of Sans Souçi in the early nineteenth century and stayed to cater to the needs of the burgeoning Russian colony. In the late nineteen-twenties, as street battles between right and left intensified throughout Germany, the family sensed that both opportunity and danger were in the air and changed its name by adding a *t*. After Hitler came to power in 1933, they had few qualms about donning brown uniforms and extending their right arms with enthusiasm. That one letter saved Putschkin's father, Helmut, from possible incarceration, but it also got him drafted into the Wehrmacht as a simple foot soldier. After Operation Barbarossa was launched in 1941, his unit was assigned to Belarus, on the edge of a swampy region infiltrated with Soviet partisans who killed his *Kameraden* at night and who, in turn, were killed by the *Kameraden* during the day. What most impressed Helmut was that there was no stopping the Belarusians. They crawled out of the mud and they crawled back into it. Despite some misgivings about killing his ethnic blood brothers, Helmut did his duty and, when necessary, shot them, some point-blank in the forehead, some in the groin, if he wanted them to confess. But they never did. Instead, when surrounded, they would burst out of their bunkers firing wildly, inviting death. Or if the situation was hopeless, they would pull the pins on their grenades or explode their guns in their mouths. They died like heroes, for a cause they believed in—and one in which he, too, soon claimed to believe. Upon liberation Helmut joined the Communist Party.

He first served as an agitator among the workers of Wedding. Then, in 1948, when the Soviet comrades made their first attempt to liberate all of Berlin from the imperialist yoke, he joined the security service, the *Staatssicherheitsdienst*. The Stasi was the front; it was where the trenches were. It was where he could atone for his sins in Belarus. Putschkin, appropriately, was born when the fascists provoked some retrograde workers to march on people's power in 1953. Joseph Vissarionovich had just died and the working class was confused. How could it live without the great leader? The fascists struck, but the people struck back. His father's first gift to Putschkin was an Order of Stalin medal, pinned to the baby carriage after the fascist diversion had been decisively rebuffed.

Helmut married his secretary in the *Staatssicherheitsdienst*. A nice plump Jewish girl from Lower Saxony, she had been in the Communist Party in the twenties, acquired Aryan airs and sided with the Nazis in the thirties, and then, as Russian tanks were lumbering from the east and the Allies were advancing from the west, had burned her party card and joined the anti-Nazi underground. The invading Soviet troops repeatedly raped her anyway, but she took that humiliation as penance for her former collaboration and emerged from the experience chastened, if no longer chaste, and firmly committed to serving socialism for the good of the proletariat and the friendship of peoples the world over.

Both parents had decided that Putschkin should follow in their footsteps. He was patient and industrious and articulate. He could have chosen to do other things, but protecting the workers and serving the Party seemed like the best way to combine self-fulfillment and duty. Putschkin volunteered to serve as an informant while he was still in middle school. He told his parents of his wishes at dinner—he remembered that they were eating a succulent Wiener Schnitzel that evening—and, although they feigned to be surprised by his desire to serve the cause, they quickly and gladly gave their assent. Next evening he accompanied them to an elegant restaurant in the Friedenssackgasse. They sat at a small corner table, diagonally across the room from the stage on which a large blonde comrade played Beethoven's incomparable Tenth on an accordion. His father ordered a string of courses as well as beer and wine and champagne. As they were eating dessert, a tall man in uniform joined them, shook their hands, bowed to Putschkin's mother, and sat down next to him. The man asked Putschkin to join him for coffee next day at Stasi headquarters. When Putschkin arrived, the man told him that his codename would be Little Koba, that he would keep his eye on suspicious activities at school, and that he should deliver his reports to his father or mother on the first Monday of every month. Putschkin was, as he put it to Volodymyr, "thrilled" by the assignment. His father said, "Now, you too are a fighter." His mother embraced and kissed him. I am in the battlefield, he thought. How can socialism possibly lose with me on its side?

But Putschkin lost his zeal after his first trip to the West. His family had moved to Moscow and he had joined the Komsomol. One day the best and the brightest of the Young Leninist League were packed into Ikarus buses and transported to Paris, to get a first-hand look at capitalist decadence and have endless meetings with French comrades star-struck by the workers' paradise. It was there that Putschkin met Berria, a brash French girl with large breasts, a name that resounded with socialist rectitude, and a passion for dialectical materialism, post-structuralist poetry, and oral sex. Putschkin had never quite experienced such a combination of the scientific and the emotional, and he quickly fell head over heels in love.

"I found Berria on Thursday," Putschkin waxed positively poetic to Volodymyr. "I don't mean to say that I had lost Berria the day before and then found her the day after. Nor do I mean to say that I met her or that we met on that Thursday, although technically that would be true. No, I found her in the sense that you find, if you're really lucky and happen to have been on the terrace at the precise moment of its conception, a lovely view, as of the valley below Karaganda, when the blackness is cut in two by a string of light moving hesitantly from left to right and leaving no trace in its wake."

"A troop transport train?" Volodymyr asked hesitantly.

"No, enemies of the people," said Putschkin.

"And then what happened?"

"I kissed Berria on Friday," Putschkin continued. "She was standing at the open window, the dark air rushing in, the tracks singing rhythmically, the gentle horizon twisting in the wind, a single constellation suspended amorously above. I pointed at the stars and, as she turned her head and stretched her neck, I lowered my lips. We reached the border on Saturday, and as the German guards checked our passports, I knew that I had fallen in love. *Enfin*, she said, as the train resumed its journey. *Endlich*, I replied."

Putschkin's unlikely encounter with Berria ended soon after he returned home. She sent him a postcard on which she wrote, "*Défense de fumer. Je t'aime, B.*" Putschkin had started smoking Gitanes in Paris, and as charmed as Berria was by his Francophile affectations, she tried to make him stop. But the dour Moscow KGB didn't get the joke, and, suspecting Berria of communicating with Putschkin by secret code, subjected the poor boy to endless rounds of interrogations in the Lubyanka. Putschkin had heard about the famed basement—the joke was that the Lubyanka was the tallest building in the Soviet Union because you could see Siberia from its greasy basement—but hearing had failed to dispel his enthusiasm for the secret police. Being there did. He also resented the KGB's lack of faith in him. After all, his parents were Stasi. He wanted to join. Their credentials were impeccable. Why should a romance with a French comrade be held against him?

Putschkin was summarily expelled from university, and his parents were transferred to lower-paying jobs in the security apparatus. It was a small step from that humiliation to depression, which evolved into anger, which eventually became, and remained, hatred of a stupid—and criminal, "yes, Volodymyr, an absolutely criminal"—regime.

In a remarkable development with striking parallels to Volodymyr's experiences with Katorga, Putschkin gives Volodymyr the dope on Bohdan Stashinsky, another man who, unbeknownst to Volodymyr, would have an immeasurably large impact on the course of his life, thereby proving that insignificant causes can have significant consequences, and vice versa

Putschkin had become a voracious reader after his break with the secret police, and he tried to get his hands on everything that smacked of nonconformist thought. At first, he just placed the books in ever larger piles scattered about his apartment, but after a while—when the floor space gradually disappeared and the books formed a level surface about one meter off the ground—it became clear even to the dissident within him that wall-length book shelves were in order. He bought them in the newly opened IKEA-Moskva for a fraction of their original cost. People had stopped reading, and although book burning was no longer quite in fashion, the poor sold their remaining copies to make money and the rich sold theirs to make room for postmodernist furniture, vertical blinds, and oversized paintings by Maxim Gorky's imitators. And since no one was buying shelves, Putschkin stocked up on cheap books and acquired the place to store them in one fell swoop.

Putschkin began his reading with the kinds of books that his parents would never have tolerated—dissident literature and exposes of Stalinism by a quartet of authors he came to refer to as the 4-H Club: Gus Hall, Enver Hoxha, Ho Chi Minh, and Eric Hobsbawm. It took very little for his hitherto unquestioning faith in communism to crumble and be replaced with an equally fanatical rejection of the entire Soviet experiment. Once that phase was over, Putschkin proceeded to the logically next step—an examination of his family's role in what he somewhat luridly came to call the "crimes of communism." That his parents were no innocents had long been clear to him. That they felt equally at home in Russia and Germany also seemed to testify to a distressingly low level of patriotism and a dreadfully high willingness to serve any Communist master. Volodymyr told Putschkin that he was being unfair, that officers of the Communist secret police—and especially of the Stasi—had to follow orders and that following orders meant serving whomever and wherever one was told to serve.

"So they were just following orders?" Putschkin sneered. "That, my dear friend, is the Eichmann defense, and I reject it. They knew exactly what they were doing. They chose to follow the criminal orders of a criminal organization."

"But," Volodymyr objected, "surely you don't think your own parents were—"

"—criminals?" Putschkin snapped. "Of course they were."

One day, Putschkin's suspicions were confirmed. After tortuous conversations with retired KGB officers, ex-diplomats, and dissidents, Putschkin uncovered the fantastic story of his father's work in East Berlin. Helmut had apparently been the Stasi case officer of one Bohdan Stashinsky—a Ukrainian assassin who had killed two Ukrainian nationalist émigrés in Munich and defected to West Berlin with his East German wife in 1961. Stashynky had been tried at a sensational trial in Karlsruhe in 1962 and, after serving time in a West German prison, had disappeared, presumably having been relocated to a safe country by the CIA. The trial had exposed the KGB's bloody methods and embarrassed its then head, Aleksandr Shelepin.

Stashinsky had been recruited in the early nineteen-fifties. After mastering German and receiving a new identity, he was assigned to the struggle against the perfidious Ukrainian bourgeois nationalists who dwelled on the ash heaps of history. In 1957, he took a flight to Munich, where he infiltrated the cafes favored by conspiratorially inclined Ukrainian émigrés. His first target was the liberal anti-Soviet nationalist, Lev Rebet, whom he killed later that year in a building on Karlsplatz, at the entrance to Munich's old town. Everyone thought Rebet had collapsed on the stairs from a massive heart attack. Two years later, Stashinsky dispatched the right-wing anti-Soviet nationalist, Stepan Bandera, in the entrance to his building in Kreittmayer Strasse. The initial diagnosis was a heart attack, but doctors discovered tiny pieces of glass in Bandera's face which led them to suspect foul play. As it turned out, Stashinsky had used a clever assassination device developed by the KGB. By squeezing two handles, he cracked open a vial and released a poisonous spray that resulted in immediate death. It was clear to Putschkin that his father must have trained Stashinsky in the use of this deadly contraption.

"My father is a murderer." Putschkin's tone was flat, almost matter of fact. "And I am the son of a killer."

"It's not your fault, Putschkin," Volodymyr pleaded. "You know that."

"But it is my responsibility to atone," Putschkin insisted.

"No," Volodymyr countered, "it is not. Why should it be?"

"Because I cannot sleep. That is why."

"For heaven's sake, Putschkin, *both* my parents are murderers! If you should atone, then what should I do?"

"Beg forgiveness," Putschkin intoned.

"For what?" Volodymyr cried. "From whom?"

Putschkin fell silent and looked out the window. "Did you know," he said, "that, after serving eight years in jail, Stashinsky was smuggled to South Africa, where he was given a new name and alias? He even married a South African woman."

"South Africa?" Volodymyr gasped. "But that's where Schwartzbard died!"

"Schwartz—who?" Putschkin asked, his face as blank as the Siberian taiga.

"You wouldn't know him," Volodymyr replied. "You said Stashinsky was tried in Karlsruhe. Do you have more information about the trial?"

"Sure," Putschkin calmly said. "Here."

As Putschkin handed him a rolled-up magazine, Volodymyr subliminally sensed that he was about to be struck by a bolt out of the blue.

Although provoked by Putschkin to learn more about a Ukrainian assassin, Volodymyr remains blissfully unaware of the suspicious similarities between his conversation with Putschkin and his conversation with Katorga and decides to make another foray into the past, in the hope that he just might be able to deflect the arrow of time by making good use of another respectable, quotable, and unimpeachable Western source[3]

The day before the Berlin Wall was built, a Russian named Bogdan Nikolaevich Stashinsky went over to the West, confessed that he was a Soviet secret agent and that years earlier he had hunted down and killed two Ukrainian anti-Red emigrés in Munich. The reason why the deaths had not attracted special attention— one was put down as a heart attack, the other as suicide—proved bizarre. His weapon, said Stashinsky, had been a single-barreled aluminum air gun that fired a pellet of liquid potassium cyanide through a fine mesh screen, releasing a poison spray. The poison caused death within 90 seconds after it was inhaled, leaving no mark on the victims.

---

[3] "Espionage: A Poor Devil," *Time*, October 26, 1962. Reprinted with permission of *Time* magazine.
<http://www.time.com/time/magazine/article/0,9171,874524,00.html?iid=chix-sphere>

Last week, in the Federal High Court in Karlsruhe, the airgun killer was on trial, and for three days he quietly explained the circumstances behind his cold-blooded crime. Oddly enough, the friends and relatives of Stashinsky's victims who crowded the courtroom felt less hate than pity for the man in the dock. His was a tale of blackmail, grief, fear and love that moved the lawyer representing the widow of one victim to define the crime as manslaughter, not murder. Added an attorney for the other widow: Stashinsky was only "a poor devil."

Struck by the decidedly different atmosphere of this trial and grateful for the absence of unnecessarily lurid modifiers, Volodymyr decides to listen attentively to the proceedings before engaging in histrionics and actually interfering in the course of time

No Choice. Stashinsky's bedevilment began innocently enough. In the summer of 1950, he was riding home on the train from Lvov, where he was studying to be a mathematics teacher, when he was picked up by Soviet transport police for traveling without a ticket. Stashinsky, the son of a poor peasant in a nearby village, was relieved when police let him go after merely asking some questions.

But the cops obviously concluded that they could use Stashinsky; a few days later, he was summoned back to police headquarters and blackmailed into becoming an informer. The area around Lvov was a hotbed of guerrilla activity by anti-Communist Ukrainian nationalists, many of whom had fought with the Nazis against the Russians during the war. Stashinsky's family, especially a younger sister, supported the guerrillas. Unless he cooperated, police told Stashinsky, his family would be sent to Siberia. Testified Stashinsky last week: "I had no choice. I wanted to see an end to the fighting. I wanted to protect my family. And I wanted to go on studying."

The new MVD recruit easily passed his first test: he asked his sister to put him in contact with a local underground group, then turned in its leaders. Soon afterward, Stashinsky was enrolled in a spy school at Kiev. Assigned to East Berlin, Stashinsky was bored with his tasks; he passed information to and from other Soviet couriers, and once he was ordered to copy down the license plate numbers of Allied military vehicles. One of Stashinsky's few excitements was a girl he met in an East Berlin dance hall, Inge Pohl, with whom he fell in love. Inge did not know her lover's real employer, thought Stashinsky was a translator.

Uncertain of how genuine bedevilments can begin innocently, Volodymyr wonders just how choice evaporates and is replaced by compulsion, especially under conditions of civil war, and then decides, perhaps a tad too hastily, to pursue the same line of attack he had perfected at an earlier trial in Paris

Volodymyr's 7th Antihistorical Intervention. And thus they continued until the defiant Frauenzimmer rose from his seat and turned to the blanched flappers, bewhiskered Hebrews, and pallid Ukrainians and, pointing accusingly at both lawyers, screamed, his eyes glistening with hysteria and fanatical exultation: "Ladies and gentlemen of the jury, the defendant wants us to believe that he was unwittingly implicated in a step-by-step process that inexorably brought him to assassination and that he bears little or no responsibility for his actions. This classic slippery-slope argument does not get the defendant off the hook. When confronted with choices, Stashinsky always said yes to the secret police. Regardless of whether those choices were simple, as they were at first, or complex, as they eventually became, he always said yes. Did the defendant have no choice, as he insists? The reality is that he had many choices, but that he always refused to make them." Then, dropping limp, he fell into his seat.

*

Stricken Conscience. In 1957 Stashinsky received orders to go to Munich, track down a Ukrainian nationalist writer named Lev Rebet and kill him; an agent sent from Moscow gave him instructions in using the poison-spray gun. The prospect mildly disturbed Stashinsky, but his belief that the Ukrainian extremists were "people of the lowest sort" stiffened his spirit. Still, when he tested the gun on a dog that was tied to a tree, Stashinsky recalled, "I felt sick. I kept telling myself this was all necessary to help other people. At moments like this you grab on to your political dogma to pull you through even when you feel it's hollow."

100

Stashinsky pulled through. While passing Rebet on the staircase of an office building, he pointed the six-inch aluminum barrel at Rebet's face and pulled the trigger. Rebet toppled without a sound, and Stashinsky did not look back as he walked to a canal and dropped the weapon into the water. Two years later, he killed another exiled Ukrainian leader, Stefan Bandera, almost as smoothly. But while watching a newsreel of Bandera's funeral in a movie theater, Stashinsky felt his conscience catching up with him. "It hit me like a hammer," he said. "From then on, I knew that I must never allow myself to be used like this again."

To his Soviet superiors, Stashinsky was a hero: he was flown back to Moscow, received the Order of the Red Banner signed personally by Marshal Kliment Voroshilov. At a lavish stag party, Secret Police Boss Aleksander Shelepin himself gave him the high award.

Beginning to appreciate that his interventions are as pointless now as they were in 1927, though not yet sure whether he should throw in the towel or continue, Volodymyr decides to raise an important moral issue that, in principle at least, should be of interest to the jury and, perhaps, even to humanity

Volodymyr's 8th Antihistorical Intervention. And thus they continued until the defiant Frauenzimmer again rose from his seat and turned to the blanched flappers, bewhiskered Hebrews, and pallid Ukrainians and, pointing accusingly at both lawyers, screamed, his eyes glistening with hysteria and fanatical exultation: "How can we fail to notice that Stashinsky felt more remorse about killing a dog than about killing a man? And how can we fail to notice that he felt guilt only after viewing a dead man on film—that is, several steps removed from life—and that this guilt did not get in the way of his enjoying a stag party? I wonder, ladies and gentlemen of the jury, whether the defendant is quite the poor victim of circumstance that he wants us to believe he is." Then, dropping limp, he fell into his seat.

*

Tragic Opportunity. That night Stashinsky announced that he intended to marry Inge Pohl. Reluctantly, Shelepin & Co.

101

agreed, though they would have preferred a Russian girl for their boy. Stashinsky was ordered to stay in Moscow and Inge, who by now knew her husband's real job, joined him there. Soon she persuaded Stashinsky to flee to the West, but it seemed impossible. Their Moscow apartment was bugged, and often they would communicate only by notes.

Tragedy finally gave them their chance to escape. When Inge became pregnant, she was allowed to go back to East Berlin to have her baby. The baby died, and the secret police, though suspicious that Inge had poisoned the child, permitted Stashinsky to return for the funeral. Before the burial, the couple shook off Soviet agents who were trailing them and took the elevated train into Berlin.

Said Stashinsky at last week's trial: "My confession is a sign of my remorse." His sentence: eight years in prison, a surprisingly light punishment, reflecting the court's opinion that Stashinsky was "an abused tool of highly placed wire-pullers" and the really guilty party was the Soviet government.

Exhausted, frustrated, despairing, and despondent, as well as increasingly persuaded that the world is deaf to his interventions, Volodymyr takes a bold leap and decides in desperation to appeal to reason and numbers, presumably in the belief that audiences will respond more readily to the authority of science than to the appeal of emotion

Volodymyr's 9th Antihistorical Intervention. And thus they continued until the defiant Frauenzimmer yet again rose from his seat and turned to the blanched flappers, bewhiskered Hebrews, and pallid Ukrainians and, pointing accusingly at both lawyers, whispered, his eyes glistening with hysteria and fanatical exultation: "Ladies and gentlemen of the jury, I beg you to reconsider your verdict. The defendant killed two men in cold blood, and for these crimes he received eight years—four per assassination. Thirty-five years ago another man was set free for killing someone he considered a dog. That comes to eight years for three deaths—or thirty-two months of punishment per corpse. I understand the motives, I understand the circumstances—but is that what human life is worth? A measly thirty-two months in jail?" Then, dropping limp, he fell into his seat.

Chapter 8

Secretly hoping that his failure to transform the past was just a one-off fluke, Volodymyr decides to go for broke by embarking on his second premeditated attempt to change history and, unsurprisingly, is again demoralized, possibly even crushed, by its uncertain results

Volodymyr cross-examines the defendant Bohdan Stashinsky in the hope of discovering just how he could have killed twice in the course of two years, thereby exceeding Sholom Schwartzbard's and most assassins' one-time interruptions of the flow of history and, not parenthetically, of life, too

Frauenzimmer: Your name?

Stashinsky: Bohdan Stashinsky.

Frauenzimmer: Your occupation?

Stashinsky: Assassin.

Frauenzimmer: Whom did you kill?

Stashinsky: Two enemies of the people—Lev Rebet and Stepan Bandera.

Frauenzimmer: And why did you kill them?

Stashinsky: I was following orders.

Frauenzimmer: Whose?

Stashinsky: The KGB's.

Frauenzimmer: So you bore no personal animus toward Rebet and Bandera?

Stashinsky: They were my ideological enemies.

Frauenzimmer: Do you kill all your ideological enemies?

Stashinsky: Of course not.

Frauenzimmer: So why did you kill these ideological enemies?

Stashinsky: I already told you. Those were my orders.

Frauenzimmer: Why do you think you were ordered to kill these two men?

Stashinsky: They were anti-Soviet leaders. They were conspiring to overthrow Soviet power. They had to be liquidated.

Frauenzimmer: You had no feelings, no emotions about killing them?

Stashinsky: I am a trained assassin. I am not supposed to have emotions.

Frauenzimmer: But you did have emotions. You were sorry to have killed a dog.

Stashinsky: It was just a helpless animal—

Frauenzimmer: —that deserved more pity than two human beings?

Stashinsky: I did feel pity for them.

Frauenzimmer: Perhaps later, *after* you killed them—but not before or during.

Stashinsky: I told you. I am a professional. And besides, they were the enemy.

Frauenzimmer: And therefore deserved to be liquidated—like vermin.

Stashinsky: I never said they were vermin.

Frauenzimmer: But you implied as much by feeling sorry for a dog, and not for them.

Stashinsky: You are putting words in my mouth.

Frauenzimmer: I am drawing the logical conclusions from your actions.

Stashinsky: I did have doubts.

Frauenzimmer: Doubts about what?

Stashinsky: About the wisdom of killing them.

Frauenzimmer: Please explain. What do you mean by wisdom?

Stashinsky: I wondered whether killing two men in Munich would really help the Soviet Union.

Frauenzimmer: But you just said they were nationalist leaders. They opposed the Soviet Union. Why shouldn't killing anti-Soviet émigrés have helped the Soviet Union?

Stashinsky: When I learned more about them, I saw they were just men, with wives and families and friends. I once saw Bandera with some woman. Was she his mistress? I thought. And he was such a small man, hardly the monster that my handlers in Moscow said he was.

Frauenzimmer: And yet you killed both.

Stashinsky: I am a professional, and I do what I am told.

Frauenzimmer: Well, not quite, isn't that so? Eventually you did defect, and you betrayed your comrades at your trial.

Stashinsky: That was later. That was after I met Inge and we fell in love. We had a child.

Frauenzimmer: And then you lost the child.

Stashinsky: It was the saddest day of my life.

Frauenzimmer: The assassin experiences tragedy and becomes a human being!

Stashinsky: If you like.

Frauenzimmer: How did you become an assassin? Was it for ideological reasons?

Stashinsky: I was caught—it was 1950, I think—riding the train without a ticket. The secret police knew that my sisters were in the Ukrainian underground. They offered me a deal: my collaboration in exchange for their safety.

Frauenzimmer: Why weren't you in the underground?

Stashinsky: I was never political, and I didn't really care— about nationalism or communism.

Frauenzimmer: But you surely knew of the fighting taking place all around you?

Stashinsky: Of course, we all did. Some supported the nationalists, some the Communists. Some, like me, tried to stay out.

Frauenzimmer: But didn't the Communists anger you? They were occupying your land, killing your people.

Stashinsky: The nationalists were doing the same. They were all ruthless. The things I saw….

Frauenzimmer: Such as what?

Stashinsky: Killings, torture—by both sides. It was horrible. And the Germans were even worse.

Frauenzimmer: But the nationalists fought for national liberation. Didn't you want that?

Stashinsky: Perhaps, maybe—I don't know. Anyway, their struggle was hopeless.

Frauenzimmer: Very well, then, it is 1950 and you've been dragooned into the ranks of the secret police. What did you do?

Stashinsky: I reported on the activities of the underground.

Frauenzimmer: Was there already talk of your becoming an assassin?

Stashinsky: No, that came later.

Frauenzimmer: Did they just say, "And now you will become an assassin"?

Stashinsky: Of course not. I had to learn German, so I knew I'd have an assignment in West Germany, and I was briefed on the émigré nationalists, so I assumed that my task would be to infiltrate them.

Frauenzimmer: But weren't they already infiltrated?

Stashinsky: Completely—the émigrés as well as the underground. We played them off against each other.

Frauenzimmer: Rebet versus Bandera, right?

Stashinsky: The hard-liners supported Bandera and the moderates supported Rebet. Our people provoked the split. Bandera accused Rebet of treason; Rebet accused Bandera of treason. They spent more time fighting each other than us. It was almost comical, actually.

Frauenzimmer: So why kill them?

Stashinsky: We had destroyed the underground in Ukraine and we had divided the émigrés. The next logical step was to decapitate them.

Frauenzimmer: Why was Rebet first? Wasn't Bandera the more radical of the two?

Stashinsky: Rebet and his pals were the intellectuals. Bandera's followers were the true believers.

Frauenzimmer: Like Bolsheviks?

Stashinsky: Yeah, like Bolsheviks. Anyway, after the underground was smashed, the ideological threat was more dangerous than Bandera's rabble-rousing.

Frauenzimmer: Let's move on to the actual assassinations. You used a device that released a fatal gas.

Stashinsky: It wasn't easy figuring out how to use the damn thing. I even had to practice on a poor dog. A gun would've been simpler, but our people didn't want to create martyrs. What could be more natural than for two excitable émigrés to die of heart attacks?

Frauenzimmer: You shot Rebet in the staircase of the building in which he worked.

Stashinsky: He was climbing the stairs and I was walking down.

Frauenzimmer: I've seen photographs in which you staged the assassination for the German police. What struck me most was that you were wearing white socks.

Stashinsky: Was I? I don't remember.

Frauenzimmer: No assassin would wear white socks. Your trainers trained you poorly.

Stashinsky: Perhaps, but Rebet never suspected anything. If he thought my socks were unusual, he said or did nothing.

Frauenzimmer: Did he die immediately?

Stashinsky: I believe he climbed another floor before collapsing.

Frauenzimmer: And what did you think when you released the gas?

Stashinsky: I don't know. I think I felt relief—that it was finally over.

Frauenzimmer: But no vindication, no happiness at the thought that an enemy of the people had been liquidated?

Stashinsky: I told you. He seemed like such an ordinary enemy, hardly worth the bother.

Frauenzimmer: And how did you kill Bandera?

Stashinsky: More or less the same way. He opened the door to his building. As he approached the staircase, I was descending. I said something like "Hello," he looked up at me, and then I squeezed the device and he fell and the bag he was carrying dropped to the floor and the tomatoes rolled out.

Frauenzimmer: Nice touch—the tomatoes. Did that really happen? Or are you just embellishing for dramatic effect?

Stashinsky: Of course it happened. I always tell the truth.

Frauenzimmer: Really? Always?

Stashinsky: I couldn't live with myself otherwise.

Frauenzimmer: I find that self-delusions are indispensable. I think you do too.

Stashinsky: Quite the contrary.

Frauenzimmer: I don't think you're being honest with yourself—and with us, with history.

Stashinsky: But I've already told you. I know what I did, and I know why I did it.

Frauenzimmer: You say it's remorse. But I wonder. If you were truly remorseful, you wouldn't insist you'd been trapped. I think it's something else. I think you know you're a criminal.

Stashinsky: I had no choice. Like Schwartzbard. *We* had no choice.

Frauenzimmer: What did you think when you killed Bandera?

Stashinsky: I'm not sure. Some relief, and some pity.

Frauenzimmer: For this enemy of the people?

Stashinsky: He was such a small man, and he was fumbling with his keys and holding a bag of groceries. What sort of enemy carries a bag of tomatoes?

Frauenzimmer: The same that is killed by an assassin in white socks.

Stashinsky: Touché.

Frauenzimmer: I've noticed something peculiar about your two assassinations.

Stashinsky: They were classic KGB wet work.

Frauenzimmer: Both times you left the scene of the crime and walked quite a distance to a stone bridge in the Hofgarten, where you dumped the device into a canal.

Stashinsky: It was out of the way—a good place to get rid of the weapon. Those were my instructions.

Frauenzimmer: Why not a sewer?

Stashinsky: Too suspicious. Why would a grown man bend over a gutter and drop a piece of metal into the sewer? Some *Hausfrau* might've thought I'm littering.

Frauenzimmer: Still, I have the feeling you were driven to that canal.

Stashinsky: Like Raskolnikov, you mean? Driven by guilt?

Frauenzimmer: A tortured conscience....

Stashinsky: Nice theory. Who knows? Could be, I suppose.

Frauenzimmer: Surely the parallel has crossed your mind.

Stashinsky: I don't care for Russian literature. Too gloomy for my taste.

Frauenzimmer: What do you read? Lenin?

Stashinsky: I may be an assassin, but I'm not crazy. No—I don't care for literature. I always wanted to build things— be an engineer.

Frauenzimmer: Well, you certainly built an interesting life.

Stashinsky: I was sucked in, trapped.

Frauenzimmer: You had no choice?

Stashinsky: None at all. Perhaps like you. Have you chosen your life? I doubt it.

Frauenzimmer: But you did eventually make a momentous decision.

Stashinsky: I met Inge, and when she began asking me who I was and what I did, I thought she must be Stasi.

Frauenzimmer: You didn't even trust the woman you loved.

Stashinsky: How could I? I had to assume that everyone I met was a spy.

Frauenzimmer: What made you trust her?

Stashinsky: I decided to test her. I'd tell her I was an assassin. She'd express horror, of course, but I felt I'd be able to tell the difference between real horror and feigned horror.

Frauenzimmer: And you did?

Stashinsky: And I did. I held her in my arms when I told her, and I could feel her heart beat more rapidly. I knew she was for real.

Frauenzimmer: So you defected for the love of a woman?

Stashinsky: I suppose so.

Frauenzimmer: Love was your downfall!

Stashinsky: Only partly. By then I had begun having doubts about my profession.

Frauenzimmer: You felt guilt?

Stashinsky: Of course, of course—I already told you so. But I also began to hate the system that had trapped me.

Frauenzimmer: Hatred was your salvation?

Stashinsky: I suppose so. Jumping ship was the best decision of my life.

Frauenzimmer: So you defected and you were put on trial and then you were imprisoned. For all of eight years. That's a pretty light sentence, considering—

Stashinsky: —the real killer was the KGB.

Frauenzimmer: And you were just following orders?

Stashinsky: Believe it or not, but yes.

Frauenzimmer: Do you really think that gets you off the moral hook?

Stashinsky: How many years did Schwartzbard get? And he didn't have to follow orders.

Frauenzimmer: So both of you are equally innocent—

Stashinsky: Exactly.

Frauenzimmer: —or equally guilty.

Stashinsky: If anything, he's more guilty than I am. No one forced him to kill.

Frauenzimmer: He says it was his conscience—that he had to avenge a crime.

Stashinsky: My KGB handlers said the same about the nationalists.

Frauenzimmer: So you served your eight years, and then they took you to South Africa, where you assumed a new identity and a new life. And where you died.

Stashinsky: Yes.

Frauenzimmer: Did you know that Schwartzbard also died in South Africa?

Stashinsky: Really? What was he doing there?

Frauenzimmer: Selling encyclopedias. Don't you see a savage irony here—that a Jewish watchmaker and a Ukrainian village boy should both come to rest in the land of apartheid?

Stashinsky: You're being poetic. That was pure chance. And it means nothing.

Frauenzimmer: Like your being caught without a ticket? One last question. Do you regret your life?

Stashinsky: What do you think?

Volodymyr interrogates the village boy's victims in the hope of figuring out just why killers kill the people they kill or, to put it more or less precisely perhaps, just why the people killed by killers are killed by the killers who kill them

Frauenzimmer: Your name?

Rebet: Lev Rebet.

Frauenzimmer: Your occupation?

Rebet: Democratic nationalist.

Frauenzimmer: And your name?

Bandera: Stepan Bandera.

Frauenzimmer: Your occupation?

Bandera: Revolutionary nationalist.

Frauenzimmer: So—you're both nationalists, but apparently of different kinds.

Rebet: I am a democrat. He is not.

Bandera: He says he's a democrat. But the people support me.

Frauenzimmer: We'll return to that later. I assume you both agree you're nationalists?

Bandera: If you mean that we both want an independent Ukraine, yes. If you mean that both of us know how to achieve this goal, then no. I do, he does not.

Rebet: Authoritarian thinking and leader cults are a dead-end.

Bandera: The pursuit of fashionable ideas of pseudo-democracy advances the Bolshevik agenda.

Frauenzimmer: I think we can agree that you disagree on some fundamental points.

Bandera: It's more than a disagreement. I am right, and he is wrong.

Rebet: And who appointed you the nation's lawgiver?

Frauenzimmer: But you can surely agree on one thing— that you were both assassinated by the same Soviet agent.

Bandera: I was the target. He was for practice. The Bolsheviks had been trying to kill me since 1945.

Rebet: That's absurd. The KGB doesn't risk its agents for practice.

Frauenzimmer: Well, why *do* you think you were killed?

Rebet: We were both nationalist leaders. The Soviets knew that our movements enjoyed great support among the Ukrainian people. They still do.

Frauenzimmer: But the Soviets say you were enemies of the people.

Rebet: That's just propaganda—

Bandera: —and lies. Ukrainians supported us.

Frauenzimmer: Your assassin, Stashinsky, was Ukrainian, you know.

Bandera: But what kind of Ukrainian?

Frauenzimmer: He says he was only following orders.

Bandera: Exactly, he's the kind of Ukrainian who blindly follows Moscow's orders. The new Ukrainian will be confident, strong, and energetic.

Rebet: And democratic.

Frauenzimmer: You talk a bit like a fascist.

Bandera: That's ridiculous. We fought the fascists in the war.

Frauenzimmer: But you were happy to collaborate with Germany before the war.

Bandera: That was geopolitics. The Soviet Union was our enemy, and only Berlin supported us. What would you have done?

Frauenzimmer: Ally myself with the democracies.

Bandera: The same democracies that approved Austria's annexation and Czechoslovakia's dismemberment?

Frauenzimmer: But the Germans were fascists!

Bandera: And we were nationalists! We led a national liberation struggle. You have to be strong to do that, and strength isn't fascism. Were the Zionists fascists? I am the Menachem Begin of Ukraine, you know. Was he a fascist because he was strong?

Frauenzimmer: I'm glad you mentioned Jews. Your movement called them Communists.

Bandera: We said that communism was a Russian-Jewish creation. Who ran the Communist Party of Western Ukraine? Jews. Who ran the Communist Party of Poland? Jews. Who ran the secret police in Soviet-occupied Ukraine? Jews. Who established the Soviet Union? Russians.

Frauenzimmer: But that's anti-Semitism!

Bandera: Nonsense! Wasn't your own father a Jew and an NKVD executioner?

Frauenzimmer: That's beside the point.

Bandera: That *is* the point!

Rebet: The real point is that many of our people hated Jews. And don't forget the pogroms.

Bandera: Pogroms? They were acts of vengeance. Your mother was present at one of those so-called pogroms. How would *you* have responded to the thousands of dead bodies the Communists dumped in pits?

Frauenzimmer: You sound like Schwartzbard.

Bandera: Why is he praised for seeking revenge? And why are we vilified for doing the same?

Frauenzimmer: Let's move on to your assassinations. Do you think you deserved to die?

112

Bandera: Only evil people deserve to die. I wasn't evil. I was an enemy of the Soviet Union.

Rebet: Does anyone deserve to die? Besides, there are procedures. You don't just take a gun and shoot.

Frauenzimmer: Like Schwartzbard?

Rebet: I can understand his rage, but he was wrong.

Frauenzimmer: He believed there was no other way to get justice.

Rebet: Perhaps, but that's still the law of the jungle. And what if one of Petliura's people had shot him? Should he have been set free too?

Frauenzimmer: Stashinsky got eight years.

Bandera: He should've been hanged.

Frauenzimmer: What were both of you thinking when Stashinsky pointed his weapon at you?

Rebet: It was wrapped in a newspaper. I thought he was pointing to something.

Frauenzimmer: Did he look like an assassin to you?

Rebet: He was nondescript.

Bandera: He greeted me after I opened the door to my building. I looked up to see a slender young man walking down the stairs with a newspaper in his hand.

Frauenzimmer: So there was nothing to alert you?

Rebet: Nothing at all.

Frauenzimmer: You had no last thoughts?

Bandera: How could I? I saw him extending his arm, and then I was dead.

Frauenzimmer: He says he's sorry he killed you.

Bandera: He should be. I was his leader, and he betrayed his nation.

Rebet: A remorseful KGB assassin? I suppose anything is possible in this day and age.

Frauenzimmer: As you look back on your lives, would you have done anything differently?

Bandera: No, nothing at all.

Rebet: Yes. We thought Germany would help us after war with the Soviets broke out. That was a mistake.

Frauenzimmer: And what of the Jews, the Poles?

Rebet: Our hatred of both was wrong—and stupid. Ukraine cannot just be for Ukrainians. We can't fight everybody.

Frauenzimmer: It was more than just hatred. There were pogroms. There was ethnic cleansing.

Bandera: There you go again! Every national liberation struggle is bloody: *every single one.* Look at the Americans, look at the Algerians, look at the Israelis. Mistakes are inevitable. Bloodshed is inevitable. Suffering is inevitable. The important thing is never to veer from one's ultimate goal. My movement never has.

Rebet: He talks like Mussolini.

Bandera: I beg to differ. I talk like Begin, like Washington.

Frauenzimmer: What do you think of Petliura?

Bandera: A great hero!

Rebet: He could have been a great man.

Frauenzimmer: And Schwartzbard?

Bandera: A Soviet agent, like Stashinsky.

Rebet: A Jewish nationalist, who made the same mistakes we made.

Frauenzimmer: What do you mean?

Rebet: Violence and vengeance, even if justified, are no solution.

Frauenzimmer: You sound like a pacifist.

Rebet: Hardly, just a realist.

Frauenzimmer: Since when?

Rebet: Getting killed concentrates the mind, you know.

Chapter 9

Once again, the master narrative rears its ugly head as Volodymyr experiences a savage bolt out of the blue and discovers the redeeming power of hatred, without fully appreciating that enlightenment, like salvation and knowledge, may actually be a dead end

Continuing to feel great anxiety and no small measure of genuine Angst, Volodymyr finally experiences something akin to relief when he espies the exceptionally great leader's fish eyes and ugly mug and senses a visceral hatred that, counterintuitively perhaps, promises faith and hope, though definitely not charity

And then the anxiety induced by ontological evaporation came to a complete halt, and it happened like this. Though speech-impaired and reality-deprived, Volodymyr remained determined to retain his reading skills and therefore took to buying all the daily papers, reading them from front to back and, with the Yiddish tabloids, from back to front. One day, as he opened the *Übermensch Revue* to the second page, he came upon a large photograph of a bald-headed man with fish eyes and tight lips. He felt an immediate sense of revulsion, of downright detestation, of the kind he had never before felt in his life. Not even his parents' worst stories had elicited so visceral a response as this bald-headed, fish-eyed, tight-lipped, mug-faced little man did. As Volodymyr stared at the photograph—one could say that he felt downright transfixed, just as Alexander may have been transfixed by the sight of the mighty Ganges—as he tried to understand just what it was about that little man that so repelled him, he experienced a bolt out of the blue. As long as he felt hatred for fish-eyes, the anxiety provoked by his disturbing encounter with the objective truth behind his parents' troubled past ceased. Indeed, as he gazed at fish-eyes with the intensity of an Impressionist painter leering at a nude, a remarkable thing happened: hesitantly at first, and then with growing confidence, he began chanting the rhythmic epithets he knew so well—

"Stupid Ukrainian pig!"

"*Dirty kike!*"

"Killer!"

"*Exploiter!*"

"Pogromchik!"

"*Usurer!*"

"Collaborator!"

"*Boot-licker!*"

"Nazi!"

"*Stalinist!*"

"Peasant!"

"*Banker!*"

"Filthy peasant!"

"*Money-grubbing banker!*"

"Vicious anti-Semite!"

"*Rabid Communist!*"

"Fascist scum!"

"*Socialist scum!*"

"Stupid Ukrainian pig!"

"*Dirty kike!*"

—and saw that they had become a source of great comfort once again. Good-bye, Charlie, he thought, I can speak again! I am cured and fish-eyes has cured me!

Who was this little man, and why did he hate him so? A few strolls with the denizens of the corridors of power revealed that he was the exceptionally great leader of Russia—the *velikii vozhd*. A former big wheel in Leningrad and a big cheese in Moscow, the great leader had abandoned *la dolce vita* after being exiled to a minor administrative post in Mother Russia's equivalent of an armpit for some infraction involving pay-offs to other big wheels and big cheeses. Upon emerging from obscurity a new man, he became an ascetic devotee of a saintly Saxon pipeline manufacturer who administered to the needs of the very poor and, to maintain God's plans for universal equilibrium, to the very rich—but never, as he put it, the filthy *nouveaux riches*. It was then that fish-eyes began his long climb back to respectability via the German secret police. He collected dissidents' soiled underpants, stored them in airtight jars, and used them to direct canine noses in the righteous struggle against ideological diversion and bourgeois subversion.

Fish-eyes did his job well, assembling a fabulous array of dirty linen that enabled him to promote, dismiss, or dispatch anybody he desired to whichever post, in this or the next world, he desired. He quickly succeeded in eliminating his rivals, promoting his cronies, and propelling himself to the very top of the power pyramid. Soon thereafter, as Russia experienced the throes of another time of troubles and presidents and prime ministers proved too drunk or too disputatious to set things right, fish-eyes seized power and declared himself the exceptionally great leader of a great and powerful and strong Russia. His success in drawing on and merging the police traditions of both Mother Russia and *Vater Deutschland* attracted the attention and admiration of international human rights organizations that lauded him for his vision and courage and convinced German chancellors, Italian prime ministers, and French presidents to grant him medals, prizes, and other commemorative humanitarian knickknacks.

His last name was Pitoon, which, Volodymyr had to smile, rhymed almost perfectly with spittoon. Was it coincidence—or was it the hand of God—that Pitoon's first name was, like that of a cigar-smoking bigwig with a platonic love of democracy, Gerhard? Volodymyr concluded that it had to be the hand of God. Like me, Volodymyr observed, Pitoon was of mixed parentage. His father was Russian and his mother was German, and, like Volodymyr, Pitoon was fluent in both languages. But that's where the similarities ended. Unlike Volodymyr, Pitoon was reputed to have engaged in fabulous exploits and to have remarkable talents. He had apparently traveled throughout much of the world, having been to the Orient, the Occident, and all points in between. He had, people said, actually gone back to Constantinople, which he claimed was far superior to Istanbul. He had jogged along the top of the Berlin Wall, done cartwheels in No-Man's Land, and swum the Straits of Magellan. Once, at some gathering in Hungary, near Lake Balaton, a distinguished woman who was known to be worth millions told him that his slight accent betrayed him as a native of Trieste. Pitoon immediately had her shot, not because she was right, but because she was dead wrong, and he took his expressions seriously. One summer, Pitoon spent several weeks living on Mount Athos, with Russian monks who still believed the tsar was alive. Pitoon assured them that they were right. While traveling by train in a third-class compartment from Kraków to Vilnius, he was offered a Polish peasant farmer's daughter in marriage, and accepted. He uncovered Etruscan ruins in Turkey and Turkish ruins in Tuscany. He could predict earthquakes by kicking the tires of an old Zhiguli and cause bull markets by spitting at a black cat. Pitoon was supposed to have made love in, his closest confidantes swore, over eighty countries with over three hundred women, all with different first names. The ladies, unsurprisingly, adored him, and he had a well-deserved reputation as a lady-killer—much to the consternation of his dowdy wife of twenty-plus years who knew of and feared his inability to distinguish between images, metaphors, and reality, if even of the imagined and constructed kind.

Much to his surprise and contrary to his expectations, his upbringing, and his beliefs, Volodymyr discovers the redeeming power of hatred and succeeds in displacing his personal neuroses onto a sacrificial lamb that, unsurprisingly though ironically, may also be a scapegoat

Notwithstanding these impressive achievements, fish-eyes's damned fish eyes gave Volodymyr no rest. They were set close together, lodged between two sharply curved eyebrows that only accentuated the deathly emptiness that emanated from the cavities. Fish-eyes's nose sloped from a narrow bridge between the dead fish eyes and expanded to a width exceeding that of either aperture. There was something unnatural, something aesthetically wrong, about that eye-and-nose ensemble: it resembled bad architecture or bad art that was made worse by a feeble attempt to lend it respectability by means of a desperate recourse to symmetry. And below the nose hovered a tightly closed mouth with a weak and drooping lower lip. Suspended above fish-eyes's fish eyes was a large rounded forehead held taut by two slivers of sweet pink flesh, his ears. Each of his features reminded Volodymyr of a dead fish—especially the kind he had seen arrayed on ice in markets along the Mediterranean—but taken together they resembled— shades of Auschwitz!—a pile of emaciated corpses. Volodymyr suspected that fish-eyes probably thought his visage was icy, but he had it all wrong. In reality, his was the face of a dead man: no, his was the face of death. It exuded neither warmth nor iciness; it exuded only emptiness. It was a void, a grave—as cold and hard and hopeless as the earth in a snow-covered graveyard on a cold, moonlit night after a sudden, brief hailstorm.

118

These feelings—of hatred, revulsion, and disgust—were new for the naturally pacific Volodymyr. Despite the awfully hackneyed nature of such bathetic sentiments, he had always believed in the redeeming power of, yes, love, but his encounter with fish-eyes opened his eyes to something that he hadn't fully appreciated before—the redeeming power of hatred. Just why he hated Pitoon so intensely seemed perfectly clear to Volodymyr. This little fishy Pitoon was ugly—which was reason enough to detest him—but he was also the embodiment of both Mother Russia and *Vater Deutschland.* This little man with fish eyes and the snout of a swine represented both the past, which had formed Volodymyr and had given him his preposterous name and criminal parents, and the present, which continued to exert what simple folk called neo-Gramscian hegemony over his browbeaten *Lebenswelt.* It was Pitoon who had, willfully or not, spawned Volodymyr's parents. It was, Volodymyr decided, Pitoon as well who bore the ultimate responsibility for everything that had gone wrong in Volodymyr's life and, indeed, for everything that had gone wrong in life.

Volodymyr understood that ascribing all the attributes he found most repellant in the universe to this fish-eyed little man made no sense, *no sense whatsoever.* Volodymyr understood that his feelings toward Pitoon—that is to say, his intense detestation of the very fiber of this little man's existence—were completely irrational, indeed, so thoroughly preposterous as to be breathtakingly preposterous. That the preposterousness of his hatred nicely complemented the preposterousness of his preposterous name and life was some consolation, suggesting during Volodymyr's more lyrical moments that something approximating poetic justice might be at work. It went without saying, of course, that Volodymyr fully understood that this hypothesis, even if correct, provided no reasonable grounds for the extent of his hatred.

No, that was absolutely visceral. That came from the depths of his soul and heart and gut. That hatred was a manifestation of his own being and it could be explained only by a primal force of which Volodymyr had not been fully aware. Until now, that is. There was only one way to explain, however feebly and unpersuasively, just why he hated fish-eyes. Pitoon had to be his alter ego. Pitoon negated Volodymyr, even if he wasn't aware, as was certainly the case, of poor Volodymyr's existence. But that fact changed nothing. Volodymyr knew that, despite the vast distance that separated him from Pitoon in space-time, the two of them could not co-exist. They were like matter and anti-matter: it was only a matter of time before they met and destroyed each other.

Despite this overabundance of complex, hyperbolic, and possibly contradictory emotions, beliefs, and suspicions, Volodymyr knew that he was on the right track, because the more he thought about Pitoon, the more insistently did the long list of lyrically engaging epithets—

Dirty Jew!

Stupid Ukrainian pig!

Dirty kike!

Killer!

Exploiter!

Pogromchik!

Usurer!

Collaborator!

Boot-licker!

Nazi!

Stalinist!

Peasant!

Banker!

Filthy peasant!

Money-grubbing banker!

Vicious anti-Semite!

Rabid Communist!

Fascist scum!

Socialist scum!

Stupid Ukrainian pig!

Dirty kike!

—undergo a magical transformation, reflected on the surface by their loss of quotation marks and italics, and come to be directed at Pitoon himself. Volodymyr couldn't even pinpoint the exact time that, like a bolt out of the blue, the vertically assembled epithets assumed horizontal form and merged into a chorus shouting, "Dirty Russian! Stupid Muscovite pig! Dirty Chekist! Killer! Exploiter! Pogromchik! Bandit! Collaborator! Boot-licker! Nazi! Stalinist! Peasant! Banker! Filthy oligarch! Money-grubbing banker! Vicious anti-Semite! Rabid Communist! Fascist scum! Socialist scum!"

Volodymyr wasn't sure that all these epithets could be applied sensibly to Pitoon, but he was struck by how his unconscious had vastly exceeded its own job description and engaged in an editorial, grammatical, and semantic shift to redirect his anger, frustration, and hatred from himself and onto fish-eyes. All at once, Volodymyr saw that his life had all the hallmarks of an ancient Greek tragedy. Emotions were raw, contradictions were open, dilemmas were painful—and he was the tragic hero who loved and hated in equal measure. It is good to hate, he concluded, it is very good—especially if a *deus ex machina* has the good sense to appear when things get out of hand.

As Volodymyr thought these thoughts, it suddenly struck him, like a bolt out of the blue, that his encounters with Sholom and Bohdan had already taught, or should have taught, him the same lessons that he had only now, belatedly alas, learned—that love is impossible without hate and that hatred of things that deserve to be hated is good. Better late than never, he thought. Nothing ventured, nothing gained. And, although absolutely all the toothpaste might never be squeezed back into the tube, it was better to scrape ninety-nine percent back in than never to have tried at all. I am learning wisdom, Volodymyr concluded. And from wisdom, he knew, there springs goodness and hope and all that other great stuff.

Inspired by a superficial reading of the classics—which may or may not be reflective of a deeper and more all-encompassing personal superficiality— Volodymyr takes a daring leap of faith and, somewhat unexpectedly perhaps, decides to become a hit man

Volodymyr knew what he had to do next. Like Hecuba, like Medea, like Clytemnestra—he had to bump off this dirty little fish-eyed bald man, whose name rhymed with spittoon and was, appropriately enough, no less preposterous than his own. Our names are birds of a feather, Volodymyr concluded solemnly. The grave-like stillness that emanated from fish-eyes's fish eyes actually comforted Volodymyr. How could he have any qualms about rubbing out someone already rubbed out? How could he have any doubts about the rightness of dealing death a death blow?

Volodymyr felt a deep sense of relief—akin to falling asleep in the Moscow metro after a hard day in the Lubyanka's basement—after realizing that his personal well-being required removing Pitoon from, as he resolved to put it, the realm of the living, but that wondrous state of harmony did not, alas, last long. After a few days Volodymyr also saw that, despite his determination to carry out a deed that reminded him of Abraham's willingness to sacrifice Isaac, he had no idea—*no idea whatsoever*—of how to bump off the great leader or any leader, regardless of size, for that matter. He had no doubt that, if Pitoon were ever to attack him, with a gun, with a switchblade, or even with his bare fists, he could defend himself. He also had no doubt that, if Pitoon were an enemy soldier pointing a rifle or manning a machine gun in some bunker, he would know how to find cover and shoot back or crawl right up to the bunker on his belly and throw a grenade inside. And Volodymyr also knew that, if he were to stumble upon Pitoon lying dead drunk in some alley amid torn newspapers, broken glass, fresh vomit, and the pitter-patter of scurrying rats' feet, he would have no qualms about unsheathing his knife and inserting it quietly into his beating heart or severing an artery in his thick neck.

All of this was doable, and some of it was even easy, in principle in any case, but doing a Gavrilo Princip was an entirely different thing. That required extensive planning. He would have to learn just how and when he'd have access to Pitoon, and since high-ranking politicians were always under heavy guard and never appeared in public alone, it was next to impossible that he would ever find Pitoon lying dead drunk in an alley or that Pitoon would attack him with his bare fists. Gavrilo had it easy, Volodymyr thought. All he needed was a revolver and a spot near the bridge where the motorcar with Franz Ferdinand would pass. Brutus only needed a dagger. But the days when fat cats cavorted in public wearing togas or ostrich-plumed hats were long gone. The shadowy Pitoon was a resident of Mother Russia's nether regions. No one knew where he lived. No one knew what his routines were. He was unpredictable and mercurial and impossible to pin down. How could Volodymyr ever get him to cry, "*Et tu, Frauenzimmer?*" if he couldn't get within earshot of him? The answer to that question appeared to resemble a malfunctioning traffic light at the end of a very long tunnel. As so often happens in life, however, Volodymyr didn't suspect that he was much closer to emerging from that tunnel than he imagined.

Thanking his stars for his serendipitous encounters with Katorga and Putschkin, Volodymyr decides to hone his hit-man skills by consulting with a Jewish watchmaker and a Ukrainian village boy about the finer points of knocking off a political opponent, especially a slippery and elusive one

Frauenzimmer: I'd like to ask you for a few tips. You've probably guessed by now that my interest in assassinations isn't purely academic.

Stashinsky: Ah, so you wish to kill someone! Who?

Frauenzimmer: The exceptionally great leader.

Schwartzbard: You want to bump off the exceptionally great leader of Mother Russia? Are you mad?

Frauenzimmer: My reasons are irrelevant.

Schwartzbard: *Au contraire, mon ami!* You must believe in what you're doing, you must be passionate—

Stashinsky: Above all, you must be *professional.*

Frauenzimmer: You're both right. So what should I do?

Schwartzbard: Don't. He's committed no crimes.

Frauenzimmer: He was head of the KGB!

Stashinsky: And I was an assassin for the KGB. Will you shoot me too? Besides, he's too well guarded. You can't just approach him in some staircase—

Schwartzbard: —or on the street. Are you ready to sacrifice your own life? You could be caught—or shot.

Frauenzimmer: I'm sure I can manage a quick getaway.

Schwartzbard: You intend to run? Only a coward runs!

Stashinsky: Only a fool does not. Do you know where you'll dump the weapon? That's rule number one.

Schwartzbard: And rule number two is: always believe in what you're doing.

Stashinsky: That's a stupid rule. No professional holds it.

Schwartzbard: Well, *do* you?

Frauenzimmer: Surely, it's not a question of belief. My soul—

Schwartzbard: —is troubled, *oui?*

Frauenzimmer: I have no peace, no rest.

Stashinsky: And how will killing the great leader help?

Frauenzimmer: When I first saw his ugly mug in the paper, I felt at peace. And I feel at peace every time I think about him.

Schwartzbard: Yes, yes, that's exactly how I felt about Petliura…

Frauenzimmer: Hatred can be such a liberating force. I never suspected.

Schwartzbard: It's far stronger than love, of course.

Stashinsky: No, it's not: believe me.

Schwartzbard: Ah, *la belle* Inge!

Stashinsky: I warn you. Stay away from emotions. Killing is serious business.

Schwartzbard: Why do you hate the exceptionally great leader? What has he done to you?

Frauenzimmer: Nothing, actually.

Stashinsky: He represents the past to you, doesn't he?

Schwartzbard: Ah, how interesting. We Jews have long memories.

Frauenzimmer: The past? *Whose* past? *My* past?

Stashinsky: The Soviet past, your people's past, and yes—*your* past. He is the evil spirit that must be exorcised.

Frauenzimmer: I don't believe in evil spirits.

Schwartzbard: Of course you do! All Jews—

Stashinsky: —and all Ukrainians—

Schwartzbard: —believe in evil spirits!

Frauenzimmer: I thought of him as a scapegoat, as a sacrificial lamb.

Stashinsky: I'm beginning to understand you, my friend. The great leader represents the past to you, and you hope to salvage that past—

Schwartzbard: I think he wants to free himself of that past.

Stashinsky: Yes, of course! You hope to free yourself of that past by killing the man who stands for it!

Frauenzimmer: I just know that killing him will save me.

Schwartzbard: You do know he wasn't responsible for that past? It wasn't the exceptionally great leader who instigated pogroms—

Stashinsky: —or killed Ukrainian peasants—

Schwartzbard: —or killed Petliura.

Frauenzimmer: You're both right. You're both wrong. I don't care. I only know I need to find peace.

Schwartzbard: I must confess something to you, *mon ami*. I found no peace after shooting Petliura.

Stashinsky: Nor I. Rebet's death disturbed me. Bandera's devastated me. I still don't know why.

Frauenzimmer: My very being cries for the great leader's death!

Schwartzbard: Spare us the melodrama, *mon ami*. It's a romantic illusion to think that vengeance brings peace to the soul. It brings only agitation.

Stashinsky: Or emptiness.

Frauenzimmer: So what are you saying?

Schwartzbard: You will still be tortured. His ghost will live on. Nothing will change.

Frauenzimmer: Nothing?

Schwartzbard: Absolutely nothing.

Stashinsky: And you won't succeed. You're an amateur. You don't have it in you to be a professional.

Frauenzimmer: So what should I do?

Schwartzbard: Go home. Tend to your garden. Grow tomatoes.

Stashinsky: Forget the past. It'll kill you if you don't.

Frauenzimmer: But it's all around me!

Schwartzbard: Then you are doomed, *mon ami*, then you are doomed.

Unsettled by his conversation with the watchmaker and the village boy, Volodymyr consults with three dead white males who, despite those ontological shortcomings, have extensive experience that they willingly share with a would-be assassin

Frauenzimmer: Your killers say I'm doomed.

Petliura: They're right.

125

Rebet: Quite.

Bandera: I agree.

Frauenzimmer: I thought you didn't fear death.

Rebet: That's besides the point. Do you have any idea of the security that surrounds the exceptionally great leader?

Petliura: He doesn't just saunter down the street to dine at a bistro, you know.

Bandera: Or drive his car—or buy his own tomatoes.

Rebet: It can't be done. Abandon this hare-brained scheme of yours.

Bandera: Of course, there *is* great glory in dying a hero's death.

Petliura: Listen to me. Do what Schwartzbard did.

Frauenzimmer: Shoot five times? I'll be lucky if I get one shot.

Petliura: His trial humiliated me and—

Frauenzimmer: You were dead!

Petliura: —yes, but he discredited me for all posterity. That really hurt.

Frauenzimmer: More than death?

Petliura: Believe me, the Rue Racine was terrible. I still recall Schwartzbard's extended hand, how I raised my cane in defense. But the trial damned me. I would have died a thousand deaths to be spared that.

Bandera: Actually, my death made me into more of a hero.

Frauenzimmer: A *dead* hero.

Bandera: Even so, a more *heroic* dead hero. Don't underestimate the power of martyrdom.

Petliura: My point exactly. Torrès turned Schwartzbard into a martyr and me into the villain.

Rebet: The real issue is practical. You'll never get close to the exceptionally great leader.

Petliura: All the more reason to take my advice.

Rebet: I'd look into his years in Germany.

Petliura: You may be on to something. Away from Moscow's peering eyes, almost in the decadent West—who knows what a boy from Leningrad would do?

Rebet: Emigrés do strange things.

Frauenzimmer: Even in Communist Germany?

Bandera: Why not? Perhaps especially there. Perhaps he had a woman? Or dealt in the black market? Or liked boys?

Frauenzimmer: That might embarrass him, but it wouldn't humiliate him.

Petliura: He'd be humiliated by even the smallest embarrassment.

Rebet: Every émigré has dirty secrets. Dig. You'll find something.

Bandera: Perhaps he had several women?

Petliura: This is Germany, not Paris!

Bandera: Perhaps he's homosexual? All Russians are. That's why the nation is dying out.

Rebet: I'd look into his sexual habits. Dictators aren't known for chastity.

Frauenzimmer: What would you have me do—loiter in the men's room of the Lubyanka?

Bandera: Not the Lubyanka. He'd be on his best behavior there. But in some restaurant? Or along the banks of the Neva—in some park?

Frauenzimmer: But even if I do humiliate him, so what? I don't want to punish him. I want to be freed of my sins.

Petliura: But you did nothing.

Bandera: You're a nobody. Your sins are trivial.

Frauenzimmer: I meant my parents' sins. I've been carrying that burden all my life and—

Petliura: It's getting impossibly heavy, right? I felt the same way.

Frauenzimmer: And I know—I *really* know—that only eliminating the exceptionally great leader can help.

Rebet: Don't you know anybody who could help you?

Frauenzimmer: A woman—she lives in Berlin. And a man—in Moscow.

Petliura: Do you trust them?

Frauenzimmer: They hate him and they led me to you.

Bandera: *They* know about *us*? How could they?

Frauenzimmer: Through Schwartzbard and Stashinsky.

Rebet: And you're certain you can trust them?

Frauenzimmer: Absolutely. I'm an excellent judge of character.

Petliura: Nothing is absolute, *mon ami*. Be very careful.

Bandera: Listen to me. Do *not* trust them. You can only trust the dead, *never* the living.

Chapter 10

Volodymyr gets a painful lesson in the school of hard knocks after being introduced to fine cuisine, a delightful floor show, and excellent conversation in a magnificent setting reflective of Mother Russia's own magnificence and, quite possibly, munificence

Mistakenly believing that his life is about to take a turn for the better, Volodymyr finally meets the man who will change his life and enable him to embark on the path of knowledge and self-knowledge and a variety of other self-reflexive poses

The immediate background to Volodymyr's ultimately sad fate is of little interest, but, in light of its extraordinarily convoluted nature, it may still be worth relating, if only as a strained metaphor for the overall condition of Volodymyr's life. It happened like this. One day, after viewing the Kaganovich Art Centre's "Go, Collectivization, Go!" exhibit of watercolors, Volodymyr decided that it'd be in keeping with the day's *Leitmotif* for him to eat lunch at the feet of the statue to Feliks Dzerzhinsky, the famed founder of the Cheka. Poor Muscovites without country dachas had responded to the exceptionally great leader's frequent exhortations to bask in the bright light of the country's great history by sunning themselves in the square. The pigeons that favored Dzerzhinsky's head could be a nuisance, of course, but the base of the pedestal reminded locals of postcards of Piccadilly Circus, and congregating at Iron Feliks's gentle feet seemed like a cheap way to experience a vicarious thrill without having to stomach English food. In time, the guitar strummers drifted elsewhere and their places were taken by Moscow's chesty babushkas, who, when the sun was high, were wont to open their coats and sweaters and blouses and bare their brassieres. The sight of so many stout women did little to titillate Volodymyr, but he appreciated the silence that so much flesh engendered and knew that, among so many oversized breasts, there was safety in numbers.

It was on that fateful day, as Volodymyr stood, leaning against the monument and hungrily devouring a popular brand of sausage, that Putschkin, Katorga, and another man emerged laughing from the Lubyanka. Surprised and delighted by the coincidence, Volodymyr waved excitedly and, as soon as they espied him, Putschkin took Katorga's hand and, together, they braved the mad traffic to run toward Volodymyr. Their elegantly attired companion followed, but at a more leisurely pace.

"This," said Putschkin, introducing a portly man in an off-white suit, silk purple scarf, and white fedora, "is our great friend, Boris Semyonovich Dostaevsky."

"That's Dostaevsky with an *a*," Dostaevsky added, extending his hand. "No relation, alas. We hail from Minsk."

Volodymyr hid the sausage in his inside coat pocket—somewhat in the manner, he inwardly laughed, of a B-film hit man concealing his rod—and shook Dostaevsky's hand. To Volodymyr's surprise, Dostaevsky's grip, unlike the plotting of his namesake's novels, was firm.

"Come," said Dostaevsky, "let's all have a drink at my place and get acquainted."

Volodymyr learns how, thanks to Dostaevsky's entrepreneurial genius and the historical legacy of the great Lenin, the fabulous Gulag got fabulous and how Dostaevsky became a household name among people of good taste, impeccable manners, and boundless good will

Tout le monde knew that the Gulag Grill served mediocre food, but the *nouvelle rousskie* set went there for other reasons—to see and be seen in the plush booths arranged in the form of a vast archipelago. When the place opened, there were some muted objections from obscure journalists and aged human rights activists, but the hubbub died down quickly. The glitterati began frequenting the joint almost immediately. They naturally attracted the paparazzi, who in turn attracted the chattering classes and the talking heads. Very soon politicians, Eurodiplomats, long-legged models, and ex-KGB officers were dining side by side, ambidextrously employing both forks and knives or sipping martinis at the curved tin bar. The exceptionally great leader would occasionally drop in unannounced, without his otherwise omnipresent entourage of leather-clad bodyguards. If Dostaevsky were around, he would greet the exceptionally great leader with a broad smile and curt handshake and escort the little man dressed inconspicuously in a black suit and black shirt toward a discrete table in the back. The exceptionally great leader preferred not to make waves and had told the management that he wanted to be left undisturbed with his friends, as often suntanned muscular youths resembling Australian surfers as lithe young blondes with thick lips and slim calves.

Dostaevsky was one of the owners of the Gulag. As a matter of fact, the place was his idea, and Putschkin still remembered when it first occurred to him—like, truth to tell, a bolt out of the blue. Dostaevsky had been reading *Mother Russia's Favorite Russian Memoirs* (the 100-page sixth volume, which featured the abridged Solzhenitsyn) as they were traveling home from a wine-tasting weekend in the verdant hills surrounding Solovki. The train had just emerged from a long tunnel, and the brightness of the snow-covered tundra had blinded them momentarily. Dostaevsky placed the book on the seat next to Putschkin, took off his glasses, and rubbed his temples. He then looked Putschkin in the eyes and said, "That would be a fabulous name for a restaurant."

"What?" Putschkin asked. "The Solzhenitsyn?"

"No, my naïve friend," Dostaevsky replied, "The Gulag."

And that was that. Being an entrepreneurial *muzhik*, Dostaevsky quickly found backers with deep pockets and neatly trimmed beards. They met a few times in St. Moritz and St. Tropez and then closed the deal before the cameras at a big press conference at the Hotel Adlon, just a few goose steps away from the Brandenburg Gate. Two of Dostaevsky's partners were Russian and two were German. The Russians were part-owners of the trendy Lee Harvey Oswald Bar in Berlin and obviously knew a thing or two about marketing; the Germans had made a fortune in the Siberian hotel business, with the Guest-Stop-Oh! chain of family-friendly hostelries. The press loved the idea of a German-Russian consortium headed by an internationally renowned intellectual declaring that the project symbolized both nations' determination to embrace the past and build a glorious future.

A picky eater with a sensitive colon, Dostaevsky rarely dined at the Gulag. But he would make an occasional appearance in the evening, usually with a slinky brunette on his arm. All eyes would then turn to him, and Dostaevsky would respond with casual waves of his hand or bear hugs and kisses, Russian style.

Muscovites still remembered the night he showed up with Galina Brezhneva, then starring in a fabulous ice show at the Bolshoi. She was bedecked with ostrich plumes and rows of flawlessly round red pearls, while Dostaevsky, as usual, wore his off-white linen suit and fedora. The place turned completely quiet—one wag joked that it was so quiet that one could hear an ice pick drop—as they descended the marble staircase. Dostaevsky visibly enjoyed watching the effect he and Galina were having. As they approached the pool, he stopped and, while slowly turning his head from left to right and from right to left, began clapping. The audience followed his lead, and the result was a rhythmic applause that continued for several minutes, until—to everybody's surprise, astonishment, and delight—Dostaevsky and Galina jumped into the pool. It was quite a splash, both literally and figuratively. What could the others do but follow? The exceptionally great leader was the first to take the plunge, doing an elegant swan dive and then proceeding to splash water at the screeching Galina. Moscow had never experienced anything like this, not even at the height of the decadent movements of pre-revolutionary times.

The heated pool was Dostaevsky's idea, of course. He sensed, correctly, that the city's fashionistas would gladly shed their designer outfits in extravagant public settings. And ever since he and Galina and the exceptionally great leader had ruffled the surface of the pool's azure waters in their evening best, Moscow's most prominent celebrities felt impelled to do the same, usually after dessert and champagne, when conversations sagged and a little bit of wet fun revived the spirit. Dostaevsky's partners had proposed that the pool encompass the entire floor of the restaurant, thereby reinforcing the archipelago theme. All the booths and tables would have been surrounded by water on at least two sides, while a few—reserved for the more intrepid and athletic guests—would have been placed on free-floating platforms meandering among the fixed settings. Dostaevsky thought the idea, though charming, was impractical, especially as it would expose the staff to potential mishaps. Just imagine, he said, the pungent smell that clumsy waiters dropping bowls of caviar into warm water would produce. That argument won the day, and the decision was made to construct a conventional restaurant *sans* too much *eau*.

It was also Dostaevsky's idea that the menu should consist of dishes named after Russia's unexceptionally great leaders, the *pares sub primum*, as it were. Beef Beria, Chicken Dzerzhinsky, Pasta Putinesca, and Baked Andropov were among the highlights, while the Goulash Archipelago was, naturally, the specialty of the house. The exceptionally great leader's own favorite was said to be Lamb Lubyanka, a delicious dish featuring a rack of lamb with sprigs of rosemary and thyme and a delicate Edelweiss sauce served on a cast iron plate. At first, the chef—a highly strung Frenchman whom Dostaevsky lured from Maxim's—objected and threw a temper tantrum. But Dostaevsky mollified his pride by offering him a substantial raise, in euros no less, and appealing to his Gallic logic. After all, how could a restaurant named after the Gulag not serve meals named after Chekist honchos?

Unsurprisingly, the Gulag took off like the Sputnik. The place was always packed and reservations were almost impossible to get. As the buzz spread like denunciations during the Great Terror, the money-making implications of Dostaevsky's stroke of business genius began to multiply in almost dizzying combinations. One popular men's magazine, *KGB GQ*, devoted a special issue to the benefits of swimming off calories immediately after finishing a hearty meal. An entrepreneurial physician in Magadan suggested to Dostaevsky that they establish Club Gulag, a chain of weight reduction spas offering a regimen of work and exercise in Spartan living conditions. In turn, Dostaevsky proposed that the good doctor develop a Gulag Diet that could be published in all the major European languages and be announced to great fanfare at the Cannes Film Festival. With a little luck and some serious money, a skinny German model might even be persuaded to let her photograph be used for the cover.

His publisher pal Deniquine, meanwhile, had the inspired idea of a Gulag cookbook with chapters devoted to camp cuisine and the cooks who developed the recipes. The volume would contain retouched photographs of both camp and spa inmates happily munching on cabbage, sipping soup, or breaking off large pieces of good old-fashioned black bread, with humorous captions running along the bottom. Dostaevsky's personal favorite, perhaps because it reminded him of his first roll in the hay in the buckwheat fields outside his village, was: "Don't tell Mamasha that Natasha loves kasha!" Dostaevsky's confessor, Father Vlassov,

loved the concept and, according to the capital city's hyperactive
rumor mills, was apparently on the verge of signing blockbuster
deals with the Gerhard Schröder Verlag and the Georges Marchais
Film Studio in Vichy.

*Volodymyr learns how Dostaevsky succeeded in business without really trying
and, inspired by his rise from rags to riches in the face of daunting
circumstances that would have demoralized a lesser man, resolves to perform his
great deed in the restaurant*

Dostaevsky had a colorful past that was the envy of all his
patrons and employees. A Russian, he had been born in a small
town near Minsk in 1921. His father, Semyon, had been a
Nepman, a member of the despised merchant class that had
emerged after Lenin introduced the New Economic Policy the year
of Dostaevsky's birth. Dostaevsky Senior bought grain from the
peasants and transported it to the Belarusian capital, where he sold
it to bakeries in the old part of town. His prices were on the high
side, but his deliveries were always punctual, and, in the chaotic
conditions of post-revolutionary Russia, any kind of regularity was
greatly appreciated and admired, especially if the handiwork of
Gentile men and gentlemen.

Boris Semyonovich Dostaevsky's childhood was
uneventful. The world around him was rapidly changing, but high
politics were of no concern to his father, and Dostaevsky had little
notion of the drama that was overtaking the Union of Soviet
Socialist Republics. Dostaevsky once told Putschkin of the
fondness with which he recalled his family's Sunday picnics in the
Kuropaty forest, the occasional treks into the big city, the
wondrous sights of the main street, and the noises and smells of
the bazaar with its old peasant faces, jars of black currants,
enormous pieces of pig fat, and bundles of fresh dill—poignant
memories that may very well have contributed to his eventual
decision to go into the restaurant business.

It was his misfortune—or fortune—that Dostaevsky came
of age during the years of high Stalinism. The Great Terror of
1936-1938 followed on the heels of the collectivization that had
devastated the Belarusian countryside. His father's business fell to
ruins. Peasants went hungry and wheat was confiscated by the

secret police, and the Nepmen, the odious intermediaries between the pathetic kulaks and the victorious proletariat, suddenly took a hike as a class. Semyon had saved some money, enough to bribe impeccably honest local officials, but not quite enough to escape the ire of the aroused working masses. His anti-people activities landed the old man in prison, from which he may or may not have ever emerged. The young Dostaevsky, in any case, never saw his dad again after 1936.

That same year Dostaevsky joined the Young Leninist League and, determined to atone for his father's misdeeds, quickly climbed the ranks to become the chief propagandist for his town. That was in 1937. Next year the teenage prodigy entered the Minsk Polytechnic Institute, where he studied engineering. He graduated just in time for Chamberlain and Hitler to have dismembered Czechoslovakia and for Molotov and Ribbentrop to have divided Poland. The next two years were spent in western Belarus, recently rescued by the USSR from the Piłsudskiite fascists, where Dostaevsky worked for the local branch of the German-Soviet Friendship Society. In 1941, when Hitler betrayed his erstwhile ally, Stalin, Dostaevsky was drafted. Several years later, as the Red Army drove the Wehrmacht out of western Belarus, Dostaevsky was reassigned to a road-construction unit in Brest.

Dostaevsky was one of the fortunate few to have defected from the Soviet Union before the onset of Leonid Brezhnev's creaky socialism loosened the doors. While on a trade mission to Vienna in March 1956, just a few weeks after Khrushchev's notorious secret speech had lowered the boom on the Generalissimo, Dostaevsky appeared at the doors of the American Embassy. He arrived in the United States a few months later. Then, after the obligatory anti-Soviet stint at Radio Liberation, for which he composed a highly touted series of broadcasts on "Why I Chose Truth and Freedom," Dostaevsky took up history at the University of Frankfurt. He completed his dissertation—on "Dialectical Theory and Socialist Construction under Stalin"—in 1961, received high honors, and immediately began teaching at the Free University of Berlin.

During the student riots of 1968, Dostaevsky sided with the most radical factions, teaching them the art of organization and mass propaganda. Rumor had it that he instigated the occupation of several buildings. Some even hinted at a more nefarious role, speaking darkly of violence and Molotov cocktails and an intimate relationship with both Markus Wolf and Ulrike Meinhof. What is certain is that Dostaevsky was arrested, fingerprinted, and released after forty-eight hours, quite possibly after the discrete intervention of the Soviet ambassador, who, apparently, reminded the authorities in Bonn of West Berlin's precarious status as an island of capitalism in a turbulent socialist sea.

Dostaevsky then moved to Vienna, where he found employment at the Nikolai Lysenko Peace Institute, located near the pension on Schönbrunnerstrasse where Joseph Vissarionovich Stalin had penned his famous treatise on the nationality question in 1913. One of Dostaevsky's more lucrative pastimes was to lead American tourist groups through Vienna's cemeteries, where he regaled them with stories of the Soviet occupation of 1945-1955 and showed them the headstones of dead Bolshevik heroes. It was on one such occasion that he met Father Vlassov, lying prostrate in the mud, his arms extended and his long hair concealing his collar, before one of the graves. "Arise, o holy man!" Dostaevsky had shouted. They fast became great friends and the good priest soon became his spiritual advisor. When Vienna's first McDonald's restaurant opened on Schwarzenbergplatz, just across from the monument to the Soviet liberators, Dostaevsky and Vlassov wept. Dostaevsky wrote an outraged letter to the editor of *Die Presse*, demonstratively quit the Socialist Party of Austria and, just as demonstratively, joined the Communists and moved back to Berlin.

That was East Berlin, of course. The intrepid Dostaevsky thrived as the head of the well-funded German-Soviet Friendship Society in the Friedrichstrasse. But then came Gorbachev, and everything went to pieces. Dostaevsky's physical appearance was the first to go, as it became increasingly clear that communism was dying and the Soviet Union might collapse. 1989 was an especially traumatic year. The socialist bloc fell apart and, soon thereafter, so did Dostaevsky. His life had lost meaning. "History is ended," he said. "We are now all slaves of capital." He divorced his wife, or, more accurately, she divorced him. She kept the large apartment near the Brecht Museum and the children; he moved into a one-room flat in Kreuzberg, near the Wall, just around the corner from an excellent, if uncharacteristically filthy, *Kneipe* and down the street from the *Puppenarzt*, who fixed broken dolls but not, alas, broken lives. Rumor had it that Dostaevsky hid in his apartment, eating horse meat and watching old Soviet war films. People claimed to see him in Monbijou Park, feeding pigeons, but, aside from the trusty Father Vlassov, few succeeded in speaking to him. The good priest once asked Dostaevsky how he was. "Oh," he replied. "I am reading, and I am enjoying it like never before." Vlassov prayed that his soul mate and friend wouldn't go down easily, and one day, while extracting a confession, he had an epiphany and saw that, verily, Dostaevsky would soon rise from the dead.

The day after his retirement from the Free University was officially announced, Dostaevsky moved to Moscow, where, thanks to Deniquine's timely intercession, he had received an appointment at the Pobedonostsev Forum, a liberal think tank located in a magnificent old building just off Red Square. He cut his hair, trimmed his fingernails, exchanged horsemeat for caviar, and, taking advantage of a hefty expense account, spent several exhausting days shopping on the Arbat. Soon thereafter, while on a trip with Putschkin he had the epiphany that led him into the restaurant business.

As Dostaevsky finished the story of his life, Volodymyr could barely contain his excitement. The exceptionally great leader liked to dine at the Gulag! Dostaevsky would know when, and he'd also know at which table he usually sat. And, most amazing of all, Dostaevsky was the exceptionally great leader's great *tovarishch*. All that he, Volodymyr, had to do was to ask Dostaevsky about the exceptionally great leader's dining habits and prepare accordingly. Volodymyr considered poisoning the food, but quickly discarded the idea upon realizing that finagling his way into the kitchen would either attract attention or require including a cook in his plot, and both courses were too risky. He also considered diving into one of the pools and shooting the exceptionally great leader with a harpoon, but that seemed impractical, if only for forcing him to get wet. He realized that, in line with the dictum that less is more, simple would be best. He would acquire a small but accurate and powerful handgun. He would reserve a table in the exceptionally great leader's vicinity. And, as all eyes were fixed on the stripper carving the Lamb Lubyanka, he would calmly point the gun and shoot—and the exceptionally great leader would be no more. The plan was perfect. It was simple, it was obvious, and it was foolproof.

Unexpectedly, but in all likelihood inevitably, Volodymyr receives a solid knock on the head, with the result that the lights go out, the flow of history is momentarily interrupted, and time stands still, metaphorically, that is, as time cannot, after all, be halted or reversed or accelerated

As luck would have it, that day's goings-on at the Grill were pitched at the city's intellectual elite. Three poets—a Great Russian, a Little Russian, and a White Russian—read simultaneously from their works, creating a magically polyphonous effect that transcended what should have been sheer cacophony, while two artists, a Berliner and a Muscovite, showed slides of their collaboratively executed paintings, oversized hyperrealist portraits of Siegfried and Ilya Muromets gazing admiringly at each other amid a dazzling display of medieval military hardware in the background. While waiting at the bar for his Martini Magadan, Volodymyr stood next to a fat man with furry eyebrows and a stained white shirt. The man drank his beer, smacked his lips, and buried his face in the goulash. Finally, exhausted by the maneuver, he leaned back on his stool and gave Volodymyr his card.

"Deniquine," he introduced himself. "Like the famous general—but with a *q*. I am a publisher."

"Publisher of what?" Volodymyr politely inquired.

"Memoirs," Deniquine said. "Not memories." He laughed into his beer.

"What's the difference?" Volodymyr asked. "I'm afraid I don't—"

"There are no memories in Russia," Deniquine smiled, "but there are plenty of memoirs." He raised the beer mug to his lips and blew at the froth. "Moscow is beautiful, *n'est-ce pas?*"

As Deniquine was telling his fifth Pitoon joke—the one about the exceptionally great leader's incestuous relationship with Mother Russia—Volodymyr excused himself and went to the lavatory, a closet-like space with dirty tiles, sticky green walls, and the oppressive smell of urine and cigarette smoke. A small window, with an impenetrably grimy pane, provided the only ventilation. As befit a five-star *établissement*, the Gulag was fully committed to verisimilitude and authenticity, regardless of cost.

"Whoa, boy," a loud voice cried from within a stall, as Volodymyr flushed the urinal, "save some for the *hoi polloi* over here." A short man in a shapeless brown suit with black elbow patches grinned at him. "Vlassov's the name, last name—like that general, but with a double-*s*. First name's—gosh, what's my first name? This stuff really goes to your head." Vlassov was holding a small vodka bottle in his hand. "Love this stuff, just love it. Oh yeah—Andrei. No relation, of course. Don't know much about guns." Vlassov ran his hand through his hair. "But I do know my sacraments. Father Vlassov"—he bowed—"at your service. Orthodox, of course. Want a swig?"

Volodymyr politely declined. At that very moment, Deniquine crept up from behind and smacked him over the head with a blackjack, and the metaphorical equivalent of lights went out—for Volodymyr, that is, and not for Deniquine, who first made use of a urinal before helping Father Vlassov collect the crumpled body of Volodymyr Frauenzimmer off the sticky bathroom floor.

Volodymyr ends up in captivity—an outcome he decidedly did not foresee—and feels a myriad of emotions, ranging from anger to fear to existential Angst, as it occurs to him, subconsciously of course, that all his efforts, like all the efforts of all people in all places, can only lead to dead ends

Volodymyr's disappearance would surely have gone unnoticed had Dostaevsky not reported it to the Moscow police. His story was simple. They had agreed to meet for a two-martini lunch at the Gulag and, when Volodymyr was over one hour late, a visibly annoyed Dostaevsky called his hotel, the fabulous Trump-Belomorkanal, but the receptionist told him, in the best broken English he usually reserved for sweet-smelling out-of-towners, that *Meester Valadeemeer* had dropped off his key card thirty minutes before his scheduled appointment. When two hours had passed, a visibly worried Dostaevsky hurriedly blew the joint. Two empty vodka bottles, several martini glasses—some with toothpicks, some without—and three plates with caviar detritus and yellowing sour cream were proof positive of how long he had battled time and ennui for the sake of a friend who, like an understaffed third-world airline, was incapable of a punctual arrival.

After a few more calls to the Belomorkanal, Dostaevsky went to the police. A bleary-eyed officer with pock-marked jowls and garlic breath took down his report and, after scratching his own face and armpits, assured the visibly distressed Dostaevsky that the people's servants would do everything they could to save the day. Dostaevsky said *spasibo*, the fat man nodded, and, after retying his scarf and adjusting his fedora, Dostaevsky called Putschkin from the public phone in the men's room at St. Basil's Cathedral.

"All's well?" Putschkin asked.

"*Vse khorosho*," Dostaevsky answered. "Do you have him?"

"*Da*," Putschkin said, "he is here, tied up like a pig."

"Do not let him squeal," Dostaevsky barked and hung up.

Volodymyr remains off stage, as Dostaevsky reflects upon modes of transport and makes a mental note of culinary contradictions, perhaps as an unconscious reference to the existential contradictions that plague sensitive persons in general and sensitive persons in this narrative in particular

Dostaevsky's interrogation by the police had gone exactly as he had expected. Despite periodic bouts of fire breathing by the exceptionally great leader, sleaze had—somewhat like Adolf Hitler's self-confidence after Munich—only increased during his tenure. Dostaevsky had known that the exceptionally great leader's frequent declarations of clean government would, when combined with increasingly autocratic rule (called, in the official parlance, the "strengthening of the power vertical"—a turn of phrase that had always struck Dostaevsky as delightfully phallic), encourage all manner of bureaucratic scum to build empires, extort money from both poor and rich, and grow fat. The thick-necked policeman who feigned concern over Volodymyr's disappearance was malodorous, but, despite his obesity and manifestly infrequent encounters with soap, he was small fry. His superiors wore cleaner clothes and lacked his fleshy folds, but Dostaevsky knew from the self-confident swagger they affected, their use of crisply enunciated verbs, and their preference for sharply pressed gabardine pants that their dedication to the art of decay was far superior to that practiced by their bumbling underlings. As much as he admired their behavioral accoutrements, Dostaevsky was glad that his only penance for being a sartorially impeccable law-abiding citizen was a prolonged encounter with body odor and sweat.

Besides, body odor and sweat were no news to Dostaevsky, inured as he was to zipping around the city on its efficient metro. Dostaevsky loved the arches and marble ceilings and the paintings and mosaics of happy peasants with abundant sheaves of wheat and muscular workers with big hammers and anvils. There was a time that he never traveled in the underground. Dostaevsky finally broke down after waiting endlessly for a cab on one snowy Christmas eve and deciding that the metro couldn't possibly be worse than stomping his feet in the blistery cold, like some unrepentant Lithuanian nationalist in a Polar concentration camp. He had enjoyed that first ride immensely, looking about him at the gilded decorations and socialist realist adornments with child-like awe. He had even pointed at the hammers and remarked to his fellow commuters how curious it was that the muscle-bound young men always came endowed with such huge instruments. "Stalin, you old goat," Dostaevsky had laughed, amused at the thought that Soviet communism was just an elaborate attempt at enthroning male genitalia. His fellow commuters, all sensitized to the subtleties of gender by the exceptionally great leader's exceptional aura of masculinity, recognized a wag when they saw one and broke out in peals of spontaneous laughter.

After leaving the police station, Dostaevsky took the metro to Putschkin's. As usual, the elevator was broken, so the intrepid Dostaevsky climbed the six flights of uneven concrete stairs and, after knocking in code on the dented metal door, opened the locks with his own keys. Putschkin was slouched in front of a Zenit television set, watching a trio of long-legged girls sing about the exceptionally great leader's many exceptional qualities and drinking a German beer. Dostaevsky could tell from the crackling sound of fried potatoes that Katorga was in the kitchen preparing dinner.

"Where is he?" Dostaevsky asked. Putschkin motioned at the bedroom door with his beer bottle.

"Any trouble?"

Putschkin shook his head and pointed at the couch. Dostaevsky removed his coat and hat and sat down.

"When do we start?" Putschkin asked.

"Let's eat first," Dostaevsky said. "Katorga!"

"*Da?*"

"Katorga, we're hungry. When will you be ready?"

She showed her head. "Soon." Then she smiled. "Have some vodka. And pour me a glass. We have much to celebrate today."

When the food finally came, Dostaevsky almost gagged. Fried potatoes were not exactly his favorite food, but fried potatoes fried in yesterday's animal fat were definitely at the bottom of the list. His stomach turned, and he almost regretted having had Caviar *à la* Yezhov with his Martini Magadan. He might have vomited, had not the buxom trio sung the refrain at that very moment: "*Ya khochu takogo kak Pitoon.*" A man like Pitoon, Dostaevsky thought, is exactly what you should want—and exactly what you shall get.

In a realization that raises as many questions as it provides answers, Volodymyr realizes that clothes, like appearance in general, do indeed make the man, especially in morally challenging and physically uncomfortable circumstances that test a man's true mettle and, possibly, even his manliness

Putschkin had no carpet or rugs or furniture, other than a long table, in the bedroom. Volodymyr lay bound and gagged on the bare wooden floor, stained from bodily fluids, repeated alcohol spills, and sloppy moppings. Dostaevsky was dressed in his usual off-white linen suit, white cotton shirt with golden cuff-links, and striped silk tie. The soles of his patent leather shoes were barely scratched, and the finely woven black socks accentuated his bony ankles in a way that few designers would have found attractive. Unsurprisingly perhaps, Volodymyr's first thought was that the black of the socks didn't quite match the off-white of the suit. It was probably testimony to his unfashionably traditional upbringing that Volodymyr kept his unflattering opinion to himself, even though he didn't know, and couldn't have known, that, but for a brief spell when the aesthetically sensitive Dostaevsky was down and out and almost on skid row, he had always tried his darndest to dress well—in the firm, if perhaps exaggerated, neo-Calvinist belief that outward appearance reflected the condition of one's soul. Indeed, ever since his success with the Gulag, Dostaevsky's yen for dashing clothes had taken off. Rumor had it that he made a point of dropping in on the fashion shows of Fendi, Armani, and his favorite, Berlusconi. Some of his colleagues—especially those with a proclivity for the dowdy and the shapeless, in clothes, women, and careers—even hinted at his having dated Italian supermodels hot off the runways of Milan.

Volodymyr couldn't help consider the impact Dostaevsky's preference for off-white suits had made on the capital city's upper crust. Some well-traveled, and well-read, intellectuals pointed out that Dostaevsky was just a pale imitation of a famous American journalist no one had ever heard of. Their snide remarks were meant to put Dostaevsky in his place, but they succeeded only in adding to his already growing mystique as an exceptionally great man of exceptionally great taste. When Dostaevsky ambled along the Arbat, he would elicit stares from sartorially challenged babushkas and whistles from short-skirted teenyboppers. Pedestrians, cabbies, and even burly truck drivers stopped dead in their tracks and watched this curiously dressed man flaunt a color that seemed completely out of place in the great Russia of the exceptionally great leader.

After all, off white provoked three associations in the multilayered mind of Mother Russia. The color reminded the older generation of the baggy suits favored by the Communist nomenklatura. Who could fail to think of Nikita Khrushchev or Konstantin Chernenko upon seeing Dostaevsky? At the same time, the white seemed to assert—almost scream out, if you thought about it—that their peccadilloes should be forgiven, a sentiment most people were all too happy to endorse, especially when the exceptionally great leader reminded them of the greatness of their great country. And who could avoid associating the white with snow, that symbol of the Russian soul, and the off white with the midnight sun that—at least according to the official version of things—would never fail to shine forever on this blessed land, even when hidden by thick Siberian clouds?

Volodymyr feels the heavy hand of injustice and the even heavier hand of betrayal, without, quite possibly, fully appreciating which is worse, or better, or whether such a distinction makes any difference in the greater scheme of things—especially if one is bound and gagged

"Place him in a chair," Dostaevsky commanded; Katorga and Putschkin did. "Remove the gag."

Volodymyr exploded with a series of epithets in Russian, German, Ukrainian, and Yiddish—sounding unintentionally like a gaggle of kulaks haggling over cigarette stubs in a cattle car lumbering eastward through pristine forests and silent tundras.

"Would you like a cigarette?" Putschkin extended a crumpled pack.

"Or some water?" Katorga added.

"You betrayed me!" the defiant Volodymyr screamed, his eyes welling up with tears.

"I guess not," Putschkin smiled. "Do you know why you are here?"

"I will," Volodymyr sniffed, "report you to the police."

"My dear Volodymyr"—Katorga seemed genuinely puzzled—"don't you know?"

"*We* are the police!" cried Putschkin.

Katorga raised her right hand—almost as if she were holding a handgun—and pointed a finger at Volodymyr's chest. "Bang, bang, bang, bang, bang," she said in a monotone that almost bordered on suppressed hysteria and fanatical exultation. Volodymyr got the reference and flinched. Putschkin then pointed a rolled-up newspaper at Volodymyr's face and, while whispering "whoosh," squeezed. Once again, fully aware of the ongoing interplay of savage intertextuality, Volodymyr flinched, but not before first holding his breath, for reasons that readers of this narrative will surely understand.

"Cigarette?" Putschkin asked. "Russian? German?"

"Water?" Katorga said.

"Vipers!" Volodymyr hissed.

"Exactly," said Putschkin, "we are vipers. And what are you?"

"A mensch," Volodymyr hissed again.

"Really?" Putschkin raised his eyebrows. "We are animals and you are merely human. Well, well, well"—Putschkin turned to Katorga and Dostaevsky with a broad smile on his face—"then who can blame us?"

"I can blame you, you traitors!" Volodymyr cried. "All of civilized humanity can blame you. And will."

"Here in Moscow?" Putschkin laughed. "Good luck, my friend."

Volodymyr spat at him, but Putschkin stepped quickly to his left and the glob dropped at his feet.

"Don't be pathetic, Volodymyr," he said. "A great man like you shouldn't spit inside someone's home."

"A great man? A great man?" Dostaevsky shouted. "Who? Volodymyr? No, our Volodymyr is a common criminal, a petty thief, a little man, a mediocrity. That's why our Volodymyr spits. That's why our Volodymyr loses his temper. Our Volodymyr is a coward, a *Zimmerfrau*. Our Volodymyr is wondering: What will they do to me? Why did they bring me here? Will they torture me? Will they kill me?" Dostaevsky spat. "Don't worry, dear Volodymyr. We will do nothing to you. The great leader only wishes to talk to you, to shine some light on you, to see you sweat—to teach you a thing or two." Dostaevsky spat again.

"And then you'll let me go?"

"What would our *velikii vozhd* do with a poor schmuck like you?" said Katorga.

Chapter 11

Bound and gagged and expecting little in the way of a happy end, Volodymyr seeks consolation in philosophical overtures to Sholom Schwartzbard about—what else?—life and death and a variety of related issues approximately located somewhere in between

Volodymyr discusses watches and time and other ontological things that may open epistemological doors to greater self-knowledge or, just as possibly, close them or, equally possibly, leave them half-open or, not inconceivably, leave them completely unaffected

Tell me, Sholom, what exactly am I doing? I've been plotting to bump off the exceptionally great leader, I've embraced violence, and I'm supposedly doing this in order to ease the pain within my soul. Does any of this make sense to you? Is this the reasonable behavior of a reasonable man? I'm beginning to have my doubts. I didn't at first. But now, after having spoken to you and Bohdan and the others, after having been betrayed by what I thought were my closest friends and comrades-in-arms, I'm no longer sure. I have doubts, Sholom, I have doubts about what I'm doing and about who I am.

Did you also have doubts, or were you always a model of cool and calm and steely determination? Did you know exactly what you had to do when you witnessed the pogroms? Did you ever weaken or lose faith? Did you ever think it might be more sensible for you to keep making watches? After all, why would a watchmaker kill? That doesn't make sense, Sholom. Even you must agree that watchmakers aren't usually assassins.

Did you work in a factory, Sholom? I can see you and your colleagues sitting at tiny tables, shoulders hunched, heads bent over minute apparatuses, goose-head lamps casting yellow light on the tables, your hands almost frozen as your nimble fingers twist and turn along the face of the device. There is silence. An occasional cough, an occasional sneeze—how disruptive of the work table a sneeze must be!—breaks the silence. No one speaks. Sometimes you mumble or whisper to yourself. Perhaps you say something like "Ah, there it goes" or "One more screw and it's done." The room is clean, but clouds of dust particles swirl in the yellow light. A dark-haired Hasidic boy moves silently from table to table, carrying a tray with tiny springs and circles and nuts and bolts. As you sit there, your shoulders hunched, your head bowed as if in prayer, what are you really thinking about? The gun? The killing? The pogroms? The look on Petliura's face? Can anyone ever make a watch again after killing a fellow human being? Can anyone who contemplates killing a human being make a watch?

It occurs to me that you must be an expert on time. And how appropriate that is for a Jew. Which people if not us has such long roots in history? Which people if not us has such a long memory? We forget nothing, not the bad and not the good. And even if some of us manage to forget, however fleetingly, how can you—surrounded as you are by the instruments of time? I see why you could never put the pogroms out of your mind. Sholom the watchmaker was Sholom the time-maker. Your memories were always alive, the past was always the present for you, and I wouldn't be surprised if it had also been your future. How terrible that must be, Sholom—to live always in the past, never to be able to escape its clutches, never to be able to live in a present and a future that are not tainted with the past.

I suppose, as you sat at your workman's table, shoulders stooped and head bent as if in prayer, your eyes focused on the insides of time itself—I suppose you saw, not the components of watches, but history itself. History itself—the history of our people, the history of their suffering throughout the ages, the history of the pogroms—must have appeared to your eyes, always marching forward, always returning to its starting point, always revolving about you. How could you stand so much history, Sholom? How could you work on your watches, day after day after day, rising from bed each morning and going to bed each night in the knowledge, in the certainty, that ten hours a day, every day, you'd be reliving history, the same history, over and over again?

I don't understand time, Sholom. I understand the concepts of before and after, of course, and I understand that strings of things can be arranged in this endless before-and-after relationship, but that's history, isn't it? Endless strings of befores and afters aren't time. We measure time not in befores and afters, but in durings. If there's too much history, if there are too many befores and afters, time disappears. It's only when history stops and the befores and afters stop, that time reasserts itself. It's only then that the durings take over.

I suppose I don't understand time because I've never experienced it. All my life, I've been living in a past that is not mine and in a present that does not exist. You probably think that you did too, but you didn't—not in the same way I did. For you history vanquished time after the Revolution. For me, history was the midwife that brought me to life. I've been saddled with history from my very first breath, from my very first cry. When I wailed and asserted myself as a living human being, history slapped me across my tender face, and it has never ceased slapping me since. My cheeks are red and swollen from these slaps, my teeth hurt, my eyes are bloodshot.

I am waxing philosophical, Sholom, but how else can I confront the dead weight of history? Mine is a primitive philosophy. It's more of an agenda, really, a cause. You see, my goal is to destroy history. That's the only way I'll be able to live in time. But what a ridiculous aspiration! Who can destroy history? One may be able to make it or remake it, but surely one cannot unmake it. The notion is preposterous, but before you dismiss me altogether, don't forget my preposterous name and my preposterous past and my preposterous parentage. I think I have all the qualifications, and every right, to insist that, if anyone can destroy history, I can.

And what would happen if I succeeded? Would humanity suffer? Would the world be any different? I think there'd be nothing but time. Every string of befores and afters would disappear and be replaced by one resounding during. Everything would be a during, Sholom, *everything!* My mother would sit in her room and I would hear only the sounds she makes, without comprehending what they mean. My father would only be a thing in space, and not a symbol with meaning. I would feed them, I would wash them. They would still wish damnation on each other, but I wouldn't understand a thing. They would remain entangled in their chains of befores and afters, while I would glide along on my durings.

But if destroying history means destroying fish-eyes, I fear that I will fail. Am I pathetic, Sholom? Are you laughing at me? Are you thinking that I was born to be a watchmaker? Can you see me sitting at a tiny table, shoulders hunched, head bent over minute apparatuses, a goose-head lamp casting yellow light on the table, my hands almost frozen as my nimble fingers twist and turn along the face of the device? Can you hear the silence, the occasional cough, the occasional sneeze? Can you hear me mumble or whisper something like "Ah, there it goes" or "One more screw and it's done"? Can you see the clouds of dust particles swirling in the yellow light, the dark-haired Hasidic boy moving silently from table to table, carrying a tray with tiny springs and circles and nuts and bolts?

Volodymyr asks technically unsophisticated, but existentially pseudo-sophisticated and epistemologically semi-sophisticated, questions about guns and hands and taking aim and how they all relate to killing and not killing

Sholom, my dear friend, I have been thinking about firearms, and I have more questions for you. You see, the absurdity of my situation has struck me—almost like a bolt out of the blue. (I shall have to tell you more about the role these bolts have played in my life, but some other time, not now.) Here I am, planning an assassination—pretending to be planning an assassination while my hands are tied and my mouth is gagged—without knowing the slightest thing about carrying out assassinations!

I do know this much. There are bombs, there are knives, there are guns, and there is poison. It's pretty clear that poisons are out of the question. I have no idea how they're made, and I cannot even imagine how I could possibly apply them to Pitoon. Bombs terrify me. I don't know where to acquire or how to construct them, and I can all too easily imagine their exploding in my hands. Knives are somewhat more appealing, but I dislike blood, I shudder at the very thought of the sound of flesh and bones being pierced, and I know that I could never get within reach of Pitoon to be able to strike a fatal blow. So that leaves guns. I know I can buy one, and I suspect I could fire off a shot without having to get too close to Pitoon.

And that brings me to you, Sholom. You fired a pistol, and you fired five shots. I suppose you had learned how to use firearms when you traveled to Ukraine and joined the Red Guard. I imagine that you rode through the countryside on horseback, with a saber strapped to your belt, a revolver in your holster, and a rifle slung over your shoulder. How did you tell friend from foe? I once read that the Bolsheviks simply examined people's hands. If they were smooth and pink, they belonged to the class enemy. If they were rough and brown, they belonged to workers. Did you shoot people with the wrong hands, Sholom? Is that what it came down to—the size and texture and appearance of one's hands? The thought terrifies me, but I can see that it would've been effective and accurate—or at least accurate enough—for your purposes. A Red Guard doesn't have the time to examine a prisoner's background in great detail. Enemies must be defeated, revolutions must be promoted, territories must be liberated! If someone has the wrong hands—too bad. He shouldn't have been caught.

Here's a question for you, Sholom. Surely, Jews would have had the wrong hands. Years of studying the Torah, years of praying, years of handling fine textiles could not have produced the craggy hands of the victorious proletariat. Were your people and mine—were they suspect, too? Is that why the Bolsheviks killed us? Was it because of our hands? When you and your comrades rode into a shtetl and saw long-bearded men in black hats and black coats and smooth hands, did you think, "Ah, enemies of the revolution! They must be liquidated!" Did our hands get us killed, Sholom? Did your unit kill our people? Did *you*?

Who were you before you joined the revolution? A watchmaker. And a watchmaker must have the smoothest of hands, the gentlest of hands, the kindest of hands. You make time, you caress time; your hands cannot be peasant hands, rough and gnarled, with thick fingers like little logs. Did you hide your hands from your comrades, Sholom? Did you wear gloves or smear your hands with dirt and grease? Did you scrape them with a bayonet? And when you saw a man with wrong hands, did it ever occur to you, perhaps at the moment that you raised your saber or pointed your gun and were able, however fleetingly, to espy the watchmaker's hand on the handle or the watchmaker's finger on the trigger, that a man with wrong hands was being killed by another man with wrong hands? How did you live with yourself— with the knowledge that your victim could just as easily have claimed, had circumstances been slightly different, had he first joined the Guard, had his horse been a jot faster and healthier than yours, that *you* were the enemy of the revolution and that *he* was its defender?

Did you kill people with the wrong hands because *you* had the wrong hands? Did you keep killing in order to justify your having killed? Or perhaps your calculation rested on fear? Perhaps you believed that killing was the only way your comrades would accept you, a man with watchmaker's hands?

I'm beginning to suspect that we are rather more alike than I had thought, Sholom. Do you know why I resolved to bump off Pitoon? I needed a sacrificial lamb, someone to assume the burden of my anguish and, in laying his bald head on the altar, to erase it forever. Did you also need such a lamb? Did you have to kill someone in order to extinguish your anguish? Did Petliura have to die because you wanted to live? Did Petliura have to die because you couldn't live with yourself? Because you had killed? Because you had failed to save your own people? Because you had watched your own people get killed? Because you had swung the saber and fired the revolver at men with long beards and curly side-locks and black hats—and wrong hands?

Sholom, how does one fire a gun at a man? I'm not asking how one shoots. I know: one points and presses the trigger and the gun goes off. And I'm not asking how one shoots at a target. Again, I know: one practices, one takes aim, one aligns the barrel of the gun with the imaginary line extending from one's eye to the target, and one shoots. No, I want to know how one takes aim at a human being. What worries me, as I contemplate my own shooting of Pitoon, is this. I raise the gun to the appropriate height, I aim at the exceptionally great leader, I begin squeezing the trigger—and then he turns his head in my direction and his fish eyes fix on mine. At that very moment, I would be aiming a gun at a man who is looking into my eyes. Can cutting down a man with a saber be any different? You raise your arm, you ready yourself for the crushing blow—and then the man with the wrong hands glances at you. What do you see in those eyes? I'm sure that Pitoon's fish eyes would evoke no pity in me, but I'm also certain that I'd hesitate and that, as my finger stopped just short of pressing the trigger or as my arm remained suspended above my head, he might escape, or I might be caught, or my horse might gallop away.

And this brings me back to the question I posed at your trial. You met Petliura in the Rue Racine. You approached him and asked him if he was Petliura. He turned to you, and then you shot. You could have shot him in the back or in the side, but you wanted him to look into your eyes and know that he'd be shot by you. You said, and I believe you, that you wanted him to know you were the avenger of our people's suffering, that you held him responsible for their deaths. I understand that, but I don't understand how you failed to hesitate when he looked you in the eyes. Instead, you fired five shots—*five*, Sholom, *five*! Even as his body was falling to the street, you kept firing. You began shooting as he looked you in the eyes, and you stopped shooting only after he could no longer look you in the eyes. Was that hatred, Sholom, or was it habit? Was that how you had killed the men with wrong hands during the Civil War? Were you reenacting the Civil War in the Rue Racine? Or was it guilt, Sholom? Did you see yourself in Petliura's eyes?

I know that if I ever pull the trigger at Pitoon, I will shoot him in the back. No eyes for me, Sholom. The lamb must be sacrificed as quickly, as treacherously, and as efficiently as possible. No eyes for me, absolutely no eyes for me.

Volodymyr ruminates about bolts out of the blue and zigzags and coincidences, while considering a variety of alternative realities, exotic counterfactuals, and tough-guy hypotheticals that suggest that his capacity to think straight just might be very seriously in doubt

Sholom, I had mentioned to you that bolts out of the blue have played a great and decisive role in my life. My impression is that yours unfolded without the sudden changes of direction that have characterized mine. I look at your life and I see continuity. Your life strikes me as simple and uncomplicated, as unfolding according to an inner logic. It's almost as if you entered a life that lived itself out, with you as the protagonist. In contrast, my life is a random collection of events. It is chaos, a constantly evolving agglomeration of things and people and developments without rhyme or reason. And within this chaos bolts will always strike out of the blue.

You are the avenger, and I can imagine that you believe you were born the avenger. You lived your life as an avenger before you had even heard of Petliura's name. It was Schwartzbard the avenger who embarked on his life's path and who happened to come across Petliura somewhere along that path. We think that your assassination of Petliura was the high point of your life, but we are mistaken. *You* were always the high point of your own life. Petliura was, I suspect, just a distraction or, better still, an opportunity for you to show the world who you were and what you were made of. Not so with me. My life zigs and zags from moment to moment; it follows no logic, no order, no plan. I have no fate; I am not subject to any unfolding narrative with a beginning, middle, and end. If your life is a path that you follow, then mine is a boundless sea with no land in sight in any direction.

My parents cast me adrift. They produced a twofold bastard—a Jew who cannot be Jewish and a Ukrainian who cannot be Ukrainian. There is no place for me to go, because I belong to nobody and to nothing. I drift and wander and run and escape, even though I'm not at all sure why I run and what I hope to escape. And it's when I'm running, my head down and my arms and legs pumping, that these bolts out of the blue strike. And when they do, I pause, I look up at the sky, and then resume my running—but usually, because of the slight pause, in a slightly different direction. I wish I could say that I'm like Saul who became Paul, but that wouldn't be accurate. It's not I who ever seems to change. I stay the same. It's the things about me that change and confuse me.

This may be the first time in my life that I'm acting with the strength you possessed. When I experienced that bolt out of the blue about fish-eyes, I knew that my life had acquired direction. It, and not just the circumstances around it, had changed. I knew what I wanted and I knew where to go. You know better than anyone that I still don't know how to get there. I still worry about the choice of weapons. I'm still uncertain about being able to approach Pitoon. But at least I know, or think I know, where I'm going. My life is finally unfolding.

Or is it? I worry that what I think is happening may not really be happening. I fear that I may be misinterpreting my life. It wouldn't be the first time. After all, that's why I've experienced so many bolts out of the blue. And who's to say that this bolt won't be followed by others, that the zigzagging won't continue, that the directionlessness of my directionless life won't reassert itself?

Any why shouldn't it? Isn't it preposterous of me to believe that a life that's lacked content, form, and direction from its very inception should suddenly acquire content, form, and direction? Isn't that just as preposterous as the course of my whole life, indeed of my very name? I am Volodymyr Frauenzimmer. The first name is fine, on its own. As is the second, but also on its own. But placed side by side, they make for the unlikeliest couple. It's as if a rich and handsome man were betrothed to a poor and ugly woman. There is no one else on earth, I wager, with this name. I've sometimes considered changing it. I could become Volodymyr Petliura or Sholom Frauenzimmer. I could then hold my head high and look people in the eye. Or could I? Alas, I could not. I am who I am, and I cannot be who I cannot be. It's as simple as that. I could wear a top hat, I could wrap myself in a kimono, I could dress as a gaucho—but I would always remain that damned elusive Volodymyr Frauenzimmer.

Perhaps I should don a fancy suit and parade down the Champs-Élysées? Or show off a shiny black tuxedo with spats and white gloves and drink an espresso on the Via Veneto? Breakfast at Tiffany's might not be such a bad idea, or a swim off Capri. Or a bullfight in Barcelona or a fish dinner off the Bosporus or a stroll along the Rue Mouffetard while smelling the cheeses and pointing at the octopus. I could cross the ocean in a ship with easy chairs and blankets and handrails and stewards in white uniforms. I could board a freighter, kibitz with the unshaven deck hands with cigarette stubs in their mouths, snap my fingers as I climb the rust-covered staircase to the captain's dining room, exchange pleasantries with the other guests, flirt with the thin woman in the maroon dress, toast the queen.

But why just toast the queen? Why not toast every president and prime minister and monarch who has ever lived? Every baron and duke and baroness and duchess and prince and princess and get rip-roaring drunk, completely stinko, utterly blotto, absolutely stupefyingly inebriated? And why just cross the Atlantic? Why not the Pacific and the Indian Ocean and the Mediterranean and the South China Sea? I could travel to North Africa, find a joint with a bartender named Django, drink Pastis, sweat, sit among the palm trees, and watch the slow fans churn the hot air. I could dance the tango with chanteuses and the fox trot with prostitutes and the swing with the black wives of Foreign Legionnaires. I could smile at the shiny Africans, admire their big white teeth, and speak to them in broken French. I could contemplate the whores with long bony fingers and paint on their sculpted cheeks. I could ask the singers to light my Cuban cigars with dollar bills.

And what if I were to junk it all and take up a career as a mug? Find myself some nice moll named Pinkie and tell her that I love her something fierce even as she's beating me with her fists? Fix her scarf as she brushes away my hands and snarls? Tells me to beat it and then takes me by the shoulders and plants a big smacker on my open lips? But why settle for second fiddle? I could be the boss. I could run the mob. I could organize the hits and arrange the pay-offs and bribe the Irish cops and sell dope to the Puerto Ricans and rob banks and shoot machine guns and escape in big black cars driven by little men with flattened noses and hairy hands grasping the wheels. I could sit back in a big leather chair, place my legs on the desk before me, and tell them to divvy up the loot, making sure that the biggest piece of the action is mine. I could nod at Spike and have him do a number on Mugsy. I could call in the boys and tell them to take to the mattresses. I could finger Louie and have him rubbed out. I could solve every problem in the world and make a million G's in the process. So why *not* become a gunslinger? Or a sergeant in this man's army? Or a centurion? Or a tank commander? Better still, why not join the revolution, hide out in the underground, write incendiary leaflets, stir up the people, fight the oppressor, assassinate collaborators, rob banks, carry false passports, wear a fake beard, sleep in safe houses, smoke cheap cigarettes, discuss ideology, argue over the program maximum, plan the uprising? Why not lead the masses into battle? Why not?

Because I am Volodymyr Frauenzimmer—that's why not.

Those bolts out of the blue are my salvation, Sholom. Whatever the reason for their occurrence, they occur and, when they do, they give me the sense, however illusory, that all is well with me, that my life will, finally, acquire purpose and direction. Every time the bolt strikes, I get hope. Every time, that hope, and I with it, is dashed. Every time, I despair. But, even in the depths of my despair, I know that another bolt will strike, someday, and

156

that this cycle of hope and despair and hope and despair will continue. Is that like time, Sholom? Is that like history? No, but I can pretend it is, can't I?

Chapter 12

Insufficiently consoled and doubtless suspecting that the end is near, Volodymyr displays a distressing lack of imagination and retreads familiar ground by talking to Bohdan Stashinsky about life and death, while wondering if talking about life and death is all there is to life and death

Despite a surfeit of clues scattered throughout the narrative, Volodymyr realizes the importance of white socks a bit late in the game, thereby inadvertently raising the question of what his fate would have been had he realized their importance sooner rather than later, in the narrative if not in real life

We had spoken about your socks before, Bohdan, but I keep thinking about them. They give me no peace. I see in my mind's eye that photograph of you in the staircase with your hand in your vest—you are reaching, presumably, for the poison air gun—one leg straight, the other bent, a serious expression on your face—and those socks, those damned white socks. Why am I obsessed with them? They clash with my image of an assassin, that's why. I see a thick-set man in a long trench coat and fedora pulled over his eyes. I see dark shoes, dark pants, and of course dark socks. Instead, you look as if you were going home from a date. You've just seen the girl to her door, she gave you a kiss, you're placing your handkerchief, which you used to wipe off the lipstick, into your inside coat pocket, and you're calmly descending the stairs, thinking about the fine time you had and the good impression your white socks must have made, especially as you twirled the night away doing the jitterbug.

Of course, you're not quite as innocent as you look. That photograph is ostensibly of you right after you killed Rebet. A man is dying, perhaps already is dead, as a result of the poison you shot into his face, and there you are, calmly walking down the stairs, one leg straight, the other bent, and your white socks proclaiming your innocence to the world. You just killed a man, you just exterminated a human being—and yet there you are, strolling casually with a devil-may-care expression on your face and your white socks ablaze on your feet.

Were the white socks a political statement, perhaps even a moral one? Were you saying that not you, but the executioners in Moscow, bore the responsibility for Rebet's death? Were you using those white socks to proclaim your innocence? But surely you know that you're *not* innocent. *You* pulled the trigger, *you* killed Rebet, *you* were the assassin, and *you*, not some shadows in Moscow, were responsible. Were you trying to assert your humanity? Were the socks meant to signify that you weren't a mere robot, a mindless, soulless machine doing the Kremlin's bidding? Were the socks a sign of your individuality? Were you simply saying that, even after having killed a man, you were still Bohdan Stashinsky, Ukrainian village boy?

I know you have nerves of steel, Bohdan. After all, you approached Rebet, you saw his face, you pointed, you squeezed, you heard what I imagine to have been a gentle whooshing sound, you saw his face freeze, you watched him crumble, you placed the device in your pocket, you swallowed an anti-poison pill—and you walked away. I would have had difficulty walking, and you just walked away. I marvel at your strength, Bohdan. But I also wonder. Didn't you pause *at all*? Not even for a millisecond? Just before you retrieved the gun from your pocket and stuck it in Rebet's terrified or puzzled or surprised face, just before you actually fired it—didn't you freeze for a tiny fraction of a second? Didn't you think to yourself: Good God, what the hell am I doing? Why am I killing this man in some staircase in some building on Karlsplatz in, of all places, Munich? How did it come to this? Why is a village boy from Ukraine killing someone in Bavaria? Didn't the absurdity of it all strike you? Didn't you think that it made no sense for you, a simple peasant boy who made the mistake of boarding a train without a ticket, to have ended up as an assassin?

Just think how different your life would have been had you bought a ticket or had the conductor been too tipsy to notice you hadn't. But he happened to do his job conscientiously on the very day that you happened to decide not to pay. And the result of that bizarre coincidence is that you are killing a man on a staircase in Munich while wearing white socks!

Good God, Bohdan, perhaps you were wearing white socks on the train? Perhaps you're the kind of man who always wears white socks? Perhaps your choice of white socks on that fateful day in Munich had nothing to do with guilt or innocence or individuality? Perhaps the conductor decided to get tough with you *because* of your white socks? Perhaps he thought you were flouting good manners and thumbing your nose at authority—at him? Perhaps he viewed those socks as a symbol of your *pride*, as a symbol of your youthful arrogance?

I've just had an epiphany, Bohdan. I bet you were wearing your only pair of socks or your only pair of clean socks. The conductor was probably eager to go home, to the wife and kids and vodka and radio. He thought he saw a freeloader, but how could he have known that your socks proclaimed your poverty and the stubborn pride of a simple village boy? A tired man makes the slightest of miscalculations, Bohdan, and here you are—calmly walking down the stairs, one leg straight, the other bent, while a floor or two above you a bald-headed man is desperately gasping for breath and dying.

Volodymyr considers good luck and bad luck and no luck in an extended rumination that ends inconclusively and suggests that we may be, at best, the playthings of happenstance incapable of exercising free will or, at worst, the playthings of happenstance capable of exercising free will

I want to talk to you about two things that have concerned me all my life—luck and timing. I've had very little of the former, but my life has been marked by many instances of the latter. That sounds odd, but what I mean is that I've noticed, or think I've noticed, that much of my life has depended on things or people or events being in the right place at the right time. Perhaps I should say coincidence, and not timing. Whatever it is and however it's called, this quality has been with me all my life. These repeated coincidences—these bolts out of the blue—have made my life bearable.

I'm also struck by how great a part both luck and coincidence have played in your life. One such coincidence gives me no peace, Bohdan. You and Inge decide to escape to West Berlin on August 12, 1961. One day later, construction on the Berlin Wall begins. Had you dawdled for just one day, had something happened to delay your decision by twenty-four hours, perhaps even fewer, you wouldn't have been able to escape! Your

161

flight to freedom took place on the very last day that it could possibly have succeeded. That's what I mean by luck, and that's what I mean by timing. That August day, you had both in spades.

It's almost as if the hand of God had guided you in your decisions. Your good fortune spared you the necessity of having to keep on killing. It spared you the anguish you began to feel after Bandera's assassination. Can you imagine employing that poisonous device a third time? Who knows how many other nationalists would have died of apparent heart attacks? Your *modus operandi* would surely have had to change. Too many dead nationalists, and all dying in stairwells or lobbies, could have stirred suspicion. Coincidence would've been heaped on coincidence to the point of undermining the very point of coincidence. I wonder what your instructions would have been. To kill them as they emerged from their cars? As they shoveled snow? As they crossed empty boulevards or sat on park benches in the summer feeding pigeons?

My life has been anything but lucky. I've looked in every corner of my life, I've explored every single minute of my life, and I've failed to find any luck at all. But there has been much good timing. I've been fortunate to have experienced some extraordinary coincidences. Meeting you, for instance. Or meeting Sholom. Or realizing that fish-eyes and I cannot coexist in the same place at the same time on this earth. These coincidences have made my life bearable. It's as if the complete lack of luck had set my life on an inexorably downward path. It's also as if these bolts out of the blue have deflected my life from that hopeless trajectory—not completely, perhaps not even significantly, but just enough to make it worth living, or perhaps to make it not worth not living.

Fish-eyes is like you, a man of good luck and good timing. He is a formidable opponent, and I fear that, however much and however thoroughly I prepare, his good luck and good timing will trump me. If you're lucky, you're lucky, and if you're not, you're not. God may help those who help themselves, but even God is powerless against luck and timing. I find some comfort in the knowledge that this gross imbalance means that I'll either succeed in my plan or not. There's not much I can do about it. I can prepare assiduously or I can approach the matter lackadaisically.

162

It's all the same. If I'm fated to be lucky on that day, I'll succeed. If I'm fated to be unlucky, I won't. It's as simple as that.

Had my parents not met in that small Ukrainian town and in Auschwitz, I wouldn't be alive. Had they not killed, I wouldn't be alive. Had they not been bloodthirsty, I wouldn't be alive. But so what? Our lives consist of chains of an infinite number of happenstances that appear, in retrospect, to look like inevitabilities. The chains appear to have beginnings, middles, and ends, and as we ponder the happenstances that comprise them, we conclude that we are what we could only have become. That makes perfect sense to me, but who knows whether it's true or not.

Let me give you an example. As I was walking down some street, a brick hit the pavement just in front of me and cracked in two. I looked up and saw some men working on the roof. One of them cried, "Are you fine?" I said nothing and kept walking. It was only a few minutes later that the momentous nature of what I had experienced hit me with full force. The very last thing on my mind was my own death—and yet I could have been killed if, say, the worker had dropped that brick half a second later or if I had slightly accelerated my pace. What if I had seen the love of my life and rushed to her? What if the worker had scratched his nose before the brick fell from his hand? Timing and luck were both on my side. But they were a hair's breadth from working against me.

Who decides these things, Bohdan? Are we slaves of happenstance and accident, or do we determine our own fates? I'd like to think it's the latter, and that's why I've decided to take my fate into my own hands, but as I look at your life and the miraculous turn it took on August 12, 1961, I suspect it's the former. Does it make any difference what we do or not do? I hope it does, but I suspect it doesn't. Of course, I have to have this hope, don't I? How else could I even contemplate doing what I intend to do? That takes guts, that takes initiative, and I have both, at least to some degree, but it also, I fear, takes what you have and I don't—luck. Were you to ask me why I'm still intent on doing what I intend to do, the only answer I could possibly give you is that, like Sholom, I have no choice. I am at wit's end. I am desperate. Nothing else can save me, even though I know—or suspect?—that nothing can save me.

One of the things that worry me, Bohdan, is that I may lack the killer instinct. It seems pretty obvious to me that anyone who decides to undertake something as serious as a rub out must have the disposition of an assassin, and I suspect that that disposition is innate and not learned. I have no proof of that assertion. For all I know, assassins are made, not born, or perhaps all of us could become assassins if the conditions, or conditioning, were right. But I suspect that assassins are born. I don't mean to say that someone looking at you as a two-year old child would've concluded that you had an assassin's disposition, but I do believe that there was already something within you that inclined you to kill without passion.

Sholom also had that disposition. How else could a watchmaker have become a killer? He claims to have been outraged by the violations he witnessed, but surely he wasn't the only one, and why did he, and no one else, pull a trigger five times? You say you witnessed nationalist outrages; you say the police trapped you. That's all true—technically, but it doesn't really explain anything. Others saw atrocities, others were caught by the police or recruited by the KGB. Only you became an assassin—or, I should say, a twice successful assassin.

I look at myself and I fear that I lack the assassin's backbone, the assassin's will. It's all about that split second before the trigger gets pulled and the bullet emerges from the chamber to do its bloody job. I've talked about that split second with Sholom, and what amazes me about his feat was that he actually fired off five whole shots. Imagine, Bohdan, *five* shots—*one, two, three, four, five*—all fired in rapid succession and without any hesitation. In your case, I'm even more dumbfounded. You managed to overcome that hesitation twice. And the second time wasn't a few minutes or a few hours or even a few days after the first. You squeezed that device two whole years after you fired it the first time. And you had pangs of doubt during those many months. You wondered why you were doing what you were doing and you even began to look for alternatives. You and Sholom are men of great will and will power. I know I'm not.

My parents also lacked that strength of will. My father slaughtered Ukrainians. He went into cells, manacled inmates, and shot them as they stood trembling and soiling their pants before him. He may have thrust a bayonet into their guts and dismembered them. He marched them to pits, ordered them to stand at their edge, and coolly placed bullets into their skulls. That seems like it requires great strength, but it doesn't. He wasn't alone. They were all shooting and stabbing and torturing in a heated frenzy. After it was over, after the moans were all that was left of the prisoners, after the blood stopped dripping from the tables and chairs, after the guns and knives and bayonets had cooled, my father and his comrades probably felt as if they'd awoken from a dream. Not so you, Bohdan. You, like Sholom, knew exactly what you were doing all the time. You were completely in control. You followed your prey, you established your position, you pointed the device, and you fired—and then you walked away, swallowed the anti-poison pill, and dumped the gun into the canal. There were no massacres, no screams, no tortures taking place around you. No blood dripped, no commands were barked, no faces were contorted in agony. And yet you overcame that hesitation and you shot.

My mother also lacked that will. As she did her rounds of the camp, she knew she could shoot whomever she wanted to— precisely because those were her orders. If a prisoner tried to escape or even approach the fence, she shot or barked a command ordering him to be killed. If she guarded a work detail, she could hit with impunity whoever fell out of step or stumbled or fell. And if she led prisoners to the gas chambers, she could do anything to keep them marching to their deaths. Moans and screams and tears and pleadings and agonized faces were part of her everyday life. She could fire at will, she could beat at will, she could spit at will. But that's just my point, Bohdan. When she killed or stabbed or spat or struck, she did so because she could do so. She may have derived great pleasure from seeing the terrified faces of emaciated Jews, but none of her actions required that steely force of will that you and Sholom displayed.

How different it was for the two of you! You acted alone. No one was there to support you, to encourage you, to ease your pain, to erase your moral qualms. You fired the poison even though your employers in Moscow were far away. You could have said no, but you overcame that split second of hesitation and said yes. For my mother, as for my father, there was no split second of hesitation to overcome.

Do you know what gives me great pleasure, Bohdan? Doing the dishes. There they are, piled up in the sink, dirty and greasy. You turn on the faucet, make sure that the water is neither too hot nor too cold, take the sponge, pour soap onto it, and wipe the plates and forks and cups and spoons clean. And then, when you rinse them under the running water, they squeal like little pigs. Finally, you place them neatly in the rack, like soldiers in an army. It's a thing of beauty.

Do you see the problem? Do you sense the irony? Here I am, trying to follow in your footsteps, even though I know I lack your strength. But I cannot do otherwise. Like you, I have no choice. I've come this far only because I've had to come this far. And I can't abandon my plans and stay where I am. I have to move forward, even though I doubt that I can. I know I can't move backward, and I know that I can't stand still. I have to try, even though I'm quite certain of failure. Does that make me the ultimate hero, Bohdan, or the ultimate fool—or the ultimate fool of God?

Chapter 13

To everyone's astonishment, the narrative comes to a more or less happy end, as Volodymyr is tried and released, while history repeats itself—neither as farce, nor as tragedy, but, perhaps because thirteen is an unlucky number, as longwinded discourses on incomprehensible notions and picayune things

Chickens come home to roost and the other shoe drops, as the exceptionally great leader opens the proceedings against the Jew who was Ukrainian—in the present tense no less, perhaps as an indication of the timelessness of his guilt or something like that

They are sitting at the mahogany table as the exceptionally great leader walks in and takes a seat at the head. Dostaevsky, the pallid Slav, is attired in his trademark off-white. Katorga, suppressing a hysterical mien, is dressed in a gray skirt and a bright red blouse. Putschkin is sporting a mustache and resembles a bewhiskered Hebrew. The saintly Father Vlassov is wearing a cassock. The blanched Deniquine has come in black trousers and a brown shirt. The jury is assembled. The exceptionally great leader presides.

"You all know why we're here," Pitoon says, "so let's start our proceedings without further ado. I shall begin."

The exceptionally great leader cross examines the Jew who was Ukrainian and hopes to teach him a thing or two in the process—about life, about politics, about guilt, about manliness, about responsibility, as well as about this and that

Exceptionally great leader: Your name?

Frauenzimmer: Volodymyr Frauenzimmer.

Exceptionally great leader: That's quite an unusual name—Vladimir the Woman.

Frauenzimmer: I am who I am.

Exceptionally great leader: Good heavens, a philosopher... Your occupation?

167

Frauenzimmer: I am the Jew who is Ukrainian.

Exceptionally great leader: Please stop with the philosophical riddles. We have no time for nonsense.

Frauenzimmer: Unemployed.

Exceptionally great leader: Why is a bum like you plotting my death? You *do* appreciate the absurdity?

Frauenzimmer: The very idea is preposterous.

Exceptionally great leader: Exactly. And yet, here you are, being tried for committing this crime.

Frauenzimmer: For planning it—not committing it.

Exceptionally great leader: I see no difference. Do you know who I am? If you did, you'd know that to plot against me is to plot against Russia.

Frauenzimmer: And that's a crime?

Exceptionally great leader: A heinous crime.

Frauenzimmer: Then I'm guilty.

Exceptionally great leader: Why do you hate Russia?

Frauenzimmer: I don't.

Exceptionally great leader: You just confessed to plotting against Russia.

Frauenzimmer: I confessed to plotting against you.

Exceptionally great leader: And you agreed that they are the same thing.

Frauenzimmer: You're twisting my words.

Exceptionally great leader: Not at all. I'm merely repeating what you said. So, let me ask you again. Why do you hate Russia?

Frauenzimmer: I hate you.

Exceptionally great leader: Because I'm the exceptionally great leader?

Frauenzimmer: No, because of your fish eyes. They remind me of a corpse.

Exceptionally great leader: I wouldn't use that word so lightly. Remember where you are.

Frauenzimmer: That changes nothing. Your eyes—

Exceptionally great leader: —are no different from other people's eyes. That's no reason. Do you have a rational reason?

Frauenzimmer: It's not just your eyes as eyes. It's what they stand for. It's what *you* stand for.

Exceptionally great leader: Russia. I stand for Mother Russia.

Frauenzimmer: No, you stand for evil, for the past, for—

Exceptionally great leader: Ah, now we're getting somewhere. And why do I stand for evil?

Frauenzimmer: You represent everything that is wrong with—

Exceptionally great leader: What? Your life? You? Don't blame me for your inadequacies.

Frauenzimmer: I don't. My inadequacies, as you call them, are mine. But they will disappear, when you do. I know that.

Exceptionally great leader: You *believe* that. You don't know anything at all.

Frauenzimmer: Believe, know—what's the difference?

Exceptionally great leader: There are no grounds for your belief. *That* is irrational. If there were, you'd possess knowledge. Your behavior would then be rational.

Frauenzimmer: You speak like an intellectual.

Exceptionally great leader: I have a higher degree.

Frauenzimmer: In engineering!

Exceptionally great leader: And you? Do you have a degree—in anything?

Frauenzimmer: I don't need a degree. I know things. I know many things.

Exceptionally great leader: You *believe* many things.

Frauenzimmer: I know my life depends on your death.

Exceptionally great leader: And why should that be so?

Frauenzimmer: It is, it just is. When I contemplate killing you, I'm at peace.

Exceptionally great leader: Then you're a pathologically ill man.

Frauenzimmer: I never claimed to be normal.

Exceptionally great leader: True enough.

Frauenzimmer: And I never claimed to be healthy.

Exceptionally great leader: So what should we do with you?

Frauenzimmer: Let me go. I can't be held responsible for my actions.

Exceptionally great leader: But then you'll just resume your plotting.

Frauenzimmer: True.

Exceptionally great leader: So we'd have to be irrational to do that.

Frauenzimmer: True, too.

Exceptionally great leader: Let's try a different approach.

Frauenzimmer: Very well.

Exceptionally great leader: Why do you say you feel at peace when you contemplate my demise? You don't know me. I've never done anything to you or your family. And you've never done anything to me. We've never even met!

Frauenzimmer: I can't explain it.

Exceptionally great leader: Why aren't you at peace?

Frauenzimmer: I told you. I am the Jew who is Ukrainian.

Exceptionally great leader: I thought that was a joke.

Frauenzimmer: It is. It's a preposterous condition to be in.

Exceptionally great leader: But you didn't choose it.

Frauenzimmer: That makes it worse.

Exceptionally great leader: Why? There are many mixed marriages in Russia, and there are many Jewish-Ukrainian offspring. All of them—*vse*—love me. Why don't you?

Frauenzimmer: It's my parents.

Exceptionally great leader: Yes, Katorga told me.

Frauenzimmer: Did she tell you who they were and how they met?

Exceptionally great leader: Putschkin told me.

Frauenzimmer: Then you also know where I was conceived.

Exceptionally great leader: In a concentration camp. So what? Many Russians were conceived in concentration camps.

Frauenzimmer: But this wasn't just any concentration camp. This was Auschwitz!

Exceptionally great leader: And why is that worse than Vorkuta? Or Magadan? Or Norilsk? Why do you claim a monopoly on suffering? My people have suffered terribly, possibly worse than you Jews and Ukrainians. But we don't complain. We get to work. Just look at Vlassov and Deniquine. Or Dostaevsky. He used to have nothing. Now he has everything. You could learn a thing or two from them.

Frauenzimmer: My mother killed! My father did too!

Exceptionally great leader: And I've killed. So what? Do you think my children have sleepless nights as a result? We all kill. Even you.

Frauenzimmer: That was my *intent.*

Exceptionally great leader: It's the same thing. We're all sinners. We're all evil. But you're also weak. You whine. That's the greatest transgression of all.

Frauenzimmer: I thought I was strong.

Exceptionally great leader: It wouldn't make any difference. We are what we are. And things are as they are.

Frauenzimmer: Can't I change history?

Exceptionally great leader: Don't kid yourself. No one can. We're all impotent.

Frauenzimmer: Can I at least find salvation?

Exceptionally great leader: Did Schwartzbard find salvation? Did Stashinsky?

Frauenzimmer: I don't think so.

Exceptionally great leader: You don't think so! Of course, they didn't. They remained tortured all their lives. Killing solves no moral dilemmas.

Frauenzimmer: But you killed.

Exceptionally great leader: I didn't say killing solves no political dilemmas.

Frauenzimmer: Now you talk like a Stalinist.

Exceptionally great leader: And what of it? He was a great man. He built a great Russia.

Frauenzimmer: And he killed millions.

Exceptionally great leader: But he did it for Russia. You want to kill me—and for whom? Yourself. Who is the better man? Besides, Stalin was on the side of history.

Frauenzimmer: And I'm not?

Exceptionally great leader: Don't be preposterous. *I* am history. Are you on my side? No. That's why you hate me, you know.

Frauenzimmer: I told you I can't explain why I hate you.

Exceptionally great leader: Nonsense. You hate me because I represent everything you're not. I build, you whine. You're not just a Frauenzimmer. You're a *Zimmerfrau*.

Frauenzimmer: A maid? Very funny.

Exceptionally great leader: More like the handmaiden of history.

Frauenzimmer: My motives for acting are more important than the effects.

Exceptionally great leader: Only the weak, the losers, believe that.

Frauenzimmer: In the end, the last shall be first.

Exceptionally great leader: Perhaps, perhaps. But who is interrogating whom? As the great Lenin said, *Kto kogo?*

Consciously choosing the language, style, and demeanor that characterize all historically critical trials, Volodymyr vigorously argues for his own innocence by, all too predictably, appealing to history, the Leitmotif of this narrative and of his life, and, just as predictably, invoking the innately violent nature of all Ukrainians

Volodymyr's 10th Antihistorical Intervention. And thus they continued until the defiant Frauenzimmer rose from his seat and turned to the blanched flappers, bewhiskered Hebrews, and pallid Ukrainians and screamed, his eyes glistening with hysteria and fanatical exultation: "Ladies and gentlemen of the jury, the defendant is innocent. This simple, good, and trustworthy Jew deserves your compassion, not your scorn. He had no choice. He is the product of circumstances beyond his control. He is the son of his people and, like his people, he is the victim of persecution. If he tried to kill the exceptionally great leader, it was only because he had to. He should not be on trial. His tormentors, his persecutors—his people's tormentors and persecutors—are the guilty ones. *They* should be on trial!"

Blood. "They are covered in blood—my blood, my people's blood—and they have been covered in our blood ever since they came to know us and to hate us for what we are. We have done nothing to them; we have lived among them, spoken their language, talked to them, joked with them, worked with them, but they never could see us as who we were and are—as simple people trying to raise their children and to marry their young and to welcome their babies and to bury their dead. Did we ever insist that they bow to us, love us, respect us, embrace us?

"We wanted only to be who we are and to live the way we wanted to live. But they never could leave us in peace. They never could just walk past our homes and our stores and our women and our children. No, they always looked at us with envy and hatred. They hated us from the moment they laid eyes on us. And they have hated us for every minute of their lives.

"Have you noticed that their hands are covered with our blood? That their feet drip with our blood? That their faces and beards and mustaches and hair are wet with our blood? They call us blood-suckers, but it is they who have always sucked our blood. They say that we sacrifice children, but it is they who have murdered our children. They needed to spill our blood, because they hated us, because that hatred gave them life and made them breathe, because that hatred defined their souls. They hate us because they must hate us."

Demon. "Deep within their souls lies a demon, a Satanic beast, an axe-murderer, a tormentor and torturer, a madman who needs to feast on the blood of innocents, a pathological killer who cannot rest, who cannot live, without destroying us—without destroying the defendant.

"Our history with them is a history of blood. It is a history of endless suffering, of endless killing, of endless blood-letting. Their heroes thrust their sabers through our bellies. They severed our necks, they dismembered our bodies, they smashed our babies against walls, they raped our women, they burned our synagogues, they desecrated our holy books. We lived peacefully, we lived simply, we lived devoutly—but peaceful, simple, and devout people were anathema to the likes of them. How could they restrain their demons when faced with such a provocation—the provocation of people who are their antithesis?"

Hate. "We have done nothing—and we have certainly done nothing to them—to deserve such hatred. But there is nothing we can do, and there is nothing they can do. Their hatred is part of them; it is lodged in their souls and in their hearts. They negate us; they destroy; they cannot let us live, because our life means their self-negation, and our death means their self-affirmation. It is them or us.

"You see now why the defendant had to kill the exceptionally great leader. He had no choice."

Still using the language, style, and demeanor that characterize all historically critical trials, Volodymyr argues for his complete innocence by, again, appealing to history, a rhetorical move that may reflect the intrinsic importance of history or only be a symptom of Volodymyr's own lack of imagination and unhealthy, if perhaps comprehensible, obsession with the past, as well as by invoking the intrinsically brutalizing behavior of all Jews

Volodymyr's 11th, and Last, Antihistorical Intervention. And thus they continued until the defiant Volodymyr rose from his seat again and turned to the blanched flappers, bewhiskered Hebrews, and pallid Ukrainians and screamed, his eyes glistening with hysteria and fanatical exultation: "Ladies and gentlemen of the jury, the defendant is innocent. This simple, good, and trustworthy Ukrainian deserves your compassion, not your scorn. He had no choice. He is the product of circumstances beyond his control. He is the son of his people and, like his people, he is a victim of persecution. If he tried to kill the exceptionally great leader, it was only because he had to. He should not be on trial. His tormentors, his persecutors—his people's tormentors and persecutors—are the guilty ones. *They* should be on trial!"

History. "They have stolen my nation's voice, and they have stolen, robbed, destroyed, and desecrated my nation's history and memory. And what is a person without a voice, a memory, a history? Nothing. What is a nation without a voice, a memory, and a history? Nothing. We are nothing because of them. We do not exist. And how can people who do not exist be responsible for anything? How can they kill and desecrate? Terrible things may have happened, but do not blame them on us. We do not exist, and it is they who made us nonexistent.

"We are invisible. They go about their lives, they write their books, they tell their stories, they write their histories, they sing their lamentations—but we are not even shadows within their stories. They live their lives and they live *our* lives. They have reduced us to slaves, to voiceless, stupid, thoughtless animals, to the oxen that plow the fields, to the horses that draw the carriages, to the sheep that are slaughtered, to the dogs that are kicked. We are their rags, we are their filthy underwear, we are their dirty floors, we are the missing soles of their old shoes."

Animals. "They made us into vicious animals and brutes. And then they wonder that the animals and brutes should behave as animals and brutes. And then they condemn us for being exactly what they made us. And then they cry that animals and brutes should be treated as animals and brutes. But, although we *are* animals and brutes, somewhere in our souls there still exist tiny sparks of humanity. There still exists some small sense of what we should have been and might have been had we not been reduced to dogs and oxen. And sometimes that small spark produces a glowing ember, and that ember produces a fire, and then, amazingly, the animal begins to suspect that it's a human being. The dog barks and is startled by its barking. The ox bellows and is surprised by the unnaturalness of the sound.

"It is at this moment that we begin to realize that the unnatural sounds we've been making all our lives are not really our voices. It's a small step from there to the realization that, just as this voice I thought was mine is not mine, so too this being that I thought was me isn't me. I do not bark and I do not bellow; once I know that, it's an even smaller step to the conclusion that I am not a dog and I am not an ox.

"What am I, if I am not an animal that makes sounds? Perhaps I am a human being? Perhaps I am just like them? Perhaps I deserve to be what they are, to have what they have, to do what they do? And imagine that I answer yes to these questions. Imagine that this animal is ready to become a human being with a human voice."

Choice. "We are not chosen—certainly not by God, and certainly not by history. We would prefer to be God's chosen people, and we would even settle for being history's chosen people, but animals and slaves and less-than-shadows cannot choose everything. But we do choose one thing—ourselves. We choose to have a voice.

"You see now why the defendant had to kill the exceptionally great leader. He had no choice."

175

*Completely befuddled by two contextually mystifying and historically
inappropriate speeches that focus on issues of no relevance to the question of
Volodymyr's guilt with respect to the exceptionally great leader of Mother
Russia, the members of the jury metaphorically throw up their hands in despair
and decide to call it a day, thereby producing an unexpectedly happy end that is,
truth to tell, utterly inappropriate for a narrative of such seriousness*

"What the hell was that all about?" cries Deniquine. "That chap's crazy."

"Completely bonkers," gasps Katorga, "completely, totally bonkers."

"I always figured the guy was nuts," roars Pitoon. "So what do we do now? We can keep on deliberating or we could just make a decision."

"Let us," says Father Vlassov, "like the good Lord, make a just decision."

"I'm with him on this one," says Deniquine.

"I've run out of patience," says Dostaevsky. "I move we let him go. He's a harmless loon."

"I second the motion," says Katorga.

"I agree," says Putschkin.

"The Lord giveth," says Father Vlassov, "and the Lord taketh away."

"Couldn't have said it better myself," adds Deniquine.

"In that case," decrees Pitoon, "thy will be done."

*Breathing the fresh air of freedom, Volodymyr commiserates with two assassins
and three victims who have few encouraging things to say but—despite what one
might expect from their historically burdened personalities and complex
national identities and political affiliations—they do manage to converse
without resorting to fisticuffs, thereby possibly proving that, while the past may
be inevitable, the present may be just a little less so*

Frauenzimmer: You betrayed me.
Schwartzbard: Not really, but what did you expect?
Stashinsky: The Order of Lenin?
Frauenzimmer: But you said you supported me!
Stashinsky: We listened.
Schwartzbard: Sympathetically—no, *empathetically.*

Stashinsky: Surely you didn't think we'd let you destroy the past.

Schwartzbard: *We* are the past. You destroy the past, you destroy us.

Frauenzimmer: But I was only trying to salvage the present!

Schwartzbard: By destroying the past?

Stashinsky: Can't be done. The past is the past and—

Schwartzbard: —the present is the present.

Stashinsky: You—your enterprise—was doomed from the start.

Frauenzimmer: Pitoon said so, too.

Stashinsky: A smart man. Perhaps you should've listened to him?

Frauenzimmer: I failed.

Schwartzbard: You tried.

Bandera: You were weak.

Petliura: You were noble.

Rebet: You were honest.

Stashinsky: But you failed. Nothing else matters.

Schwartzbard: I disagree. The moral impetus is all that matters.

Bandera: Exactly.

Stashinsky: Pitoon was right, you know. Volodymyr is a weakling. And weaklings are history's losers.

Schwartzbard: Justice is all that matters. The criminals must be punished. The innocent must be avenged.

Stashinsky: To what end?

Schwartzbard: It's an end in itself.

Frauenzimmer: And then what? There will always be criminals and there will always be innocents. When will it stop?

Schwartzbard: It won't. Life is about vengeance.

Bandera: Life is about victory.

Petliura: Life, alas, is about defeat. We all lose, eventually.

Frauenzimmer: So what's the point?

Schwartzbard: Ignominy awaits some of us. Honor awaits the rest.

Frauenzimmer: But what's the point of honor?

Stashinsky: Exactly. Who needs an Order of Lenin? Who needs a ceremony in the Kremlin? I'll tell you something, my friends. My happiest moments were with Inge. And my saddest were when our child died. Everything else is *Scheisse*.

Petliura: I sometimes feel I'm up to my neck in it.

Schwartzbard: Well, I've certainly managed to retain my integrity.

Petliura: For most people integrity is just a meaningless—

Frauenzimmer: —word?

Petliura: For you it seems to be more than that.

Rebet: You *seem* to act with integrity.

Petliura: Appearances can be deceiving. My detractors say I acted without integrity. My supporters say the opposite. Who's right? Who's wrong? Who knows?

Stashinsky: Integrity's at stake only when you have to choose. I had no choice.

Frauenzimmer: Of course you did. You chose to kill.

Stashinsky: I *had* to shoot.

Frauenzimmer: But you chose to step onto the slippery slope. Once you were on it, you were bound to slip.

Stashinsky: Why can't one resist slipping down?

Petliura: Because one can't. I know.

Stashinsky: Perhaps *you* couldn't? Perhaps you're generalizing from your own experience? Perhaps you're just looking for an excuse?

Petliura: Then I wouldn't be tragic. I'd be pathetic.

Stashinsky: Why shouldn't your experience be only yours?

Petliura: Because everyone I know started out believing what you believe—and they've all ended up where I am. Or worse. At least I'm aware of my moral lapses.

Frauenzimmer: You're all up to your necks in *Scheisse*, you know. You're all on that slope. How can you live with yourselves?

Schwartzbard: We're dead. That's how.

Frauenzimmer: Why didn't you just quit? Become a dishwasher—or stay a watchmaker?

Schwartzbard: For many reasons: justice, struggle, truth. But I'll tell you something, *mon ami*. I don't think that's really it.

Frauenzimmer: Then what is?

Stashinsky: He likes living in sin. He likes knowing that every choice he makes, every move he makes, moves him up or down that slope. All of life becomes a moral challenge.

Bandera: And you enjoy being pulled in two directions?

Schwartzbard: It makes me free.

Bandera: You call that freedom? I pity you if you believe that. Freedom is certainty.

Schwartzbard: No, *mon ami*, freedom is struggle.

Rebet: Here your watchmaker's shop, there the concentration camp. So what if you struggle? The camp always remains.

Schwartzbard: My moral lapses aren't comparable to his.

Rebet: But the strategy is the same. You embrace the good *and* the bad.

Frauenzimmer: Exactly. You compartmentalize, but that solves nothing.

Petliura: And you pretend. You live *as if* the slope were flat. Except that it's *not*. It's a slope, and you're on it.

Schwartzbard: I know it's a slope, and I know I'm on it. But I'm not *only* on it. There are other aspects of my life, and they're not slopes. In some of them, I live with myself quite nicely. In others—I'd say in most—there are no moral choices to be made.

Bandera: Like buying tomatoes.

Rebet: And this isn't just an elaborate rationalization?

Schwartzbard: Are *you* sure it's *just* an elaborate rationalization?

Bandera: You all talk too much and—

Stashinsky: *I* act.

Bandera: —think too much.

Frauenzimmer: And know too much. There are things I know that I wish I didn't. My parents, my life, my past—they're a terrible weight on my shoulders.

Stashinsky: You will have to learn to carry it, my friend. If I could learn, so can you.

Schwartzbard: We must all carry our sins *and* the sins of the world.

Frauenzimmer: The weight is too heavy.

Schwartzbard: You'll manage. Everyone does. And besides, it's not like pushing a rock up a hill.

Stashinsky: Sisyphus did nothing else. We can actually live our lives—well, metaphorically, of course.

Petliura: And the world will turn without us.

Frauenzimmer: Is that it? Nothing will ever change?

Petliura: *Exactement, mon ami,* nothing will ever change.

Bandera: The past cannot be altered. Only the future can.

Frauenzimmer: But it doesn't exist!

Petliura: *That* is the catch.

Frauenzimmer: Then we are all doomed!

Rebet: I wouldn't say that. We do what we can. We make watches, we buy tomatoes.

Frauenzimmer: But the large questions—the killings, the massacres, the pogroms, the annihilations—will never be answered?

Stashinsky: Did *I* change anything?

Schwartzbard: Or *I?*

Petliura: The point is to be true to yourself—regardless of what others believe.

Frauenzimmer: But then you and Sholom are both right! You say you did what you could, and he says he did what he had to.

Stashinsky: We used to call that the dialectic.

Frauenzimmer: Then we should all follow Pitoon. Forget the past, forget right and wrong—and just have a good meal at the Gulag. I can't accept that.

Bandera: Neither can I, of course. On the other hand, one must eat.

Rebet: There are no good choices.

Frauenzimmer: So what do you choose?

Stashinsky: Well, you *could* choose white socks.

Schwartzbard: Or smooth hands.

Petliura: And what's wrong with a fine meal?

Close to despair, but determined to avoid the appearance of despondence on the very last page of the last chapter of his narrative, Volodymyr, somewhat unpredictably, at first seeks solace, refuge, and comfort in expletives, which can offer answers to vexing questions precisely because they, like great art, can be expressed directly and simply and without recourse to obscure and obscurantist symbols, signs, and other confusing semiotic devices, but then, mirabile dictu, pauses, only to realize that expletives are a poor substitute for the sounds produced by his name, by smoothly rounded pebbles that recede pell-mell into the ocean with a gentle wave, or by the chant—stupidukrainian pigdirtykikekillerexploiterpogromchikusurercollaboratorbootlickernazistalinistp easantbankerfilthypeasantmoneygrubbingbankerviciousantisemiterabidcommuni stfascistscumsocialistscumtupidukrainianpigdirtykike—that, like poetry, can transport him to higher levels of reality and enable him, the Jew who was Ukrainian, to acquire a deep appreciation of the rhythmic substratum of humanity's existence, the benign indifference of the universe, and the unconditional relevance thereto of the Moral of the Popcorn and, thus empowered with a certainty that transcends all doubt and all Angst, easily conclude his rip-roaring romp through an existential wasteland on a relatively up-beat, if ultimately inconclusive, note that may, or may not, be reflective of the condition of humanity or of the intractability of history or of the inalterability of the past or of the irrelevance, or possibly relevance, of all these highfalutin' things to the present, which goes by faster than the blink of an eye, or to the future, which doesn't exist until the moment it turns into the present and, like the blink of an eye, becomes immediately transformed into the past—all considerations that lead Volodymyr to wonder whether his rip-roaring romp through an existential wasteland was worth taking after all or whether he might have spent the time, more usefully and more fruitfully and certainly more profitably, going into the restaurant business or dressing well or buying tomatoes or something like that

Addendum

Volodymyr's 12th, and Definitely Last, Antihistorical Intervention

Having failed to comprehend the moral of the story, Volodymyr makes one last desperate attempt to escape narrative logic and change the course of history, unsuccessfully of course, thereby proving beyond reasonable doubt that history always repeats itself as both tragedy and farce

Volodymyr debates the incomparably great Vladimir Illich Lenin and, despite the enormous odds against him, almost convinces the father of proletarian internationalism not to board the sealed train for the Finland Station, cause mayhem, and unleash terrible though nameless forces on the poor and unsuspecting, though possibly deserving, world

Frauenzimmer: Excuse me, may I join you?

Lenin: *Ja?*

Frauenzimmer: I didn't mean to disrupt your luncheon, but—

Lenin: *Ja?*

Frauenzimmer: —I must speak to you about an important matter.

Lenin: Indeed?

Frauenzimmer: It concerns the fate of the world.

Lenin: Indeed!

Frauenzimmer: Just five minutes of your time, Herr Lenin. I'm not meshugge.

Lenin: *Nu?*

Frauenzimmer: I have a request, Herr Lenin, a simple request. I'd like you to reconsider your trip to Petrograd.

Lenin: *You* know about my trip?

Frauenzimmer: Tomorrow. In a sealed train. The German High Command is sending you.

Lenin: No one knows that. Not even my closest comrades. Who are you, Herr—?

Frauenzimmer: Frauenzimmer. Volodymyr Frauenzimmer.

Lenin: *Sie sind Jude?*

Frauenzimmer: Half-Jewish and half-Ukrainian.

Lenin: Ah, a bourgeois nationalist twice over!

Frauenzimmer: *Nein*, Herr Lenin, I am completely apolitical.

Lenin: No one is apolitical, Herr Frauenzimmer. May I ask how you've come to know about my trip?

Frauenzimmer: It's common knowledge.

Lenin: Are you a Menshevik?

Frauenzimmer: A what?

Lenin: So, you are not a Zionist or a Ukrainian bourgeois nationalist or a Menshevik—and yet you happen to know the exact details about a state secret.

Frauenzimmer: I am not a spy. I wish only to change the world.

Lenin: Don't we all?

Frauenzimmer: That's just it, Herr Lenin. I'd like you to refrain from changing the world for a short while. I'd like you to stay in Zürich for a few weeks.

Lenin: Impossible! The fate of the revolution depends on me.

Frauenzimmer: Exactly. But it will all go wrong. There will be so much bloodshed, so much suffering.

Lenin: There already is.

Frauenzimmer: Millions will die!

Lenin: Millions *are* dying.

Frauenzimmer: Millions more will die.

Lenin: Then millions more will die—but there will be communism.

Frauenzimmer: There will be *no* communism, Herr Lenin. Those millions will have died in vain.

Lenin: You're mistaken.

Frauenzimmer: You will unleash terrible forces. Jews will die, Ukrainians will die, Russians will die.

Lenin: They already are dying. And they'll keep on dying unless I stop it.

Frauenzimmer: But you will only make things worse!

Lenin: Once again, you're mistaken.

Frauenzimmer: How can you be so certain?

Lenin: How can *you*? The teachings of Marx are my guide to the future.

Frauenzimmer: They will fail.

Lenin: You make an excellent prophet. Unfortunately, I'm not a religious man.

Frauenzimmer: Lives could be saved.

Lenin: And capitalism would continue. As would the war—and all capitalist wars.

Frauenzimmer: But they will continue even if you seize power and transform Russia.

Lenin: But not *in* Russia.

Frauenzimmer: But so many will perish! Ukrainians and Jews will kill each other, Herr Lenin—and their deaths will do nothing to change the world.

Lenin: Why will they kill each other? Surely not because I'll board a train for Petrograd tomorrow!

Frauenzimmer: You'll convince your comrades to start a revolution. Without you they wouldn't.

Lenin: True.

Frauenzimmer: And you'll seize power and create a dictatorship—

Lenin: —the dictatorship of the *proletariat*!—

Frauenzimmer: —and that will throw the country into chaos—

Lenin: —or impose order—

Frauenzimmer: —and unleash terrible forces!

Lenin: Again those terrible forces! And I'm supposed to unleash them! These forces of yours—are they like mad dogs? If they are, they'll escape on their own—without my intervention.

Frauenzimmer: Are you saying that nothing can stop the killings?

Lenin: You must look at their causes. Am *I* their cause? Is my return to Petrograd their cause?

Frauenzimmer: And if you're not, then what is?

Lenin: You must look deeper—at history.

Frauenzimmer: And change it?

Lenin: Of course not. As Marx said, we can only hasten the birth pangs of history—not change it.

Frauenzimmer: Then everything is inevitable.

Lenin: Not at all: everything is determined.

Frauenzimmer: And there is no free will.

Lenin: Of course there is. It is the recognition of necessity.

Frauenzimmer: Is it necessary that innocent Jews and Ukrainians die?

Lenin: If they die, then it will have been necessary. But is it necessary for them to die? I don't know. And neither do you. Nor *can* you.

Frauenzimmer: How do you know you'll hasten those birth pangs?

Lenin: And how do you know that delaying my trip will save your Jews and Ukrainians?

Frauenzimmer: If you're wrong, delaying your trip might save thousands. And if you *are* right, then what difference does a slight delay make?

Lenin: You are being pigheaded again. Enough. We are going in circles. Excuse me, but I must pack.

Frauenzimmer: You leave me no choice, Herr Lenin. *Hände hoch!*

Lenin: A gun? Please put it away before you shoot yourself. And don't forget to pay the bill.

Frauenzimmer: But, but, I am—

Lenin: —a *Zimmerfrau*, alas. I know. But if it's any consolation, you are who you are, and I am who I am. *Auf Wiedersehen*, Herr Zimmerfrau. I'll send you a postcard from Mother Russia.

ABOUT THE AUTHOR

Alexander J. Motyl (b. 1953, New York) is a writer, painter, and professor. He is the author of four novels, *Whiskey Priest, Who Killed Andrei Warhol, Flippancy,* and *The Jew Who Was Ukrainian*; his poems have appeared in *Counterexample Poetics, Istanbul Literary Review, Orion Headless, The Battered Suitcase, Red River Review,* and *New York Quarterly.* Motyl's artwork has been exhibited in solo and group shows in New York, Philadelphia, and Toronto. He teaches at Rutgers University-Newark and lives in New York.